I'd Tell
You I
Love You,
But Then
I'd Have to
Kill You

a l l y   c a r t e r

HYPERION

NEW YORK

Acknowledgments

This book would not have been possible without the help and encouragement of many wonderful people. I thank the tremendously talented Donna Bray and Arianne Lewin for all their kindness, professionalism, and support. I owe a lot to my wonderful friends and family, who have always stood by me. But mostly, for this book, I thank Kristin Nelson, who sent the e-mail that started it all.

First Edition

1 3 5 7 9 10 8 6 4 2

Printed in the United States of America

This book is set in 12-point Goudy.

Library of Congress Cataloging-in-Publication Data on file.

ISBN 1-4231-0003-4

Reinforced binding

Visit www.hyperionteens.com

In memory of

Ellen Moore Balarzs,

a true Gallagher Girl

Chapter One

I suppose a lot of teenage girls feel invisible sometimes, like they just disappear. Well, that's me—Cammie the Chameleon. But I'm luckier than most because, at my school, that's considered cool.

I go to a school for spies.

Of course, technically, the Gallagher Academy for Exceptional Young Women is a school for *geniuses*—not *spies*—and we're free to pursue any career that befits our exceptional educations. But when a school tells you that, and then teaches you things like advanced encryption and fourteen different languages, it's kind of like big tobacco telling kids not to smoke; so all of us Gallagher Girls know lip service when we hear it. Even my mom rolls her eyes but doesn't correct me when I call it spy school, and *she's* the headmistress. Of course, she's also a retired CIA operative, and it was her idea for me to write this, my first Covert Operations Report, to summarize what happened last semester. She's always telling us that the worst part of the spy life isn't the danger—it's the paperwork. After all, when you're on a plane home from Istanbul with a nuclear warhead in a hatbox, the last thing you want to do is write a report about it. So that's why I'm writing this—for the practice.

If you've got a Level Four clearance or higher, you probably know all about us Gallagher Girls, since we've been around for more than a hundred years (the school, not me—I'll turn sixteen next month!). But if you don't have that kind of clearance, then you probably think we're just an urban spy myth—like jet packs and invisibility suits—and you drive by our ivy-covered walls, look at our gorgeous mansion and manicured grounds, and assume, like everyone else, that the Gallagher Academy for Exceptional Young Women is just a snooty boarding school for bored heiresses with no place else to go.

Well, to tell you the truth, we're totally fine with that—it's one of the reasons no one in the town of Roseville, Virginia, thought twice about the long line of limousines that brought my classmates back to campus last September. I watched from a window seat on the third floor of the mansion as the cars materialized out of the blankets of green foliage and turned through the towering wrought-iron gates. The half-mile-long driveway curved through the hills, looking as harmless as Dorothy's yellow brick road, not giving a clue that it's equipped with laser beams that read tire treads and sensors that check for explosives, and one entire section that can open up and swallow a truck whole. (If you think that's dangerous, don't even get me started about the pond!)

I wrapped my arms around my knees and stared through the window's wavy glass. The red velvet curtains were drawn around the tiny alcove, and I was enveloped by an odd sense of peace, knowing that in twenty minutes, the halls were going to be crowded; music was going to be blaring; and I was going to go from being an only child to one of a hundred sisters, so I knew to savor the silence while it lasted. Then, as if to prove my point, a loud blast and the smell of burning hair came floating up the main stairs from the second-floor Hall of History, followed by Professor Buckingham's distinguished voice crying, "Girls! I told you not to touch that!" The smell got worse, and one of the seventh graders was probably still on fire, because Professor Buckingham yelled, "Stand still. Stand still, I say!"

Then Professor Buckingham said some French swear words that the seventh graders probably wouldn't understand for three semesters, and I remembered how every year during new student orientation one of the newbies will get cocky and try to show off by grabbing the sword Gillian Gallagher used to slay the guy who was going to kill Abraham Lincoln—the first guy, that is. The one you never hear about.

But what the newbies aren't told on their campus tour is that Gilly's sword is charged with enough electricity to . . . well . . . light your hair on fire.

I just love the start of school.

* * *

I think our room used to be an attic, once upon a time. It has these cool dormers and oddly shaped windows and lots of little nooks and crannies, where a girl can sit with her back against the wall and listen to the thundering feet and squeals of hello that are probably pretty standard at boarding schools everywhere on the first day after summer break (but they probably stop being standard when they take place in Portuguese and Farsi). Out in the hall, Kim Lee was talking about her summer in Singapore; and Tina Walters was declaring that "Cairo was super cool. Johannesburg—not so much," which is exactly what my mom had said when I'd complained about how Tina's parents were taking her to Africa over the summer whereas *I* was going to have to visit my dad's parents on their ranch in Nebraska—an experience I'm fairly sure will never help me break out of an enemy interrogation facility or disarm a dirty bomb.

"Hey, where's Cammie?" Tina asked, but I wasn't about to leave my room until I could come up with a fish story to match the international exploits of my classmates, seventy percent of whom are the daughters of current or former government operatives—aka spies. Even Courtney Bauer had spent a week in Paris, and *her* parents are both optometrists, so you can see why I wasn't especially eager to admit that I'd spent three months plopped down right in the middle of North America, cleaning fish.

I'd finally decided to tell them about the time I was experimenting with average household items that can be used as weapons and accidentally decapitated a scarecrow (who knew knitting needles could do that kind of damage?), when I heard the distinctive thud of luggage crashing into a wall and a soft, Southern, "Oh, Cammie . . . come out, come out, wherever you are."

I peered around the corner and saw Liz posing in the doorway, trying to look like Miss Alabama, but bearing a greater resemblance to a toothpick in capri pants and flip-flops. A very *red* toothpick.

She smiled and said, "Did you miss me?"

Well, I *did* miss her, but I was totally afraid to hug her.

"What happened to you?"

Liz rolled her eyes and just said, "Don't fall asleep by a pool in Alabama," as if she should have known better—which she totally should have. I mean, we're all technically geniuses and everything, but at age nine, Liz had the highest score on the third-grade achievement tests *ever*. The government keeps track of that kind of thing, so the summer before seventh grade, her parents got a visit from some big guys in dark suits and three months later, Liz was a Gallagher Girl—just not the kill-a-man-with-her-bare-hands variety. If I'm ever on a mission, I want Bex beside me and Liz far, far away, with about a dozen computers and a chessboard—a fact I couldn't help but remember when Liz tried to fling her suitcase onto the bed, but missed and ended up knocking over a bookcase, demolishing my stereo and flattening a perfectly-scaled replica of DNA that I'd made out of papier-mâché in eighth grade.

"Oopsy daisy," Liz said, throwing her hand to her mouth.

Sure, she knows cuss words in fourteen different languages, but when faced with a minor catastrophe, Liz says *oopsy daisy*. At that point I didn't care how sunburned she was—I had to hug my friend.

At six thirty exactly, we were in our uniforms, sliding our hands over the smooth mahogany banisters, and descending down the staircases that spiral gracefully to the foyer floor. Everyone was laughing (turns out my knitting needle story was a big hit), but Liz and I kept looking toward the door in the center of the atrium below.

"Maybe there was trouble with the plane?" Liz whispered. "Or customs? Or . . . I'm sure she's just late."

I nodded and continued glancing down at the foyer as if, on cue, Bex was going to burst through the doors. But they stayed closed, and Liz's voice got squeakier as she asked, "Did you hear from her? I didn't hear from her. Why didn't we hear from her?"

Well, I would have been surprised if we *had* heard from her, to tell you the truth. As soon as Bex had told us that both her mom and her dad were taking a leave of absence to spend the summer with her, I knew she wasn't going to be much of a pen pal. Leave it to Liz to come to a completely different conclusion.

"Oh my gosh, what if she dropped out?" Liz cranked up the worry in her voice. "Did she get *kicked* out?"

"Why would you think that?"

"Well . . ." she said, stumbling over the obvious, "Bex always has been kind of *rules-optional*." Liz shrugged, and, sadly, I couldn't disagree. "And why else would she be late? Gallagher Girls are never late! Cammie, you know something, don't you? You've got to know *something*!"

Times like this are when it's no fun being the headmistress's daughter, because A) it's totally annoying when people think I'm in a loop I'm not in, and B) people always assume I'm in partnership with the staff, which really I'm not. Sure, I have private dinners with my mom on Sunday nights, and *sometimes* she leaves me alone in her office for five seconds, but that's it. Whenever school is in session, I'm just another Gallagher Girl (except for being the girl to whom the aforementioned A and B apply).

I looked back down at the front doors, then turned to Liz. "I bet she's just late," I said, praying that there would be a pop quiz over supper (nothing distracts Liz faster than a pop quiz).

As we approached the massive, open doors of the Grand Hall, where Gilly Gallagher supposedly poisoned a man at her own cotillion, I involuntarily glanced up at the electronic screen that read "English—American" even though I knew we always talk in our own language and accents for the welcome-back dinner. Our mealtime conversations wouldn't be taking place in "Chinese—Mandarin" for at least a week, I hoped.

We settled at our usual table in the Grand Hall, and I finally felt at home. Of course, I'd actually been back for three weeks, but my only company had been the newbies and the staff. The only thing worse than being the only upper-classman in a mansion full of seventh graders is hanging out in the teachers' lounge watching your Ancient Languages professor put drops in the ears of the world's foremost authority on data encryption while he swears he'll never go scuba diving again. (Ew, mental picture of Mr. Mosckowitz in a wet suit! Gross!)

Since a girl can only read so many back issues of *Espionage Today*, I usually spent those pre-semester days wandering around the mansion, discovering hidden compartments and secret passageways that are at least a hundred years old and haven't seen a good dusting in about that long. Mostly, I tried to spend time with my mom, but she'd been super busy and totally distracted. Remembering this now, I thought about Bex's mysterious absence and suddenly began to worry that maybe Liz had been onto something. Then Anna Fetterman squeezed onto the bench next to Liz and asked, "Have you seen it? Did you look?"

Anna was holding a blue slip of paper that instantly dissolves when you put it in your mouth. (Even though it *looks* like it will taste like cotton candy, it doesn't—trust me!) I don't know why they always put our class schedules on Evapopaper—probably so we can use up our stash of the bad-tasting kind and move on to the good stuff, like mint chocolate chip.

But Anna wasn't thinking about the Evapopaper flavor when she yelled, "We have Covert Operations!" She sounded absolutely terrified, and I remembered that she was probably the only Gallagher Girl that Liz could take in a fist-fight. I looked at Liz, and even *she* rolled her eyes at Anna's hysterics. After all, everyone knows sophomore year is the first time we get to do anything that even approaches actual fieldwork. It's our first exposure to *real* spy stuff, but Anna seemed to be forgetting that the class itself was, sadly, kind of a cakewalk.

"I'm pretty sure we can handle it," Liz soothed, prying the paper from Anna's frail hands. "All Buckingham does is tell horror stories about all the stuff she saw in World War Two and show slides, remember? Ever since she broke her hip she's—"

"But Buckingham is out!" Anna exclaimed, and *this* got my attention.

I'm sure I stared at her for a second or two before saying, "Professor Buckingham is still here, Anna," not adding that I'd spent half the morning coaxing Onyx, her cat, down from the top shelf of the staff library. "That's got to be just a start-of-school rumor." There were always plenty of those—like how some girl got kidnapped by terrorists, or one of the staff members won a hundred grand on *Wheel of Fortune*. (Though, now that I think of it, that one was actually true.)

"No," Anna said. "You don't understand. Buckingham's doing some kind of semiretirement thing. She's gonna do orientation and acclimation for the newbies—but that's it. She's not teaching anymore."

Wordlessly, our heads turned, and we counted seats

at the staff table. Sure enough, there was an extra chair.

"Then who's teaching CoveOps?" I asked.

Just then a loud murmur rippled through the enormous room as my mom strolled through the doors at the back of the hall, followed by all the usual suspects—the twenty teachers I'd been looking at and learning from for the past three years. Twenty teachers. Twenty-one chairs. I know I'm the genius, but you do the math.

Liz, Anna, and I all looked at each other, then back at the staff table as we ran through the faces, trying to comprehend that extra chair.

One face *was* new, but we were expecting that, because Professor Smith always returns from summer vacation with a whole new look—literally. His nose was larger, his ears more prominent, and a small mole had been added to his left temple, disguising what he claimed was the most wanted face on three continents. Rumor has it he's wanted by gun smugglers in the Middle East, ex-KGB hit men in Eastern Europe, and a very upset ex-wife somewhere in Brazil. Sure, all this experience makes him a great Countries of the World (COW) professor, but the best thing Professor Smith brings to the Gallagher Academy is the annual anticipation of guessing what face he will assume in order to enjoy his summer break. He hasn't come back as a woman yet, but it's probably just a matter of time.

The teachers took their seats, but *the chair* stayed empty as my mother took her place at the podium in the center of the long head table.

"Women of the Gallagher Academy, who comes here?" she asked.

Just then, every girl at every table (even the newbies) stood and said in unison, "We are the sisters of Gillian."

"Why do you come?" my mother asked.

"To learn her skills. Honor her sword. And keep her secrets."

"To what end do you work?"

"To the cause of justice and light."

"How long will you strive?"

"For all the days of our lives." We finished, and I felt a little like a character on one of my grandma's soap operas.

We sat down, but Mom remained standing. "Welcome back, students," she said, beaming. "This is going to be a wonderful year here at the Gallagher Academy. For our newest members"—she turned to the table of seventh graders, who seemed to shiver under her intense gaze— "welcome. You are about to begin the most challenging year of your young lives. Rest assured that you would not have been given this challenge were you not up to it. To our returning students, this year *will* mark many changes." She glanced at her colleagues and seemed to ponder something before turning back to face us. "We have come to a time when—" But before she could finish, the doors flew open, and not even three years of training at spy school prepared me for what I saw.

Before I say any more, I should probably remind you that I GO TO A GIRLS' SCHOOL—that's *all* girls, *all* the time, with a few ear-drop-needing, plastic-surgery-getting male faculty members thrown in for good measure. But when we turned around, we saw a man walking in our midst who would have made James Bond feel insecure. Indiana Jones would have looked like a momma's boy compared to the man in the leather jacket with two days' growth of beard who walked to where my mother stood and then—horror of horrors—winked at her.

"Sorry I'm late," he said as he slid into the empty chair.

His presence was so unprecedented, so surreal, that I didn't even realize Bex had squeezed onto the bench between Liz and Anna, and I had to do a double take when I saw her, and remembered that five seconds before she'd been MIA.

"Trouble, ladies?" she asked.

"Where have you been?" Liz demanded.

"Forget that," Anna cut in. "Who is *he*?"

But Bex was a natural-born spy. She just raised her eyebrows and said, "You'll see."

Chapter two

Bex had spent six hours on a private jet, but her cappuccino-colored skin was glowing, and she looked as if she'd just walked out of a Noxzema commercial, so I really wanted to be petty and point out that the sign in the foyer said we were supposed to be speaking English with *American* accents during the Welcome Back Dinner. But as the only non–U.S. citizen Gallagher Girl in history, Bex was used to being an exception. My mom had bent some serious rules when her old friends from England's MI6 called and asked if their daughter could be a Gallagher Girl. Admitting Bex had been Mom's first controversial act as headmistress (but *not* her last).

"You have a good holiday, then?" Throughout the hall, girls were beginning to eat, but Bex just blew a bubble with her gum and grinned, daring us to ask her for the story.

"Bex, if you know something, you've got to tell us," Liz demanded, even though it was totally pointless. *No one* can make Bex do *anything* she doesn't want to do. I may be a chameleon, and Liz may be the next Einstein, but when it comes to general stubbornness, Bex is the best spy ever!

She smirked, and I knew she'd probably been planning this scene since she was halfway over the Atlantic Ocean (in addition to being stubborn, Bex is also quite theatrical). She waited until all eyes were on her—holding the silence until Liz was about to explode, then she took a warm roll from the basket on the table and nonchalantly said, "New teacher." She tore the bread in half and slowly buttered it. "We gave him a ride from London this morning. He's an old pal of my father's."

"Name?" Liz asked, probably already planning how she was going to hack into the CIA headquarters at Langley for details as soon as we were free to go back to our rooms.

"Solomon," Bex said, eyeing us. "Joe Solomon." She sounded eerily like the black, teenage, female James Bond.

We all turned to look at Joe Solomon. He had the scruffy beard and restless hands of an agent fresh off a mission. Around me, the hall filled with whispers and giggles—fuel that would have the rumor mill running on high by midnight—and I remembered that, even though the Gallagher Academy is a school for girl geniuses, sometimes the emphasis should be kept on the *girl*.

The next morning was torture. Absolute torture! And that's *not* a word I use lightly, considering the family business. So maybe I should rephrase: the first day of classes was *challenging*.

We didn't exactly go to bed early . . . or even a little late . . . or even at all, unless you count lying on the faux-fur rug in the common room with the entire sophomore class sprawled around me as the basis for a good night's sleep. When Liz woke us up at seven, we decided we could either primp for an hour and skip breakfast, or throw on our uniforms and eat like queens, before Professor Smith's 8:05 COW lecture.

B.S. (Before Solomon), waffles and bagels would have won out for sure. But today, Professor Smith had a lot of eyelined and lip-glossed girls with growling stomachs listening to him talk about civil unrest in the Baltic States when 8:30 rolled around. I looked at my watch, the ultimate pointless gesture at the Gallagher Academy, because classes run precisely on time, but I had to see how many seconds were standing between me and lunch. (11,705, just in case you're curious.)

When COW was over, we ran up two flights of stairs to the fourth floor for Madame Dabney's Culture and Assimilation lessons which, sadly, that day did not include tea. Then it was time for third period.

I had a pain in my neck from sleeping funny, at least five hours' worth of homework, and a newfound realization that woman cannot live on cherry-flavored lip gloss alone. I dug in the bottom of my bag and found a very questionable breath mint, and figured that if I was going to die of starvation, I should at least have minty-fresh breath for the benefit of whatever classmate or faculty member would be forced to give me CPR.

Liz had to go by Mr. Mosckowitz's office to drop off an extra-credit essay she'd written over the summer (yeah, she's *that* girl), so I was alone with Bex when we reached the base of the grand staircase and turned into the small corridor that was one of three ways to the Subs, or subfloors, where we'd never been allowed before.

Standing in front of the full-length mirror, we tried hard not to blink or do anything that might confuse the optical scanner that was going to verify that we were, in fact, sophomores and not freshmen trying to sneak down to the Subs on a dare. I studied our reflections and realized that I, Cameron Morgan, the headmistress's daughter, who knew more about the school than any Gallagher Girl since Gilly herself, was getting ready to go deeper into the vault of Gallagher secrets. Judging from the goose bumps on Bex's arm, I wasn't the only one who got chills at the thought of it.

A green light flashed in the eyes of a painting behind us. The mirror slid aside, revealing a small elevator that would take us one floor beneath the basement to the Covert Operations classroom and—if you want to be dramatic about it—our destinies.

"Cammie," Bex said slowly, "we're in."

We were sitting calmly, checking our (synchronized) watches, and all thinking the exact same thing: something is definitely different.

The Gallagher mansion is made of stone and wood. It has carved banisters and towering fireplaces a girl can curl up in front of on snowy days and read all about who killed JFK (the *real* story), but somehow that elevator had brought us into a space that didn't belong in the same century, much less the same building, as the rest of the mansion. The walls were frosted glass. The tables were stainless steel. But the absolute weirdest thing about the Covert Operations classroom was that our teacher wasn't in it.

Joe Solomon was late—so late, I was beginning to get a little resentful that I hadn't taken the time to go steal some M&M's from my mom's desk, because, frankly, a two-year-old Tic Tac simply doesn't satisfy the hunger of a growing girl.

We sat quietly as the seconds ticked away, but I guess the silence became too much for Tina Walters, because she leaned across the aisle and said, "Cammie, what do you know about him?"

Well, *I* only knew what Bex had told me, but Tina's mom writes a gossip column in a major metropolitan newspaper that shall remain nameless (since that's her cover and all), so there was no way Tina wasn't going to try to get to the bottom of this story. Soon I was trapped under an avalanche of questions like, "Where's he from?" and "Does he have a girlfriend?" and "Is it true he killed a Turkish ambassador with a thong?" I wasn't sure if she was talking about the sandals or the panties, but in any case, I didn't have the answer.

"Come on," Tina said, "I heard Madame Dabney telling Chef Louis that your mom was working on him all summer to get him to take the job. You had to hear something!"

So Tina's interrogation did have one benefit: I finally understood the hushed phone calls and locked doors that had kept my mother distracted for weeks. I was just starting to process what it meant, when Joe Solomon strolled into class—five minutes late.

His hair was slightly damp, his white shirt neatly pressed—and it's either a tribute to his dreaminess or our education that it took me two full minutes to realize he was speaking in Japanese.

"What is the capital of Brunei?"

"Bandar Seri Begawan," we replied.

"The square root of 97,969 is . . ." he asked in Swahili.

"Three hundred and thirteen," Liz answered in math, because, as she likes to remind us, math *is* the universal language.

"A Dominican dictator was assassinated in 1961," he said in Portuguese. "What was his name?"

In unison, we all said "Rafael Trujillo."

(An act, I would like to point out, that was *not* committed by a Gallagher Girl, despite rumors to the contrary.)

I was just starting to get into the rhythm of our little game, when Mr. Solomon said, "Close your eyes," in Arabic.

We did as we were told.

"What color are my shoes?" This time he spoke in English and, amazingly, thirteen Gallagher Girls sat there quietly without an answer.

"Am I right-handed or left-handed?" he asked, but didn't pause for a response. "Since I walked into this room I have left fingerprints in five different places. Name them!" he demanded, but was met with empty silence.

"Open your eyes," he said, and when I did, I saw him sitting on the corner of his desk, one foot on the floor and the other hanging loosely off the side. "Yep," he said. "You girls are pretty smart. But you're also kind of stupid."

If we hadn't known for a scientific fact that the earth simply can't stop moving, we all would have sworn it had just happened.

"Welcome to Covert Operations. I'm Joe Solomon. I've never taught before, but I've been doing this stuff for eighteen years, and I'm still breathing, so that means I know what I'm talking about. This is *not* going to be like your other classes."

My stomach growled, and Liz, who had opted for a full breakfast and a ponytail, said, "Shhh," as if I could make it stop.

"Ladies, I'm going to get you ready for what goes on." He paused and pointed upward. "Out there. It's not for everyone, and that's why I'm going to make this hard on you. Damn hard. Impress me, and next year those elevators might take you one floor lower. But if I have even the slightest suspicion that you are not supremely gifted in the area of fieldwork, then I'm going to save your life right now and put you on the Operations and Research track."

He stood and placed his hands in his pockets. "Everyone starts in this business looking for adventure, but I don't care what your fantasies look like, ladies. If you can't get out from behind those desks and show me something other than book smarts, then none of you will ever see Sublevel Two."

Out of the corner of my eye, I saw Mick Morrison following his every word, almost salivating at the sound of it, because Mick had been wanting to hurt someone for years. Unsurprisingly, her beefy hand flew into the air. "Does that mean you'll be teaching us firearms, sir?" she shouted as if a drill sergeant might make her drop and do push-ups.

But Mr. Solomon only walked around the desk and said, "In this business, if you need a gun, then it's probably too late for one to do any good." Some of the air seemed to go out of Mick's well-toned body. "But on the bright side," he told her, "maybe they'll bury you with it—that's assuming you get to be buried."

My skin burned red. Tears filled my eyes. Before I even knew what was happening, my throat was so tight I could barely breathe as Joe Solomon stared at me. Then, as soon as my eyes locked with his, he glanced away.

"The lucky ones come home, even if it *is* in a box."

Although he hadn't mentioned me by name, I felt my classmates watching me. They all know what happened to my dad—that he went on a mission, that he didn't come home. I'll probably never know any more than those two simple facts, but that those two facts were all that mattered. People call me The Chameleon here—if you go to spy school, I guess that's a pretty good nickname. I wonder sometimes what made me that way, what keeps me still and quiet when Liz is jabbering and Bex is, well, *Bexing*. Am I good at going unnoticed because of my spy genetics or because I've always been shy? Or am I just the girl people would rather not see—lest they realize how easily it could happen to them.

Mr. Solomon took another step, and my classmates pulled their gazes away just that quickly—everyone but Bex, that is. She was inching toward the edge of her chair, ready to keep me from tearing out the gorgeous green eyes of our new hot teacher as he said, "Get good, ladies. Or get dead."

A part of me wanted to run straight to my mother's office and tell her what he'd said, that he was talking about Dad, implying that it had been his fault—that he wasn't *good enough*. But I stayed seated, possibly out of paralyzing anger but more probably because I feared, somewhere inside me, that Mr. Solomon was right and I didn't want my mother to say so.

Just then, Anna Fetterman pushed through the frosted-glass doors and stood panting in front of the class. "I'm sorry," she said to Mr. Solomon, still gasping for breath. "The stupid scanners didn't recognize me, so the elevator locked me in, and I had to listen to a five-minute prerecorded lecture about trying to sneak out of bounds, and . . ." Her voice trailed off as she studied the teacher and his very unimpressed expression, which I thought was a little hypocritical coming from a man who had been five minutes late himself.

"Don't bother taking a seat," Mr. Solomon said as Anna started toward a desk in the back of the room. "Your classmates were just leaving."

We all looked at our recently synchronized watches, which

showed the exact same thing—we had forty-five minutes of class time left. Forty-five valuable and never-wasted minutes. After what seemed like forever, Liz's hand shot into the air.

"Yes?" Joe Solomon sounded like someone with far better things to do.

"Is there any homework?" she asked, and the class turned instantly from shocked to irritated. (Never ask *that* question in a room full of girls who are all black belts in karate.)

"Yes," Solomon said, holding the door in the universal signal for *get out*. "Notice things."

As I headed down the slick white hallway to the elevator that had brought me there, I heard my classmates walking in the opposite direction, toward the elevator closest to our rooms. After what had just happened, I was glad to hear their footsteps going the other way. I wasn't surprised when Bex came to stand beside me.

"You okay?" she asked, because that's a best friend's job.

"Yes," I lied, because that's what spies do.

We rode the elevator to the narrow first-floor hallway, and as the doors slid open, I was seriously considering going to see my mother (and not just for the M&M's), when I stepped into the dim corridor and heard a voice cry, "Cameron Morgan!"

Professor Buckingham was rushing down the hall, and I couldn't imagine what would make the genteel British lady speak in such a way, when, above us, a red light began to whirl, and a screaming buzzer pierced our ears so that we could barely hear the cries of the electronic voice that pulsed with the light, "CODE RED. CODE RED. CODE RED."

"Cameron Morgan!" Buckingham bellowed again, grabbing Bex and me by our arms. "Your mother needs you. NOW!"

Chapter THREE

Instantly, the corridors went from empty to overflowing as girls ran and staff members hurried and the red lights continued to pulse off and on.

A shelf of trophies spun around, sending the plaques and ribbons commemorating winners in the annual hand-to-hand combat and team code-breaking competitions to the hidden compartment behind the wall, leaving a row of awards from swim meets and debate contests in its place.

Above us, in the upper story of the foyer, three gold-and-burgundy *Learn Her Skills*, *Honor Her Sword*, and *Keep Her Secrets* banners rolled miraculously up and were replaced by handmade posters supporting someone named Emily for student council president.

Buckingham dragged Bex and me up the sweeping staircase as a flock of newbies ran down, screeching at the top of their lungs. I remembered what those sirens had sounded like the first time I'd heard them. It was no wonder the girls were acting like it was the end of the world. Buckingham yelled, "Girls!" and silenced them. "Follow Madame Dabney. She's going to take you to the stables for the afternoon. And ladies"—she snapped at a pair of dark-haired twins who seemed to be especially frantic—"composure!"

And then Buckingham whirled and raced up the staircase to the second-story landing, where Mr. Mosckowitz and Mr. Smith were trying to wheel a statue of Eleanor Everett (the Gallagher Girl who had once disabled a bomb in the White House with her teeth) into a broom closet. We swept through the Hall of History, where Gillian's sword slid smoothly into the vault beneath its case like Excalibur returning to the Lady of the Lake, and was replaced by a bust of a man with enormous ears who was supposedly the school's first headmaster.

The entire school was in a state of organized chaos. Bex and I shared a questioning look, because we were supposed to be downstairs, helping the other sophomores check the main level for anything spy-related that someone might have left lying around, but Buckingham turned and snapped, "Girls, hurry!" She sounded less like the soft, elderly teacher we knew and more like the woman who had single-handedly taken out a Nazi machine gun on D-day.

I heard a crash behind us, followed by some Polish expletives, and knew that the Eleanor Everett statue was probably in a billion pieces; but at the end of the Hall of History, my mother was leaning against the double doors of her office, dropping an M&M into her mouth as calmly as if she were waiting to pick me up from soccer practice, acting like it was just an ordinary day.

Her long dark hair fell across the shoulder of her black pants suit. A wisp of bangs brushed across a flawless forehead that she swears I'll have, too, just as soon as my hormones stop waging war with my pores.

Sometimes I'm seriously glad that we live ninety percent of our lives inside the mansion, because whenever we do leave, I have to watch men drool over my mom, or (ick) ask if we're sisters, which totally freaks me out, even though I know I should be flattered that anyone would think I was related to her at all.

In short, my mom's a hottie.

"Hey, Cam, Rebecca," she said before turning to Buckingham. "Thanks for bringing them, Patricia. Come inside a sec."

Inside her office, thanks to its soundproofed walls, the mayhem of the rest of the school completely faded away. Light streamed through leaded windows and flashed upon mahogany paneling and floor-to-ceiling bookcases that were, even as we spoke, spinning around to hide tomes like *Poisons Through the Ages* and *A Praetorian's Guide to an Honorable Death*, replacing them with a flip side of volumes like *Educating the Upper Echelon* and *Private Education Monthly*. There was a photo on her desk of the two of us on vacation in Russia, and I watched in awe as we hugged and smiled in the frame while, in the background, the Kremlin was replaced by Cinderella's Castle at Disney World.

"Holographic, radio-synthesized photo paper," mom said, when she saw my gaping mouth. "Dr. Fibs whipped up a batch in his lab over the summer. Hungry?" She held her cupped hand toward Bex and me. Amazingly, I'd forgotten all about my empty stomach, but I took a green piece for good luck. Something told me we were going to need it.

"Girls, I need you to do a tour."

"But . . . we're sophomores!" Bex exclaimed, as if my mother had mysteriously forgotten.

Mom's mouth was full of chocolate, so Buckingham explained, "The juniors are beginning their semester with interrogation tactics, so they are all under the influence of sodium pentothal at the moment, and the seniors are being fitted with their night-vision contacts, and they won't un-dilate for at least two hours. This is most unfortunate timing, but Code Reds are such for a reason. We don't know when they'll happen and, well, one is happening now."

"What do you say?" Mom asked, smiling. "Can you help us out?"

There are three things a person has to be before they show up uninvited on the doorstep of the Gallagher Academy for Exceptional Young Women: persistent, powerful, and completely out of other options. After all, most potential students never make it past the "We are not accepting applications at this time" speech they get whenever they call or write; you have to be turned down by every prep school in the country before you actually drive all the way to Roseville, hoping that an in-person visit will change our minds. But no amount of persistence or desperation can get you through the gates. No, for that, it takes real power.

That's why Bex and I were standing on the front steps, waiting on the black stretch limousine that carried the McHenry family (yes, *those* McHenrys—the ones on the cover of last December's *Newsweek*) to drive down the winding lane. They were the kind of people who aren't easily turned away, and we learned a long time ago that the best place to hide is in plain sight, so Bex and I were there to welcome them to Gallagher Academy for Exceptional Young Women. Our mission: make sure they never know just *how* exceptional we really are.

The man who stepped out of the limo wore a charcoal gray suit jacket and power tie; the woman looked like the cosmetics heiress she was—not a hair or lash out of place—and I wondered if my cherry lip gloss would impress her. Judging from the scowl on her face, it didn't.

"Senator," Bex said, extending her hand toward the man, sounding as American as apple pie and loving the charade. "Welcome to the Gallagher Academy. It's an honor to have you with us today." I thought she was laying it on a little thick until Senator McHenry smiled and said, "Thank you. It's wonderful to be here," as if he didn't realize she couldn't vote.

"I'm Rebecca," Bex said. "This is Cameron." The senator glanced at me then looked quickly back to Bex, who looked like a picture-perfect model of an elite education.

"We're happy to show you and . . ." And that's when Bex and I both realized that their daughter hadn't appeared. "Is your daughter going to be . . ."

But just then, a black combat boot emerged from the limousine.

"Darling," the senator said, pointing toward the stables, "come look. They have horses."

"Oh, is *that* what I smell?" Mrs. McHenry said with a shudder. (For the record, our school smells just fine, unless of course your smelling ability has been irreparably damaged by a lifetime of sniffing perfume samples.)

But the senator glared at his wife and said, "Macey loves horses."

"No, Macey *hates* horses," Mrs. McHenry said, narrowing her eyes and glancing toward Bex and me as if to remind the senator not to contradict her in front of the help. "She fell off one and broke her arm."

I was thinking about disrupting this little display of domestic bliss to tell them both that there weren't any horses in the stables—just freaked-out seventh graders and a former French spy who had invented a way of sending coded messages in cheese, when a voice said, "Yeah, they make great glue."

Now, I don't know this for a fact, but I'm pretty sure Macey McHenry had never touched a horse in her life. Her legs were long and athletic; her clothes, though punk and rebellious, were definitely high-end, and the diamond in her nose was at least a carat and a half. Her hair might have been stark black and bluntly cut, but it was also thick and shiny, and it framed a face that belonged on the cover of a magazine.

I've seen enough TV and movies to know that if a girl like Macey McHenry can't survive high school, then someone like me would probably get eaten alive. And yet, something had driven her to our gates—making us her last resort. Or so her parents thought.

"We're . . ." I stammered, because I may be a whiz at poison-concocting, but good at public speaking—I'm not! "We're really happy to have you here."

"Then why did you keep us sitting"—Mrs. McHenry cocked her head toward the iron gates—"out there for over an hour?"

"I'm afraid that's standard protocol for people who come without appointments," Bex said in her most honor-student-y voice. "Security is a top concern here at the Gallagher Academy. If your daughter were to go here, you could expect that same level of protection."

But Mrs. McHenry's hands were on her hips when she snapped, "Don't you know who he is? Do you know—"

"We were on our way back to D.C.," the senator stepped in, cutting his wife off. "And we just couldn't resist bringing Macey by for a visit." He sent his wife a *this is our last chance, don't blow it* look as he added, "And the security is most impressive."

Bex opened the front doors and welcomed them inside, but all I could do was watch them go and think, *Senator, you have no idea.*

Bex and I got to sit in Mom's office as she went through her standard speech about the school's "history." Really, it's not all that different from the truth, just *abridged*. A lot.

"We have graduates working all over the world," Mom said, and I thought, *Yeah, as spies.* "We focus on languages, math, science, and culture. Those are the things our graduates tell us they've needed most in their lives." *As spies.* "By admitting only young women, our students develop a sense of empowerment, which enables them to be highly successful." *As spies.*

I was just starting to enjoy my little game, when Mom turned to Bex and said, "Rebecca, why don't you and Cammie show Macey around?" and I knew it was showtime.

Bex glowed, but all I could do was think about how we'd only had one half of a covert operations course, yet we were already going on a mission! How was I supposed to know how to act? Sure, if Macey wanted to conjugate Chinese verbs or break KGB codes, I was perfectly trained, but our mission was to act normally, and that's something I'm totally not qualified to do! Luckily, Bex just likes to act. Period.

"Senator," Bex said, gripping his hand, "it was an *honor* meeting you, sir. And you, too, ma'am." She smiled at Mrs. McHenry. "So glad that you both—"

"*Thank you*, Rebecca," Mom cut Bex off with her don't-overdo-it voice.

Macey stood and, with a flurry of her ultra-miniskirt,

was through the door and into the Hall of History without even a glance at her parents.

Macey was leaning against a cabinet that normally chronicled the history of the gas mask (a device on which the Gallagher Academy holds the patent, thank you very much), lighting up a cigarette, when we caught up. She took a long confident drag and then blew smoke toward a ceiling that probably held a dozen different kinds of sensors, the least of which was for smoke.

"You've got to put that out," Bex said, entering the make-sure-she-knows-she'd-be-miserable-here phase of the operation. "At the Gallagher Academy, we value personal health and safety."

Macey looked at Bex as if she'd been speaking Chinese. I had to think for a moment to make sure she hadn't.

"No smoking," I translated as I pulled an empty aluminum can from a recycling bin at the top of the stairs and held it toward her.

She took another drag and then looked at me as if to say she'd stub out her cigarette when I forced her, which I *could*, of course, but she wasn't supposed to know that. "Fine," I said, and turned to stalk off. "Your lungs."

But Bex was glaring at her and, unlike me, she actually looked capable of throwing someone off the landing; so with one last drag, our guest dropped the cigarette into the empty Diet Coke can and followed me down the stairs as a wave of girls pushed past us.

"It's lunchtime," I explained, realizing that the green

M&M had gotten together with the Tic Tac in my stomach and were trying to convince me that they would like some company. "We can go eat if you want—"

"I don't *think* so!" Macey cried with a roll of her eyes.

But stupid me jumped to say, "Really, the food here is great," which totally didn't serve our mission objective, since gross food is usually a pretty good turnoff. But our chef *is* amazing. He actually worked at the White House before this incident involving Fluffy (the First Poodle), a gastronomical chemical agent, and some very questionable cheese. Luckily, a Gallagher Girl saved poor Fluffy's life, so to show his appreciation, Chef Louis came to us and brought his awesome crème brûlée with him.

I started to mention the crème brûlée, but then Macey exclaimed, "*I* eat eight hundred calories a day."

Bex and I looked at each other, amazed. We probably burned that many calories during one session of P&E (Protection and Enforcement) class.

Macey studied us skeptically, then added, "Food is *so yesterday*."

Unfortunately, that was the last time I'd had some.

We reached the foyer, and I said, "This is the Grand Hall," because that sounded like a school tour-y thing to say, but Macey acted like I wasn't even there as she turned to Bex (her physical equal) and said, "So *everyone* wears those uniforms?"

I found this to be particularly offensive, having been on the uniform selection committee, but Bex just fingered her knee-length navy plaid skirt and matching white blouse and said, "We even wear them during gym class." Good one, I thought, taking in the horror on Macey's face as Bex stepped toward the east corridor and said, "Here we have the library—"

But Macey was heading down another hallway. "What's down here?" And just like that she was gone, passing classrooms and hidden passageways with every step. Bex and I jogged to keep up with her, throwing out pieces of made-up trivia like "That painting was a gift from the Duke of Edinburgh" or "Oh, yes, the Wizenhouse Memorial Chandelier," or my personal favorite, "This is the Washington Memorial Chalkboard." (It really is a nice chalkboard.)

Bex was in the middle of a pretty believable story about how, if a girl gets a perfect score on a test, she's allowed to watch one whole hour of television that week, when Macey plopped down in one of my favorite window seats, pulled out a cell phone, and proceeded to make a call right in front of us without so much as an excuse me. (Rude!) The joke was on her, though, since, after dialing in the number, she held the device out in front of her in bewilderment.

Bex and I glanced at each other, and then I tried to sound all sympathetic as I said, "Yeah, cell phones don't work here." *TRUE.*

"We're too far from a tower," Bex added. *FALSE.* We'd actually have great cell reception if it weren't for the monster jammer that blocks any and all foreign transmissions from campus, but Macey McHenry and her Capitol Hill father certainly didn't need to know that.

"No cell phones?" Macey said as if we'd just told her all students were required to shave their heads and live on bread and water. "That's it. I'm *so* out of here." And then she turned and stormed back toward my mother's office.

At least she *thought* that was the way to my mother's office. She was nearing the doors that lead down to the Research and Development department in the basement. I was pretty sure Dr. Fibs would have everything in Code Red form, but in the tradition of mad scientists everywhere, Dr. Fibs had a tendency to be a little, shall we say, accident prone. Sure enough, as we turned the corner, we saw Mr. Mosckowitz, who happens to be the world's foremost authority on data encryption, but he didn't look like a mega-genius just then. No. He looked like the resident alcoholic. His eyes were bloodshot and watering, his face was pale, and he was totally stumbling and slurring his words as he said, "*Hello!*"

Macey stared at him in disgust, which was actually a good thing, because that way she didn't notice the thick fog of purple smoke that was seeping beneath the stairwell doors behind him. Professor Buckingham was shoving towels in the cracks, but every time she got near the purple fog she'd start sneezing uncontrollably. She kicked the towel with her foot. Dr. Fibs appeared with a roll of duct tape and started trying to seal the cracks around the doors. (How's that for superspy technology?)

Mr. Mosckowitz kept swaying back and forth, maybe because the purple stuff had messed with his sense of balance or maybe because he was trying to block Macey's view, which would have been tough, considering he can't be an inch taller that five foot five. He said, "I understand you're a potential student."

But just then, Dr. Fibs's tall, lanky frame crashed onto the floor. He was out cold, and the purple smoke was growing thicker.

Bex and I looked at each other. *This is seriously NOT GOOD!*

Buckingham hauled Dr. Fibs into a teacher's chair and started rolling him away, but I didn't have a clue what to do. Bex grabbed Macey's arm. "Come on, Macey. I know a short—"

But Macey only wrenched her arm out of Bex's grasp and said, "Don't touch me, b———." (Yeah, that's right, she called Bex the B word.)

Now see, here's where the whole private-school thing puts a girl at a disadvantage. MTV will lead us to believe that the B word has become a term of endearment or slang among equals, but I still mainly think of it as the insult of choice for the inarticulate. So, either Macey hated us or respected us, but I looked at Bex and knew that she was betting on the former.

Bex stepped forward, shaking off her happy schoolgirl persona and putting on her superspy face.

This is SERIOUSLY not good, I thought again, just as a white shirt and khaki pants appeared in my peripheral vision.

Never again would I wonder if the only reason we thought Mr. Solomon was hot was because we'd been grading on the girls'-school curve; one look at Macey McHenry made it perfectly clear that even beyond the walls of the Gallagher Academy, Joe Solomon was gorgeous. And *she* didn't even know he was a spy (which always makes a guy hotter).

"Hello." It was the exact same thing Mr. Mosckowitz had said, but *oh* was it different. "Welcome to the Gallagher Academy. I hope you're considering joining us," he said, but I'm pretty sure Macey, Bex, and I all heard, *I think you're the most beautiful woman in the world, and I'd be honored if you'd bear my children.* (Really, truly, I think he said that.)

"Are you enjoying your tour?" he asked, but Macey just batted her eyelashes and went all seductive in a way that totally didn't go with her combat boots.

Maybe it was the cloud of purple smoke wafting toward me, but I thought I might barf.

"Do you have a second?" Mr. Solomon asked, but didn't wait for her to respond before he said, "There's something on the second floor that I'd love to show you."

He pointed her toward a circular stone staircase that had once been a fixture in the Gallagher family chapel. Stained-glass windows stood two stories tall and colored the light that landed on Mr. Solomon's white shirt as we climbed. When we reached the second floor, he held his arms out at the grand, high-ceilinged corridor that was awash in a kaleidoscope of color.

It was, in a word, beautiful, and yet I'd never really noticed it until then—there had always been classes to get to, assignments to finish. I heard Mr. Solomon's lecture again—*notice things*—and I couldn't help feeling that we'd just had our first CoveOps test. And we'd failed.

He walked us all the way to the Hall of History before turning and strolling back toward that gorgeous wall of stained glass. As Macey watched him go, she muttered, "Who was *that*?"

It was the first enthusiastic thing Macey had said since crawling out of the limo and maybe long before that—probably since realizing that her father would sell his soul for a vote and her mother was the B word as used in its traditional context.

"He's a new teacher," Bex answered.

"Yeah," Macey scoffed. "If you say so."

But Bex, who hadn't forgotten the B-word incident, wheeled around and said, "I *do* say so."

Macey reached for her pack of cigarettes but stopped short when Bex's glare hardened.

"Let me lay it out for you," Macey said, like it was some big favor. "Best-case scenario: all the girls go ga-ga for him and lose focus, which I'm sure is very important at the *Gallagher Academy*," she said with mock reverence. "Worst-case scenario: he's an inappropriate-conduct case looking for a place to happen." I had to admit that, so far, Macey the B word was making some sense. "The only people who teach at these places are freaks and geeks. And when you've got a headmistress who looks like that"—she pointed to my mom in all her hotness, who stood talking to the McHenrys thirty feet away—"it's easy to see what Mr. Eyecandy was hired for."

"What?" I asked, not understanding.

"You're the *Gallagher Girl*," she mocked again. "If you can't figure that out, then who am *I* to tell you."

I thought about my mother—my beautiful mother, who had recently been winked at by my sexy CoveOps teacher, and I thought I would never eat again.

Chapter Four

There are many excellent things about having three girls sharing a four-girl suite. The first, obviously, is closet space—followed by shelf space, followed by the fact that we had an entire corner of the room devoted to beanbag chairs. It was a very sweet setup (if you'll pardon the pun), but I don't think any of us really appreciated what we had until two guys from the maintenance department knocked on our door and asked where we wanted the extra bed.

Now, in addition to our teachers and our chef, the Gallagher Academy has a pretty extensive staff, but it's not the kind of place that advertises in the want ads (well . . . you know . . . except for coded messages). There are two types of people who come here—students looking to get into the AlphaNet (CIA, FBI, NSA, etc.), and staff members looking to get out. So when two men built like refrigerators show up with long metal poles and vise grips, it's fairly likely that those have been the tools of their trade for a while now—just in a *very different* context.

That's why we didn't ask any questions that night. We just pointed to a corner and then the three of us made a bee-line for the second floor.

"Come in, girls," my mother yelled as soon as we entered the Hall of History—long before she could have seen us. Even though I'd grown up with her, sometimes her superspy instincts scared me. She walked to the door. "I've been expecting you."

I'd been working on a doozy of a speech, let me tell you, but as soon as I saw my mother silhouetted in the door frame I forgot it. Luckily, Bex never has that problem.

"Excuse me, ma'am," she said, "but do you know why the maintenance department has delivered an extra bed to our room?"

Anyone else asking that question in that tone might have seen the wrath of Rachel Morgan, but all my mom did was cross her arms and match Bex's scholarly inflections.

"Why, yes, Rebecca. I do know."

"Is that information you can share with us, ma'am? Or is it need-to-know?" (If anyone had a need—it was us. We were the ones losing our beanbag corner over the deal!)

But Mom just took a step and gestured for us to follow. "Let's take a walk."

Something was wrong, I realized. It had to be, so I was on her heels, following her down the grand staircase, saying, "What? Is it blackmail? Does the senator have something on—"

"Cameron," Mom said, trying to cut me off.

"Is he on the House Armed Services Committee? Is it a funding thing, because we could start charging tuition, you—"

"Cammie, just walk," Mom commanded.

I did as I was told, but I still didn't shut up. "She won't last. We can get rid of—"

"Cameron Ann Morgan," Mom said, playing the middle-name card that all moms keep in their back pockets for just such an occasion. "That's enough." I froze as she handed the large manila envelope she'd been carrying to Bex and said, "Those are your new roommate's test scores."

Okay, I'll admit it—they were good. Not *Liz*-good, or anything, but they were far better than Macey McHenry's 2.0 GPA would indicate.

We turned down an old stone corridor, our feet echoing through the cold hall.

"So she tests well," I said. "So—"

Mom stopped short, and all three of us nearly ran into her. "I don't run decisions past you, do I, Cammie?" Shame started brewing inside me, but Mom had already shifted her attention toward Bex. "And I do make controversial decisions from time to time, *don't I, Rebecca?*" At this, we all remembered how Bex came to us, and even she shut up. "And, Liz." Mom shifted her gaze one last time. "Do *you* think we should only admit girls who come from spy families?"

That was it—she had us.

Mom crossed her arms and said, "Macey McHenry will bring a much-needed level of diversity to the Gallagher

Academy. She has family connections that will allow en.
into some very closed societies. She has an underutilized
intellect. And . . ." Mom seemed to be pondering this next
bit. ". . . she has a *quality* about her."

Quality? Yeah, right. Snobbery is a quality, so is elitism,
fascism, and anorexicism. I started to tell my mom about the
eight-hundred-calorie-a-day thing, or the B-word thing, or to
point out that Code Reds were fake interviews, not real ones.
But then I looked at the woman who had raised me and who,
rumor has it, once sweet-talked a Russian dignitary into
dressing in drag and carrying a beach ball full of liquid nitro-
gen under his shirt like a pregnant lady, and I knew I was
sufficiently outgunned, even with Bex and Liz beside me.

"And if that isn't enough for you . . ." Mom turned to
look at an old velvet tapestry that hung in the center of the
long stone wall.

Of course I'd seen it before. If a girl wanted to stand
there long enough, she could trace the Gallagher family tree
that branched across the tapestry through nine generations
before Gilly, and two generations after. If a girl had better
things to do, she could reach behind the tapestry, to the
Gallagher family crest imbedded in the stone, and turn the
little sword around, then slip through the secret door that
pops open. (Let's just say I'm the second type of girl.)

"What does this have to do with . . ." I started, but Liz's
"Oh my gosh" cut me off.

I followed my friend's thin finger to the line at the bottom of the tapestry. I'd never known that Gilly had gotten

married. I'd never known she'd had a child. I'd never dreamed that child's last name was "McHenry."

And all this time I thought *I* was a Gallagher legacy.

"If Macey McHenry wants to come here," Mom said, "we'll find a place for her."

She turned and started to leave, but Liz called after her, "But, ma'am, how's she gonna . . . you know . . . catch up?"

Mom considered this to be a fair question, because she folded her hands and said, "I admit that, academically, Ms. McHenry will be behind the rest of the sophomore class. For that reason, she will be taking many of her courses with our younger students."

Bex grinned at me, but even the thought of Macey's supermodel legs stretching her high above a class full of newbies couldn't change the fact that two guys with bald heads (that may or may not have prices on them) were at that very moment making room for her in our suite. The question on my mother's face was whether we would make room for her in our lives.

I looked at my best friends, knowing that our mission, should we choose to accept it, was to befriend Macey McHenry. The good girl inside of me knew that I should at least *try* to help her fit in. The spy in me knew I'd been given an assignment, and if I ever wanted to see Sublevel Two, I'd better grin and say "Yes, ma'am." The daughter in me knew there wasn't any choosing involved here.

"When does she start?" I asked.

"Monday."

That Sunday night I met Mom in her office for Tater Tots and chicken nuggets. We had one hard-and-fast rule about Sunday night suppers—Mom had to make them herself, which is nice and all, but not exactly good for my digestion. (Dad always said the most lethal thing about her was her cooking.) Directly beneath us, my friends were dining on the finest foods a five-star chef could offer, but as my mom walked around in an old sweatshirt of my dad's, looking like a teenager herself, I wouldn't have traded places with them for all the crème brûlée in the world.

When I first came to the Gallagher Academy, I felt guilty about being able to see my mother every day when my classmates had to go months on end without their parents. Eventually, I stopped feeling bad about it. After all, Mom and I don't have summers together. But mostly, we don't have Dad.

"So how's school?" She always asked as if she didn't know—and maybe she didn't. Maybe, just like every good operative, she wanted to hear all sides of the story before making up her mind.

I dipped a Tater Tot in some honey mustard dressing and said, "Fine."

"How's CoveOps?" the mother asked, but I knew the headmistress was in there somewhere, and she wanted to know if her newest staff member was making the grade.

"He knows about Dad."

I don't know where the sentence came from or why I spoke it. I'd spent six days dreading Macey McHenry's arrival into our little society, but *that* was what I said when I finally had my mother alone? I studied her, wishing Mr. Solomon would have covered *Reading Body Language* that week instead of *Basic Surveillance*.

"There are people in this world, Cam—people like Mr. Solomon—who are going to know what happened to him. It's their *job* to know what happened. I hope someday you'll get used to the look in people's eyes as they put two and two together and try to decide whether or not to mention it. Am I right to assume Mr. Solomon mentioned it?"

"Kinda."

"And how did you handle it?"

I hadn't yelled, and I hadn't cried, so I told my mother, "Okay, I guess."

"Good." She smoothed my hair, and I wondered for the millionth time if she had one set of hands for work and another for moments like this. I imagined her keeping them in a briefcase and swapping them out, silk for steel. Dr. Fibs could have made them—but he didn't.

"I'm proud of you, kiddo," she said simply. "It'll get easier."

My mom's the best spy I know—so I believed her.

When we woke up the next morning, I remembered that it was Monday. I forgot that it was *The* Monday. That's why I stopped cold on my way into breakfast when I heard Buckingham's powerful "Cameron Morgan!" echo through the foyer. "I'll need you and Ms. Baxter and Ms. Sutton to follow me, please." Bex and Liz looked as lost as I felt, until Buckingham explained, "Your new roommate has arrived."

Buckingham *was* pretty old, and we *did* have her outnumbered three-to-one, but still I didn't see many alternatives. We followed her up the stairs.

I thought it would just be Mom and Macey in her office—Macey's parents having already been sent away in the limo if they'd bothered coming at all (which they hadn't)—but when Buckingham threw open the door I saw Mr. Solomon and Jessica Boden sharing the leather couch. He looked so completely bored I almost felt sorry for him, and Jessica was perched eagerly on the edge of the sofa.

The guest of honor was seated across the desk from my mother, wearing an official uniform but looking like a supermodel. She didn't even turn around when we walked in.

"As I was saying, Macey," my mom said, once Liz, Bex, and I had positioned ourselves in the window seat at the far side of the room while Buckingham stood at attention in front of the bookshelves, "I hope you'll be happy here at the Gallagher Academy."

"Humph!"

Yeah, I know *heiress* isn't one of the languages I speak, but I'm pretty sure that translates into *Tell it to someone who cares because I've heard it all before, and you're only saying that because my father wrote you an enormous check.* (But that's just a guess.)

"Well, Macey," an utterly repulsive voice chimed. I'm not sure why I hate Jessica Boden, but I'm pretty sure it has something to do with the fact that her posture is way too up-and-down, and I don't trust someone who doesn't know how to properly slouch. "When the trustees heard about your admittance, my mother—"

"Thank you, Jessica." *How much do I love my mother? Very much.* Mom opened a thick file that lay on her desk. "Macey, I see here that you spent a semester at the Triad Academy?"

"Yeah," Macey said. (Now, *there's* a girl who knows how to slouch.)

"And then a full year at Wellington House. Two months at Ingalls. *Ooh*, just a week at the Wilder Institute."

"Do you have a point?" Macey asked, her tone just as sharp as the letter opener-slash-dagger that Joe Solomon had been absentmindedly fingering while they spoke.

"You've seen a lot of different schools, Macey—"

"I wouldn't say there was anything *different* about them," she shot back.

But no sooner had the words left her mouth than the letter-opening dagger went slicing through the air, no more than a foot away from her glossy hair, flying from Mr. Solomon's hand directly toward Buckingham's head. It all happened so fast—like blink-or-you'll-miss-it fast. One second Macey was talking about how all prep schools are the same, and the next, Patricia Buckingham was grabbing a copy of *War and Peace* from the bookshelf behind her and holding it inches from her face just as the dagger pierced its leather cover.

For a long time, the only sound was the subtle vibration of the letter opener as it stuck out of the book, humming like a tuning fork looking for middle C. Then my mom leaned onto her desk and said, "I think you'll find there are some things we teach that your other schools haven't offered."

"What . . ." Macey stammered. "What . . . What . . . Are you crazy?"

That's when my mom went through the school history again—the *unabridged* version—starting with Gilly and then hitting highlights like how it was Gallagher Girls giving each other manicures who had figured out the whole no-two-fingerprints-alike thing, and a few of our more highly profitable creations. (Duct tape didn't invent itself, you know.)

When Mom finished, Bex said, "Welcome to spy school," in her real accent instead of the geographically neutral drawl, which is all Macey had heard until then, and I could tell she was about to go into serious information overload, which, of course, wasn't helped by Jessica.

"Macey, I know this is going to come as a big adjustment to you, but that's why my mother—she's a Gallagher Trustee—has encouraged me to help you through this—"

"Thank you, Jessica," Mom said, cutting her off yet again. "Perhaps I can make things a little more clear." Mom reached into her pocket and pulled out what looked like an ordinary silver compact. She flipped up the lid and touched her forefinger to mirror inside. I saw the small light scan her fingerprint, and when she snapped the compact closed, the world around Macey McHenry shifted as the whole Code

Red process went into reverse. The bookshelves had been facing wrong-way-out for a week, but now they were spinning around to show their true side. Disney World disappeared in the photo on Mom's desk; and Liz broke out her Portuguese long enough to say, *"Sera que ela vai vomitar?"* But I had to shake my head in response because I honestly didn't know whether or not Macey was going to throw up.

When everything stopped spinning (literally) Macey was surrounded by more than a hundred years of covert secrets, but she wasn't stopping to take it all in. Instead, she screamed, "You people are psycho!" and bolted for the door. Unfortunately, Joe Solomon was one step ahead of her. "Get out of my way!" she snapped.

"Sorry," he said coolly. "I don't believe the headmistress is finished quite yet."

"Macey." My mom's voice was calm and full of reason. "I know this must come as quite a shock to you. But we're really just a school for exceptional young women. Our classes are hard. Our curriculum unique. But you may use what you learn here anywhere in the world. In any way you see fit." Mom's eyes narrowed. Her voice hardened as she said, *"If* you stay."

When Mom stepped forward, I knew she wasn't talking as an administrator anymore; she was talking as a mother. "If you want to leave, Macey, we can make you forget this ever happened. When you wake up tomorrow, this will be a dream you don't remember, and you'll have one more dismal school experience on your record. But no matter your decision, there is only one thing you have to understand."

Mom was moving closer, and Macey snapped, "What?"

"*No one* will *ever* know what you have seen and heard here today." Macey was still staring daggers, but my mom didn't have a copy of *War and Peace* handy, so she reached for the next best thing. "Especially your parents."

And just when I'd thought I'd never see Macey McHenry smile . . .

Chapter five

By the third week of school, my backpack was heavier than me (well, maybe not me, but probably Liz), I had a mountain of homework, and the sign above the Grand Hall was announcing that we'd all better dust off our French if we intended to make small talk over lunch. Plus, it was almost a full-time job keeping rumors separated from facts. (No big surprise who the rumors were all about.)

Macey McHenry had gotten kicked out of her last school because she was pregnant with the headmaster's baby. RUMOR. At her first P&E class, Macey kicked a seventh grader so hard she was out cold for an hour. FACT. (And also the reason Macey's now taking P&E with the eighth graders.) Macey told a seventh grader that her glasses make her face look fat, a senior that her hair looks like a wig (which it *is*, thanks to a very unfortunate plutonium incident), and Professor Buckingham that she really should try control-top panty hose. FACT. FACT. FACT.

As we walked between Madame Dabney's tea room and the elevator to Sublevel One, Tina Walters told me for about the tenth time, "Cammie, you don't even have to steal the file. . . . Just take a little—"

"Tina!" I snapped, then whispered because a crowded hallway full of future spies isn't the best place to have a covert conversation, "I'm not going to steal Macey's permanent record just to see if she really set the gym on fire at her last school."

"*Borrow*," Tina reminded me. "*Borrow* the permanent record. Just a peek."

"No!" I said again, just as we turned into the small, dark corridor. I saw Liz standing there, staring into the mirror that concealed the elevator as if she didn't recognize her own reflection. "What's wrong with . . ." Then I saw the little slip of yellow paper. "What? Is it out of order or—"

And then I *read* the little slip of yellow paper.

SOPHOMORE C.O. CLASS CANCELED.
MEET OUTSIDE TONIGHT. 7:00.
DON'T WEAR YOUR UNIFORMS!
                              —SOLOMON

Bex's reflection appeared beside mine, and our eyes locked. I started to rip the note from the mirror, to save it as a piece of Gallagher Academy history, because two things were extraordinary about it. First, I'd never even *heard* of a class being canceled, much less witnessed it myself. Second,

Joe Solomon had just invited fourteen girls to go on what amounted to a moonlight stroll.

Things were about to get interesting.

I've seen Liz freak out about assignments before, but that day at lunch, she was as white as the salt in the shaker as she went over every tiny, perfectly punctuated line of her CoveOps notes—stopping occasionally to cinch her eyes together as if she were trying to read the answers on the top of her head. (Maybe she was. With Liz's head, *anything* is possible.)

"Liz, *est-ce qu'il-y-a une épreuve de CoveOps dont je ne connais pas?*" I asked, thinking that if there was a CoveOps test I didn't know about, someone should really bring me into the loop. But Liz thought I was trying to be funny.

"*Tu ne la considéras pas sérieuse?*" she nearly yelled. "*Tu sais qu'est-ce qui se passe ce soir!*"

Of course I *was* taking it seriously, but Liz wasn't about to believe that, so I abandoned our French assignment and whispered, "No, Liz, I *don't* know what's going to happen tonight."

"*Exactement!*" she cried, leaning closer. "Anything in these books could be *out there!*" she said, as if we were dropping into an actual war zone and not our own backyard. "Or it could be something"—she looked around and then leaned closer—"*not in the books!*"

I seriously thought she might throw up, especially when Bex leaned over and said, "I bet we're going to bust up a drug cartel that's operating out of a nightclub." (Because she saw that once on an episode of *Alias*.)

Liz gulped, and her knuckles went white as she gripped a flash card. "It won't be anything like that, Liz," I whispered. But by this time the entire sophomore class was staring.

"Why?" Tina demanded. "What do you know? Did your mother tell you something?"

"No!" I said, wishing I hadn't gotten them started. "I don't know anything."

"So Solomon didn't ask your mother for two helicopters, three stun guns, and a dozen Brazilian passports?"

But before I could respond to Tina's ridiculous question, the main doors opened, and the seventh-grade class came in, doing a lot of *bon jour*ing—"hello" being one of the few phrases they knew—and the sophomore class forgot about me and went back to doing what it had been doing for a week—watching Macey McHenry.

She was the first person to ever combine black fingernail polish with a Peter Pan–collared white blouse (that's not verified or anything—just a guess), and her diamond nose ring looked like a twenty-thousand-dollar zit, but to an outsider, Macey McHenry might have seemed like one of us. She walked through the Grand Hall like she owned the place (as usual), picked up a plain green salad with no dressing (as usual), and walked to our table. Then she plopped down next to Bex and said, "The munchkins annoy," which was totally *not* usual.

Up to that point, I'd mainly heard Macey say things like

"You're in my light," and "If you're gonna have plastic surgery, you might want to try my mother's guy in Palm Springs." (Needless to say, Mr. Smith didn't write down the number.) But there she was, sitting with us, talking with us. Acting like one of us!

Liz said, *"Je me demande pourquoi elle a décidé a parler à nous aujourd'hui. Comme c'est bizarre!"* But I didn't know why Macey was feeling so talkative, either.

Before I could respond, Macey turned to Liz and snapped, "I don't want to talk to you either, freak."

I was just starting to process the fact that even cosmetic heiresses who get kicked out of a lot of private schools speak pretty good French, when Macey leaned closer to Liz, who leaned away.

"Tell me," Macey said in the worst imitation Southern accent I've ever heard, "how can someone who's supposed to be so smart sound so stupid?"

Liz's pale face turned instantly red as tears came to the corners of her eyes. Before I knew what was happening, Bex had flown from her seat, pinned Macey's right arm behind her back with one hand, and grabbed that diamond nose ring with the other so fast that I said a quick prayer of thanks that the British are on our side (well, assuming we never revisit the Revolutionary War).

"I know you're three years late, but let me give you a real quick, important lesson," Bex said in English (probably because it's harder to sound scary in French). But the strangest thing was happening—Macey was smiling—almost laughing, and Bex totally didn't know what to do.

The rest of the hall was going slowly quiet, as if someone somewhere was turning the volume down. By the time the teachers stopped talking, Bex still had ahold of Macey, I had leaned across the table to grab ahold of Bex, and Liz had a death grip on a flash card that listed the top five places you should go to look for black market explosives in St. Petersburg.

"Rebecca," said a male voice. I turned away from the tight-lipped smirk that was spreading across Macey's face to see Joe Solomon standing behind me, speaking across the table to Bex, who was slowly allowing blood to creep back into Macey's arm. "I understand you could get into trouble for that," he said.

It's true. Gallagher Girls don't fight in the hallways. We don't slap and we don't shove. But mostly, we don't use the skills of the sisterhood against the sisters. Ever. It's a testament to how universally despised and viewed as an outsider Macey was that Bex wasn't immediately jumped from ten directions. But Mr. Solomon was an outsider, too. Maybe that's why he said, "If you're so eager to show off, you and your friends can take point tonight." He looked at Liz and me. "Good luck."

It wasn't a cheery, break-a-leg "good luck," though. It was a watch-out-or-you'll-have-your-legs-broken "good luck."

Liz went back to her flash cards, but Bex and I stared at each other across the table as our faces morphed from sheer terror to uncontrolled excitement. For Gallagher Girls, leading a mission is no punishment—that's the gold-freaking-star! Only a little of the dread lingered in the back of my mind as I realized that we were about to play with live ammo— maybe in both the literal and figurative senses of the word.

Macey returned to her salad while Mr. Solomon added, *"Et n'oubliez pas, mesdemoiselles, ce soir vous êtes des civils— ressemblez-y."*

Oh, yeah, just what I needed—fashion advice from Joe Solomon himself. The Grand Hall went back to normal, but I doubt that any of the sophomores, besides Macey, took another bite. As if we hadn't known it before, Joe Solomon had just reminded us that we'd soon be venturing out from behind our comfortable walls, operating on our own for the first time in our superspy lives.

Four years of training had all come down to this, and I for one didn't have a thing to wear.

I'm not sure how it happened, but at some point between one P.M. and six forty-five, the sophomore class from the Gallagher Academy for Exceptional Young Women morphed from a group of spies-in-training into a bunch of teenage girls. It was pretty scary.

Liz spent her afternoon becoming the textbook version of what an undercover operative should look like, copying everything from the patent leather purse to the pillbox hat. (It was a pretty old textbook.) Then the hallways started reverberating with terrifying yells of "Have you seen my black boots?" and "Does anyone have any hair spray?"

I was seriously starting to worry about the fate of national security. In our suite, Bex looked awesome (as usual), Liz looked ridiculous (but try telling her that), and Macey was looking at an old *Cosmo* as if determining whether green is the new black was a matter of life or death. All I could do was sit on my bed in my old jeans and a black knit top my mom once wore to parachute onto the top of the Iranian Embassy, and watch the clock tick down.

But then Tina came busting into our room. "Which one?" she asked, holding a pair of black leather pants and short skirt in front of her. I was on the verge of saying, *neither*, when Eva Alvarez ran in.

"Do these go? I don't know if these go!" Eva held up a pair of high-heeled boots that made my feet hurt just by *looking* at them.

"Um, Eva, can you run in those?" I asked.

But before Eva could answer, I heard someone say, "They're all the rage in Milan." I looked around. I counted heads. And then it dawned on me who was speaking. Macey stared at us over the top of her magazine, and added, "If you want to know."

Within minutes, half the sophomore class was in our little suite, and Macey was telling Tina, "You know, lip liner is supposed to go *on* the lips," and Tina was actually listening! I mean, this is the same girl who had single-handedly started the Macey-is-Mr. Smith's-illegitimate-daughter rumor. Little did we know she was one fashion emergency away from turning to the enemy!

Courtney was borrowing earrings; Anna was trying on jackets; and I wasn't sure if I would ever feel safe going into hostile territory with any of them ever again.

"You know, Eva, what blends in Milan might stick out in Roseville," I tried, but she didn't care.

"You know, guys, hiding in plain sight requires looking plain!" I said, but Kim Lee was wriggling out of a halter top and nearly knocked my head off with her flailing arms.

"You know, I really don't think he's taking us to the prom!" I shouted, and Anna put Macey's gorgeous formal gown back into the closet.

I'm the chameleon! I wanted to cry. *I'm the CoveOps legacy!* I'd been preparing for this night my entire life—doing drills with my dad, asking my mom to tell me stories, becoming the girl nobody sees. But now I was drifting deeper and deeper into the shadows until I was standing in the middle of my own room, watching my closest friends swarm around our gorgeous new guest, and I was completely invisible.

"Lose the earrings," Macey said, pointing to Eva. "Tuck in the shirt," she told Anna, then turned to Courtney Bauer and said, "What *died* in your hair?" (Courtney does have a tendency to over-gel sometimes.)

Bex was sitting with Liz on her bed, and they both looked as amazed as I felt.

"Hey!" I cried again, to no avail, so I called upon my superspy heritage, and seconds later I was whistling loudly enough to make the cows come home (literally—that's why Grandpa Morgan taught me how to do it).

My classmates finally turned away from Macey, and I said, "It's time."

A silence had fallen over the room, but then a longer, deeper quiet stretched out.

We were through playing dress-up, and everyone knew it.

"Hello, ladies."

The words were right, but the voice coming to us through the shadows was wrong in so many ways that I can't possibly describe it here. Really, it would be cruel to all the trees who would have to give their lives for me to explain what it was like to be expecting Joe Solomon and get Mr. Mosckowitz.

"Don't you all look very . . ." He was staring, mouth gaping, as if he'd never seen push-up bras or eyeliner before. ". . . nice," he finally said, then slapped his hands together, I guess to stop the nervous shaking. But he still couldn't steady his voice as he said, "Well, very big night. Very big. For . . ." He hesitated. ". . . all of us."

Mr. Mosckowitz pushed his glasses up the bridge of his nose and stared beyond the lighted driveway of the mansion. Even *I* didn't know exactly what lay in that dark abyss. Sure, there are woods and jogging trails and a lacrosse field that is handy during Code Reds (and doubles as a great underground storage facility for the helicopters), but everyone knows the Gallagher Woods are a minefield—maybe literally—and I started shaking in my sensible shoes.

What if there are snipers? Or attack dogs . . . or . . . but before I could finish that thought, I heard crunching gravel and squealing tires, and turned around to see an Overnight Express truck roaring toward us. Gee, what's the package emergency? I wondered. But when the driver's-side door flew open and Mr. Solomon jumped out and yelled, "Get in!" I realized *we* were the package.

Instantly, my mind flashed back to one of Liz's note cards. COVERT OPERATION RULE #1: DON'T HESITATE. Mr. Mosckowitz opened the cargo doors and I climbed inside, imagining that the truck was like our teachers—it had led a fascinating and dangerous life before it retired and came to us. But I didn't see a wall of monitors and headsets—none of the stuff the trucks have in movies—only crates and crates of packages. That's when the truck became even cooler, because I'm pretty sure Mr. Solomon had stolen it!

"First rule," he warned as we settled inside, "don't touch any of the packages."

Then Mr. Solomon crawled in behind us, leaving Mr. Mosckowitz outside looking up at him like a water boy who'd just been asked to hold the star quarterback's helmet.

"Harvey?" Mr. Solomon said impatiently but still soft enough that he sounded like a pretty nice guy, "clock's ticking." He tossed Mr. Moskowitz the keys.

"Oh!" This seemed to wake him up. "Yep. Sure thing. I'll see you"—he pointed toward all of us—"out there."

"No, you won't, Harvey," Mr. Solomon said. "That's the idea."

Call me crazy, but this wasn't how I'd always pictured the first time I'd be in the dark with a guy who looks like Joe Solomon. (And I'm pretty sure I speak for the entire sophomore class on that one.)

"Operatives in deep cover will be given false histories," he fired at us through the dark. "These histories, including names, dates of birth, and favorite kindergarten teachers, and are called . . ."

"Legends!" Liz blurted. A test is a test, in Liz's mind, and as long as there was a Q&A, she could handle this mission business.

"Very good, Ms. Sutton," he said, and even in the dark I knew Liz was a number two lead pencil away from heaven. "For this mission, ladies, you will be posing as normal teenage girls. Think you can handle that?"

I'm not sure, but I think that might have been Joe Solomon's idea of a joke—but it was *soooo* not funny because, if there's one thing we're not, it's normal. But he obviously didn't care about any of that, because he just plowed on. "When conducting manual surveillance on a subject in a three-man rotation, the person with visual contact is the . . ."

"Eyeball!"

"Correct. The person within sight of the eyeball is the . . ."

"Backup."

"And the final person . . ."

"The reserve."

"Very good. Now remember, rotate frequently, but not too frequently. Vary your pace and spacing, and above all . . ."

I felt the truck come to a stop. The engine turned off.

Above all, what? I wanted to cry. *The most important night of my life, and he forgets the punch line!* A small light came on in the ceiling of the truck, bathing us in an eerie, orange-yellow glow, and I heard music, the kind a merry-go-round makes, and I wondered if my whole life from that point on would be a house of mirrors.

Mr. Solomon moved a television monitor to one of the shelves and fiddled with some wires. I was expecting a view of the world outside (or at least something from the WB), but instead I saw what I'd been seeing for years—the fourteen faces of the sophomore class.

"In the field, ladies, you can never expect to have things go as planned. I fully expect you to master the ability to improvise. For example, tonight's mission requires a vehicle not owned by the Gallagher Academy. So"—he motioned around us—"I made alternative arrangements." (Yep. He *definitely* stole it!)

He passed earpieces to Bex, Liz, and me, and said, "Basic comms units. Don't be afraid to use them." Then he showed us a pair of tortoiseshell eyeglasses, an I ❤ Roseville button, and a necklace with a silver cross. "There are cameras contained within these three items, which will allow us to follow and critique your progress." The cross swung from his forefinger and, on the screen, the image of my classmates swayed back and forth. *"These* are for *our* benefit tonight—not yours. It's a just teaching exercise, ladies, but don't expect us to come to your rescue."

Okay, I'll admit it. I was starting to get a little freaked out at that point, but seriously, who can blame me? We were all feeling it—I could tell by the way Bex's leg twitched and Liz kept wringing her hands. Every girl in the back of that truck was on edge (and not just because we were up close and personal with Mr. Solomon, either). Even though Liz, Bex, and I were the only ones going outside, we were all more than Gallagher Girls right then—we were operatives on a mission, and we knew there would come a day when way more than grades would be riding on what we were about to learn.

The carnival music suddenly got louder as the back door opened, and the first thing I saw was a bright orange cap as Mr. Mosckowitz peeked in. "They're close," he said.

Mr. Solomon plugged a wire into a speaker, and in the next second I heard my mother's voice joining the carnival music. "It's great weather for running."

My blood went cold. *Anyone but Mom,* I prayed. *Anyone but Mom.*

You know the phrase *Be careful what you wish for?* Oh yeah, I'm now a really big believer in that one, because no sooner had the words crossed my mind than Mr. Solomon turned to us and said, "There are three types of subjects who will always be the most difficult to surveil." He ticked them off on his fingers. "People who are trained. People who suspect they may be followed. And people you know." He paused. "Ladies, this is your lucky night." He pulled a black-and-white photo from the pocket of his jacket and held it up. The face was new to us, but the voice that came blaring through the speaker saying, "Yes. I should probably get back into that habit myself," was one we knew well.

"Oh, bollocks!" Bex exclaimed, and Liz dropped her note cards.

"Smith!" I cried. "You expect us to recon Professor Smith?"

I couldn't believe it! Not only was it our first mission ever, but he honestly expected us to tail a man who had thirty years of experience, and who had seen us every school day since seventh grade, and who, worst of all, was the single most paranoid human being on the planet! (Seriously. I mean, he's got the plastic surgery bills to prove it.)

A team of CIA all-stars would probably get made within twenty minutes. Three Gallagher Girls didn't stand a chance. After all, once a guy's heard you give a report on the trade routes of Northern Africa, he's probably gonna wonder why you're sitting behind him on the merry-go-round!

"But . . . but . . . but . . . he never leaves the grounds," I protested, finally finding my words. "He would never enter an unsecured area on a whim." Oooh, good one, I thought, as I struggled to recall Liz's flash cards. "This goes against the subject's pattern of behavior!"

But Mr. Solomon only smiled. He knew it was an impossible mission—that was why he'd given it to us. "Trust me, ladies," he said with somber respect, "*no one* knows Mr. Smith's patterns of behavior." He tossed a thick file folder toward us. "The one thing we do know is that tonight is the Roseville town carnival, and Mr. Smith, for good or bad, is a man who loves his funnel cakes."

"Well, have fun!" My mother's voice came blaring through the speakers. I imagined her waving at her colleague as he turned at the edge of town. I heard her breathing become deeper, almost felt her cross trainers as they struck the dark pavement.

"Your mission," Mr. Solomon said, "is to find out what he drinks with those funnel cakes."

I'd been waiting my whole life for my first mission and it all came down to what? Carbonated beverages?!

"Subject's at the firehouse, Wise Guy," Mom whispered. "He's all yours." And then, just like that, my mother and her watchful eyes were gone, leaving us alone in the dark with Joe "Wise Guy" Solomon and a mathematician in a bright orange cap.

Mr. Solomon thrust the necklace toward me and said, "In or out?"

I grabbed the cross, knowing I would need it.

Chapter Six

I love Bex and Liz. Seriously, I do. But when your mission is to go unnoticed at the Roseville town carnival while trailing an operative who's as good as Mr. Smith, a genius in Jackie O shades and a girl who could totally be Miss America (even though she's British) are not exactly what I'd call ideal backup.

"I have eyeball," Bex said, as I lurked across the town square by the dunking booth. Every minute or so, I'd hear a splash and applause behind me. People kept walking by carrying corn dogs and caramel apples—lots of calories on sticks—and I suddenly remembered that while our chef makes an awesome crème brûlée, his corn dogs really do leave something to be desired.

So I bought one—a corn dog, that is. Now, here's where you might start thinking—Hey, who is she to eat during a mission? Or, isn't it careless to stand there smearing mustard all over a deep-fried weenie when there are operatives to tail?

But that's the thing about being a pavement artist (a term first used to describe me when I was nine and successfully tailed my father through the mall to find out what he was going to buy me for Christmas), you can't be ducking behind Dumpsters and dodging into doorways all the time. Seriously, how covert is that? Real pavement artists don't hide—they blend. So when you start craving a corn dog because every third person you see is eating one, then bring on the mustard! (Besides, even spies have to eat.)

Bex was on the far side of the square, milling around outside the library while the Pride of Roseville marching band warmed up. Liz was supposed to be behind me, but I couldn't see her. (Please tell me she didn't bring her molecular regeneration homework. . . .) Mr. Smith was probably thirty feet in front of Bex, being Joe Ordinary, which was totally creeping me out. Every few moments I'd catch a flash of his black jacket as he strolled along the streets, looking like a soccer dad who was worried about the mortgage, and I remembered that of all the false facades at the Gallagher Academy, the best belonged to its people.

"How you doing up there, Duchess?" I asked, and Bex shot back, "I hate that bloody code name."

"Okay, Princess," I said.

"Cam—" Bex started, but before she could finish her threat, I heard Liz's voice in my ear.

"Chameleon, where are you?" Liz complained. "I lost you again."

"I'm over by the dunk tank, Bookworm."

"Wave your arms or something." I could almost hear Liz standing on tiptoes, peering through the crowd.

"That kind of defeats the purpose now, doesn't it?" Bex noted.

"But how am I supposed to follow you, following Smith if I can't— Oh, never mind," Liz said. "I see you."

I looked around and thought, Oh, yeah, I can see why I'd be tough to spot. I was sitting on a bench in plain sight. Seriously. I couldn't have been more out in the open if I'd had a big neon sign over my head. But that's the thing most people don't get about surveillance. No one—not even one of my best friends—was going to look twice at an ordinary-looking girl in last year's clothes sitting on a park bench eating a corn dog. If you can be still enough, and common enough, then it's really easy to be invisible.

"He's flipping," Bex said softly, and I knew it was show-time. Roseville might look like Mayberry, but Professor Smith wasn't taking any chances. He was doubling back, so I got off my bench and eased toward the sidewalk, knowing Smith was heading toward me on the opposite side of the square, past Bex, who managed to duck her head and act nonchalant. That's when a lot of people would have lost it. An amateur would have looked at her watch and spun around as if she'd just remembered some place she needed to be, but not Bex—she just kept walking.

Half the town must have turned out for the carnival, so there was lots of pedestrian cover on the sidewalk between Mr. Smith and me (a very good thing). People don't see *things* nearly as quickly as they see *motion*, so when Professor Smith turned, I stayed perfectly still. When he moved, I waited five seconds, then followed. But mostly, I remembered what my dad always said about how a tail isn't a string—it's a rubber band, stretching back and forth, in and out, moving independently of The Subject. When something interested me, I stopped. When someone said something funny, I laughed. When I passed an ice-cream stand, I bought some, all the while keeping Mr. Smith at the edge of my vision.

But that's not to say it was easy. No way. In all the times I'd imagined my first mission, I'd always thought I'd be retrieving top secret files or something. Never once did I imagine that I'd be asked to tail my COW professor through a carnival and find out what he drinks with his funnel cakes. The crazy thing was that this was *SO MUCH HARDER!* Professor Smith was acting as if those KGB hitmen were already on their way to Roseville—using every countersurveillance technique in the book (or at least the books I've seen), and I realized how exhausting it must be to be him. He couldn't even go out for funnel cakes without "flipping" and "corner clearing" and "breadcrumbing" all the time.

Once, things got really toasty, and I thought for sure he was going to make me, but I fell in behind a group of little old women. But then one of the women stumbled at the curb, and, instinctively, I reached out to help her. Ahead of us, Professor Smith stopped in front of a darkened storefront, staring at the reflection in the glass, but I was twenty feet behind him and shrouded by a sea of gray hair and poly-ester—which was a good thing. But then the women all turned to face me—which was a bad thing.

"Thank you, young lady," the older woman said. She squinted at me. *"Do I know you?"*

But just then, a voice blared in my ear. "Did we rotate?" Liz sounded close to panic. "Did we rotate the eyeball?"

Professor Smith was getting away, heading back in Bex's direction, so I answered, "Yes," but that only made the woman cock her eyebrow and stare harder.

"I don't remember seeing you before," the old woman said.

"Sure you do, Betty," one of the other women said, patting her friend on the arm. "She's that Jackson girl."

And that's why I'm the chameleon. I am the girl next door (it's just that our doors have fingerprint-reading sensors and are bulletproof and all . . .).

"Oh! Is your grandmother out of the hospital yet?" the more fragile of the women asked.

Okay, so I didn't know the Jacksons, much less how Granny was feeling, but Grandma Morgan had taught me that Chinese Water Torture is *nothing* compared to a grand-mother who really wants to know something. I saw Professor Smith nearing Bex, but over my comms unit, Bex was laugh-ing, saying, "Yeah, man. Go, Pirates!" as if she lived for Friday night football. Sure, Bex's definition of football might have been soccer, but boys were always boys, and a crowd of jersey-clad testosterone was assembling across the street. I didn't need surveillance photos to know who was at the center of the mob.

The old women were staring at me as if I were a needle they were trying to thread, and I said the only thing I could think of. "Dr. *Smith* says she needs to go south—that she needs to be *toasty*." I looked past the mob surrounding me and toward the one surrounding Bex, hoping she'd heard and understood that trouble was heading her way.

My hopes dwindled, though, when I heard her say, "Yeah, I *love* tight ends."

"Isn't that nice?" the old woman said. "Does she know where she's going?"

I saw Mr. Smith's dark jacket disappear past the pillars of the library's main entrance and then out of sight.

"You know she's such a *bookworm*," I said, hoping Liz was listening. "She can't wait to be near the *library*, just around the corner from the *library*, in fact," I said through gritted teeth, just as static and chaos filled my ears.

I heard Bex mutter, "Oh, no!"

Ahead of me, the football boys were heading in a pack down the street, but Bex wasn't with them. As far as I could see, Bex wasn't anywhere, and neither was Smith.

"Sorry, ladies. Gotta go," I snapped and hurried away. "Bookworm," I said, "do you have them? I have lost visual with The Subject and the eyeball. I repeat. I have lost visual with The Subject and the . . ."

I reached the library and looked in the direction where I'd last seen Mr. Smith, but all I saw was a long line of yellow streetlights. I weaved back through the crowd, circling the entire square, until I wound up right back where I'd started, in a vacant lot between a shoe store and City Hall, right behind the dunk tank.

I should have been more aware of my surroundings, I know—Spy 101 and all that—but it was too late. We'd been so close . . . *soooo* close. I hadn't wanted to admit it to myself, but about the time I polished off that ice-cream cone, I'd honestly started imagining what it would feel like to have Joe Solomon say, "Nice job."

But now they were gone—everyone—Smith, Bex, and Liz. I couldn't turn tail and run back to school—not then. We'd come too close. So I darted toward the funnel-cake stand, the one place we felt certain Smith would have to visit before the night was through, but I didn't pay attention to where I was going or how completely the Deputy Chief of Police filled the little seat above the dunk tank. I heard the crack of a baseball hitting metal, sensed movement out of the corner of my eye, but all the P&E training in the world wasn't enough to help me dodge the tidal wave that crashed over my shoulders.

Yeah, that's right. My first covert operations mission was also my first wet T-shirt contest, and as I stood there shivering, I knew it would probably be my last of both. People were rushing toward me, offering towels, asking if they could give me a ride home.

Yeah, I'm stealthy, I thought, as I thanked them as unmemorably as possible and darted away. Halfway down the sidewalk, I pulled a soggy twenty-dollar bill from my pocket, bought a Go Pirates! sweatshirt, and pulled it on.

In my ear, the comms unit had gone from crackling static to dense nothing, and I realized with a thud that my little silver cross, though state-of-the-art, wasn't the waterproof edition. Bex's band of football jocks strolled by, but not a single eye looked my way. As a girl, I wouldn't have minded a little corner-of-the-eye checking out, but as a spy, I was totally relieved that the whole drowned-chic look didn't undermine my covertness too much. I walked toward the funnel-cake stand, knowing that at any minute I could turn the corner on disaster—and I guess in a way, I did.

Bex and Liz were sitting together on a bench as Mr. Smith paced before them, and boy, was he scary just then. His new face had always seemed strong, but I hadn't appreciated its hard lines until he leaned over Liz and yelled, "Ms. Sutton!"

Liz started shrinking, but Bex crossed her arms and looked totally bored.

"I want to know what you are doing here!" Smith demanded.

"Ms. Baxter"—he turned to Bex—"you are going to tell me why you and Ms. Sutton have left campus. You are going to explain why you've been following me for thirty minutes, and . . ." I watched his expression change as something dawned on him. "And you are going to tell me where Joe Solomon is right now."

Bex and Liz looked at each other for a long time before

Bex turned back to Mr. Smith. "I had a craving for a corn dog."

Well, I have already pointed out the corn dog inadequacy of the Gallagher Academy food service team, but Mr. Smith didn't buy her argument, which was just as well. He wasn't supposed to. He'd heard her real message loud and clear—Bex and Liz weren't talking.

Those are my girls.

Then I remembered that I was probably supposed to be doing something! After all, the mission wasn't over yet—not really. There was still hope. Surely I could salvage some of it. Surely . . .

I was really starting to hate Joe Solomon. First he sends us out to tail a guy who was almost bound to catch at least one of us, and then he doesn't teach us what to do when we get caught! Was I supposed to cause a diversion and hope Bex and Liz could slip away? Was I supposed to find a weapon and jump Smith from behind? Or was I simply supposed to stroll across the street and take my rightful place beside them on that bench of shame?

From the corner of my eye, I saw the Overnight Express truck cruise by. It could have stopped and an army could have swarmed in and saved the day, but that didn't happen; and I instantly knew why. The street was full of people who could never know the power of the girls on the bench. I could have saved the sisters, but not at the risk of the sisterhood.

"Get up," Mr. Smith told Liz. He tossed a Dr Pepper

bottle into a nearby trash can. "We'll finish this discussion back at school."

I stayed in the shadows and watched Bex and Liz walk by. You know you're stealthy if your two best friends in the universe can pass within twenty feet of you and don't have a clue you're there. But it was for the best, I figured. After all, I was still a girl on a mission.

I waited until they turned the corner, then I strolled across the street. No one looked twice at me. Not a soul stopped to ask my name or tell me how much I looked like my mother. I didn't have to see the look of instant, uncomfortable sadness in anyone's eyes as they realized I was Cammie Morgan—one of *the* Morgans—that I was the girl with the dead dad. On the streets of Roseville I was just a regular girl, and it felt so good I almost didn't want to pull a Kleenex from my pocket, reach into the trash can, and carefully retrieve the bottle Mr. Smith had thrown away—but I did it anyway.

"Mission accomplished," I whispered. Then I turned, knowing it was time to go back to the world where I could be invisible, but never unknown.

And that's when I saw him—a boy across the street—seeing me.

Chapter Seven

In shock, I dropped the bottle on the street, but it didn't break. As it rolled toward the curb, I bolted forward and tried to pick it up, but another hand beat me to it—a hand that was pretty big and decidedly boylike, and I'd be lying if I said there wasn't some inadvertent pinkie-brushing, which led to a tingly sensation similar to the one I get when we use Dr. Fibs's temporary fingerprint modification cream (only *way* better).

I stood up, and the boy extended the bottle toward me. I took it.

"Hi, there." He had one hand in the pocket of his baggy jeans, pressing down, as if daring the pants to slide off his hips and gather around his Nikes that had that too-white, first-day-of-school glow about them. "*So, do you come here often?*" he asked in a slightly self-mocking way. I couldn't help myself—I smiled. "See, you don't even have to answer that, because I know all the trash cans in town, and while *this* is a very nice trash can, it doesn't look like the kind of trash can a girl like you would normally scavenge from." I opened my mouth to protest, but he went on. "Now, the trash cans on Seventh Street, those are some very nice trash cans."

Mr. Solomon's lesson from the first day of class came back to me, so I noted the details: the boy was about five foot ten, and he had wavy brown hair, and eyes that would put even Mr. Solomon's to shame. But the thing I noticed most was how easily he smiled. I wouldn't even mention it except it seemed to define his entire face—eyes, lips, cheeks. It wasn't especially toothy or anything. It was just easy and smooth, like melting butter. But then again, I wasn't the most impartial judge of such things. After all, he was smiling at *me*.

"That must not be an ordinary bottle," he said (while smiling, of course).

I realized how ridiculous it must have looked. Under the warmth of that smile, I forgot my legend, my mission—everything—and I blurted the first thing that popped into my mind, "I have a cat!"

He raised his eyebrows, and I imagined him whipping out a cell phone to notify the nearest mental institution that I was on the loose in Roseville.

"She likes to play with bottles," I rambled on, speaking ninety miles an hour. "But her last one broke, and then she got glass in her paw. Suzie! That's my cat's name—the one with the glass in her paw—not that I have any other ones—cats, I mean, not bottles. That's why I needed this bottle. I'm not even sure she'll want another bottle, what with the—"

"Trauma of having glass in her paw," he finished for me.

I exhaled, grateful for the chance to catch my breath. "Exactly."

Yeah, this is how a highly trained government operative behaves when intercepted on a mission. Somehow, I think the fact that the interceptor looked like a cross between a young George Clooney and Orlando Bloom might have played into that a little bit. (If he'd looked like a cross between Mr. Clooney and, say, one of the hobbits, I probably would have been far more capable of coherent thought.)

From the corner of my eye I saw the Overnight Express truck turn into an alley. I could sense it idling there—waiting on me—so I turned and started down the street, but not before the boy said, "So, you're new to Roseville, huh?" I turned back to him. Mr. Solomon probably wouldn't lay on the horn to tell a girl to hurry up, but even through my busted comms unit I could feel his frustration, hear the ticking clock.

"I'm . . . um, how did you know that?"

He raised his shoulders up and down an inch or two as he shoved his hands farther into his pockets. "I've lived in Roseville all my life. Everyone I *know* has lived in Roseville all their life. But I've never seen you before."

Maybe that's because I'm the girl no one sees, I wanted to say. But *he* had seen me, I realized, and that thought took my breath away as surely as if I'd been kicked in my stomach (a comparison I'm perfectly qualified to make).

"But . . . hey . . ." he said, as if a thought had just occurred to him. "I guess I'll be seeing you at school."

Huh? I thought for a second, wondering how a *boy* could ever get accepted at the Gallagher Academy (especially when Tina Walters swears there's a top secret boys' school somewhere in Maine, and every year she petitions my mom to let us take a field trip).

Then I remembered my legend—I was a normal teenage girl—one he wasn't going to see around the halls of Roseville High, so I shook my head. "I'm not in the public school system."

He seemed kind of surprised by this, but then he looked down at my chest. (Not THAT way—I was totally wearing a sweatshirt, remember? Plus, let me tell you, there's not that much to stare at.) I glanced down to see the silver cross glistening against my new black sweatshirt.

"What . . . are you homeschooled or something?" he asked, and I nodded. "For what, like, religious reasons?"

"Yes," I said, thinking that sounded as good as anything. "Something like that." I took a backward step toward the truck, toward my classmates, toward my home. "I have to go."

"Hey!" he cried after me. "It's dark. Let me walk you home—you know—for protection."

I'm fairly certain I could have killed him with that pop bottle, so I might have laughed if his offer hadn't been so sweet. "I'll be fine," I called back to him as I hurried down the sidewalk.

"Then for *my* protection."

I couldn't help myself—I laughed as I yelled, "Go back to the carnival!"

Ten more steps and I would have turned the corner; I would have been free, but then the boy shouted, "Hey, what's your name?"

"Cammie!" I don't know what made me say it, but the word was already out there, and I couldn't take it back, so I said again, "My name is Cammie," as if trying the truth on for size.

"Hey, Cammie . . ." He was taking long, lazy steps, backing away from me, toward the lights and sounds of the festival in full swing. ". . . tell Suzie she's a lucky cat."

Have sexier words ever been spoken? I seriously think not!

"I'm Josh, by the way."

I started running as I yelled, "Good-bye, Josh." But before the words even reached him, I was gone.

The Overnight Express truck was waiting at the end of the alley when I got there, lights off. I felt Mr. Smith's pop bottle in my hand, and for a second I couldn't remember why I would be carrying such a thing. I know. I'm almost ashamed of it now—the fact that ten seconds with a boy had driven my mission from my mind. But I *did* look at it, and I did remember who I was—why I was there—and I knew it was time to forget about boys and trash cans and cats named Suzie; I remembered what was real and what was legend.

As I pulled open the back door of the truck, I expected to see my classmates sitting there, envying my mission-accomplishing superspy-ness, but all I saw were packages and packages—even the television was gone, and instead of cries of congratulations, I heard the words *Tell Suzie she's a lucky cat* echoing in my head then growing silent as I realized something was wrong.

I spun in the street. I looked in the cab of the truck, where a bright orange cap lay on the dashboard, probably where the rightful driver had left it. We had come and gone without a trace, and now all that was left was that bottle and a long run home.

I told myself that having to run two miles in wet jeans was just karmic payback for having indulged in both the corn dog *and* the ice cream, but as I reached the edge of town, I wasn't so sure. As I ran, my mind was free. I was back on the street with Josh. I was watching Liz and Bex disappear around a corner with Mr. Smith. I was talking to an old woman about a grandmother I didn't know. I was just another girl at the party.

The lights of the school cut through the leaves of the trees in the distance as my boots beat a heavy rhythm on the pavement. Damp denim rubbed against my legs. Sweat poured down my back. Mom is always saying that a spy should trust her gut, and right then my gut was telling me that I didn't want to go back to the mansion, that I didn't want to be anywhere near Joe Solomon and Mr. Smith, and by the time I reached the main gates, I would have given just about anything not to have to go through them.

"Big night, Cam?" A stocky man with a buzz cut and a perpetual mouth full of bubble gum appeared at the guardhouse door. He knew my name, but I'd never been introduced to him. If I had, I probably would have called him something other than Bubblegum Guard. But as it was, he was just another guy on the staff who worked for my mom, who probably went on missions with my dad, who knew all the details about my life, while I knew none about his.

I suddenly missed my bench in Roseville. I longed for the noisy, anonymous chaos of the square.

I started down the driveway, but Bubblegum Guard called out to me, "Hey, Cam, you want a ride?" He gestured toward a ruby red golf cart that sat behind the guardhouse.

"No, thanks." I shook my head. "Good night."

I'm sorry I don't know your name.

When I reached the main foyer, I started for the stairs. I wanted a shower. I wanted my bed. I wanted to shake free of the uneasy feeling that had settled in my gut from the moment I saw that orange cap lying on the dashboard—abandoned. I had the bottle in my hands, but somehow I knew that wasn't really the point.

Then I heard footsteps and a cry of "Wait!" as Mr. Mosckowitz rushed after me.

"Hi, Mr. M. Great driving tonight," I said. I remembered that it had been his first mission, too.

Something important must have made him chase me

down, but for a second his features shifted. He actually glowed (but not like the time he tested that flame-retardant skin gel for Dr. Fibs).

"You think?" he asked. "Because, well, at that second stop sign, I think I might have hesitated a little too long. Forty-eight hours or less," he said, with a punch at the air, "that's the Overnight Express motto; I just don't think a real driver would have waited so long."

"Oh." I gave him a nod. "I thought it was just right— nothing causes delays like an accident, you know."

His face brightened again. "You think?"

"It was perfect."

I turned again and started up the stairs, but Mr. Mosckowitz said, "Oh, gee, wait. I was supposed to tell you . . ." He paused, and I imagined him churning through the gigabytes of his brain. ". . . that you are supposed to go to the CoveOps class for a debrief."

Of course I am, I thought as I gripped the bottle. Of course it isn't over.

As the optical scanners swept over my face I heard Mr. Mosckowitz ask, "So, hey, Cammie, it *was* fun. Wasn't it?" And I realized that one of the most brilliant men in the world needed me to verify that he'd had fun.

This place never ceases to amaze me.

Chapter eight

Sublevel One was dark as I got out of the elevator. I followed the maze of frosted glass through the light of emergency exit signs and the flickering computer screens. I passed a library filled with facts too sensitive for a seventh grader to know. I walked along a balcony that overlooks a massive three-story room the size of a gymnasium that comes complete with movable walls and fake people, so Bex and I call it the dollhouse—it's where spies come to play.

As I got closer to the classroom, the hallway got brighter, and soon I was looking through one wall of illuminated glass at the silhouettes of my classmates. No one was talking. Not Mr. Solomon. Not any of the girls. I crept toward the open door—saw my classmates in their usual seats and Mr. Solomon perched on a low bookcase at the back of the room, his hands gripping the dark wood as he leaned casually back.

I stood there for a long time, not knowing what to do. Finally, I said, "I got the bottle."

But Joe Solomon didn't smile. He didn't say "well done." He didn't even look at me as he leaned against that bookcase, staring at the white tiles on the floor.

"Come in, Ms. Morgan," he said softly. "We've been expecting you."

I headed for my desk on the far side of the room, and then I saw them—the two empty chairs. I searched for the eyes of my classmates, but not one of them looked back.

"They should be back by . . ." I began, but just then Mr. Solomon picked up a remote control and punched a button, and the room went dark except for a long sliver of light that shone from a projector beside him. I was standing in the center of its path, silhouetted against the image glowing on a screen.

In the picture, Bex was sitting on the wall in front of the Roseville library. Then I heard a click and the image changed. I saw Liz peeking around a tree, which is really bad form, but Mr. Solomon didn't comment. His silence seemed totally worse. Another click. Bex was looking over her shoulder, crossing a street. Click. Liz was next to a funnel-cake stand.

"Ask the question, Ms. Morgan," he said, his voice carrying ominously through the dark room. "Don't you want to know where they are?"

I *did* want to know, but I was almost afraid to hear the answer. More images flashed on the screen, surveillance photos taken by a well-trained, well-placed team. Bex and Liz hadn't known they were there—*I* hadn't known they were there—and yet someone had stalked our every step. I felt like prey.

"Ask me *why* they're not here," Mr. Solomon demanded. I saw his dim outline. His arms were crossed. "You want to be a spy, don't you, *Chameleon?*" My code name was nothing more than a mockery on his lips. "Now tell me what happens to spies who get made."

No, I thought.

Another click.

Is that Bex? Of course it wasn't—she was with Mr. Smith; she was safe, but I couldn't help but stare at the dark, gritty image on the screen—the bloody, swollen face that stared back at me—and tremble for my friend.

"They won't start with Bex, you know," he went on. "They'll start with Liz."

Another click and then I was looking at a pair of thin arms bound behind a chair and a cascade of bloody blond hair. "These people are very good at what they do. They know Bex can take the punches; what hurts Bex most is listening to her friend scream."

The projector's light was warm as it danced across my skin. He was moving closer. I saw his shadow join mine on the screen.

"And she *is* screaming—she will be for about six hours, until she becomes so dehydrated she can't form sounds." My gaze was going blurry; my knees were weak. Terror was pounding in my ears so loudly that I barely heard him when he whispered, "And then they start on

Bex." Another click. "They have *special things* in mind for her."

I'm going to be sick, I thought, unable to look him in the eye.

"This is what you're signing up for." He forced me to face the image. "Look at what is happening to your friends!"

"Stop it!" I yelled. "Stop it." And then I dropped the bottle. The neck snapped, shattering, sending shards of glass across the floor.

"You lost two-thirds of your team. Your friends are gone."

"No," I said again. "Stop."

"No, Ms. Morgan, once this starts—it doesn't stop." My face was hot and my eyes were swollen. "It *never* stops."

And it doesn't. He was right and I knew it all too well.

I sensed, rather than saw, Mr. Solomon turn to the class and ask, "Who wants to be a spy now?"

No one raised a hand. No one spoke. We weren't supposed to.

"Next semester, ladies, Covert Operations will be an optional field of study, but this semester, it's mandatory. No one gets to back out now because they're scared. But you won't ever be as scared as you are right now—not this semester. On that you have my word."

The overhead lights came on, and twelve girls squinted against the sudden glare. Mr. Solomon moved toward the door, but stopped. "And ladies, if you aren't scared right now, we don't want you anyway."

He slid aside a glass partition, revealing Bex and Liz, who sat behind it, unharmed. Then he walked away.

We sat in silence for a long time, listening to his footsteps fade.

Up in our room, we were greeted by a pile of clothes and accessories that had seemed so important at the start of our night—but seemed so insignificant now.

Macey was asleep—or pretending to be—I didn't care. She had a pair of those really expensive Bose sound-eliminating headphones (probably so she wouldn't be kept awake by the sound of air whizzing past her nose ring), so Bex and Liz and I could have talked or screamed. But we didn't.

Even Bex had lost her swagger, and that was maybe the scariest thing of all. I wanted her to crack a joke. I wanted her to reenact everything Smith had said on their long walk home. I wanted Bex to call out for the spotlight so that our room wouldn't be so dark. But instead, we sat in silence until I couldn't take it anymore.

"Guys, I—" I started, needing to say I was sorry, but Bex stopped me.

"You did what I would have done," she said, then looked at Liz.

"Me, too," Liz agreed.

"Yeah, but . . ." I wanted to say something else, but what, I didn't know.

In her bed, Macey rolled over, but she didn't open her

eyes. I looked at the clock and realized it was almost one in the morning.

"Was Smith mad?" I asked after a long time.

Liz was in the bathroom brushing her teeth, so Bex was the one who answered, "I don't think so. He's probably having a good laugh about it now, don't you think?"

"Maybe," I said.

I pulled on my pajamas.

"He said he never even saw you, though," Bex said, as if she'd just remembered.

Liz came in and added, "Yeah, Cammie, he was really impressed when he heard you'd been out there. Like, *really* impressed."

I felt something cold against my chest, so I reached up to feel the tiny silver cross still dangling around my neck, and I remembered that someone *had* seen me. Until then, the boy on the street had faded almost completely from my mind.

"So," Liz asked, "what happened with you after we left?"

I fingered the cross, but said, "Nothing."

I don't know why I didn't tell them about Josh. I mean, it should have been significant—a random civilian initiating contact during an operation—that's the kind of thing you totally tell your superiors, let alone your best friends. But I kept it to myself—maybe because I didn't think it mattered, but probably because, in a place where everyone knew my story, it was nice to know there was a chapter that only I had read.

Chapter nine

Culture and Assimilation isn't like our other classes, so I guess that's why Madame Dabney's tea room isn't like our other classrooms. French silk lines the walls. The lighting fixtures are crystal. Everything in that room is beautiful and refined and reminds us that we don't just have to be spies— we have to be ladies.

Sometimes I hate it and spend hours thinking what a waste it is to teach us things like calligraphy and needlepoint (aside from the obvious coded message usages, of course). But other times I love listening to Madame Dabney as she floats through the room with a monogrammed handkerchief in her hand, talking about what flowers are in season or the history of the waltz.

The day after our first mission was one of those days. I might have blown the mission, but I was still a whiz at setting tables, so I was actually sad to hear Madame Dabney say, "Oh, dear, girls, look at the time." I didn't want to put away the good china. I didn't want to go down-stairs and face Mr. Solomon again.

"But before you leave today, girls," Madame Dabney said in an expectant, excited tone that held my attention, "I have an announcement to make!" The sounds of clattering china all but ceased as everyone took Madame Dabney in. "It's time for you to expand your education here at the Gallagher Academy, so . . ." She adjusted her glasses. ". . . beginning today after school, I am going to be teaching Driver's Ed!"

Oh my gosh! I'd completely forgotten about Driver's Ed! Sure, we're allowed to toss each other over our shoulders or concoct antidotes for rare poisons for extra credit, but when it comes to tricky stuff like adjusting rearview mirrors and knowing who has the right-of-way at four-way stops, the Gallagher Trustees don't take any chances. Plus, there's that whole discount-on-your-car-insurance thing to consider.

Madame Dabney said, "We'll be going out in groups of four—by suite." She consulted a piece of paper then looked directly toward Liz, Bex, and me. "Beginning with the four of you."

Liz looked at Bex and me, not understanding. "Four?" she whispered, just as a light seemed to dawn, and from the back of the room we heard Macey say, "*Sounds like fun.*"

(Do I really need to say she was being sarcastic?)

That afternoon, we strolled down the steps of the rear portico and toward the motor pool, where an old Ford Taurus was waiting for us, its yellow STUDENT DRIVER triangle gleaming in the sun.

Mom tells me Madame Dabney spent most of her career in deep cover, working the underground Nazi cells that remained active in France after World War II, but at times like this I have a really hard time believing her—especially when the woman in question shows up wearing a *Give Safety a Brake!* T-shirt.

"Ooooh, girls! This is going to be such a delight!" she said, and then proceeded to do things like point to the brake and say, "That makes the car stop," and the accelerator, "That makes the car go." But the craziest thing of all was that Liz was taking notes.

She has a photographic memory! She joined Mensa at the age of eight! And yet she felt compelled to draw a diagram of the steering column and note exactly which button turned on the windshield wipers.

"Be sure you write down that the steering wheel is round," I said, and she seriously had the W-H-E of wheel written in her little notebook before she realized I was joking.

"Cammie, don't make fun," Liz said, the way she always did. But just then, Macey mocked, "*Yeah, Cammie, don't make fun.*" Even Liz wanted to deck her.

"Now, girls," Madame Dabney said, "let's focus." She drew her hands into a position of prayer as she turned to Bex. "Rebecca, dear, how do you feel about starting us out?"

I gasped. Don't get me wrong; I love Bex. She's my best friend. But I've been driving since I could see over the wheel and work the pedals at the same time (something Grandpa

Morgan swears is a milestone in every farm kid's life), so why should Bex, a native Londoner who spent her formative years riding the Tube and waving down taxis, be the first to tackle Highway 10?

I consoled myself by thinking that Bex *is* my best friend, and she *is* good at everything, or so I thought until she pulled out onto the highway ON THE WRONG SIDE OF THE ROAD! Now all this might have been funny except there's a hill there—did I mention that? A great big can't-see-the-semi-until-it's-about-to-hit-you-head-on hill. But I was the only one who noticed, because Madame Dabney was writing on her clipboard, Liz was doing bio-chem homework, and Macey was having a fingernail emergency.

I tried to yell, but I must have temporarily lost the power of speech, and Bex was the only other person paying attention to the road, and she thought she was on the right side of it—or left side—or whatever (you get what I mean).

My voice returned just in time for me to yell "BEX!" and she said, "What?" turning and sending us swerving into the other lane, which under normal circumstances would have been disastrous, but in this case really saved our lives. Fate is tricky that way—something I guess every spy figures out eventually.

Then Bex calmly righted the car and headed into town, completely unfazed.

When Bex hung a left at the Piggly Wiggly and nearly took out a crossing guard from Roseville Elementary School, Madame Dabney made her pull into the grocery store parking lot and trade places with Macey. But Bex didn't seem mad, which in itself was a little scary. Instead, she had a really pleased look on her face as she opened my door and made me push Liz into the seat Macey was vacating, which was harder than it sounds, since Liz had become kind of . . . *oh, what's the word?* . . . petrified.

Madame Dabney had obviously learned her lesson with Bex, because there were lots of *Easy on the accelerator, dear*s and *Okay, there's a stop sign over there, darling*s coming from the front seat as Macey eased onto the streets.

Things were starting to get pretty calm. I mean, really, it was almost nice, being driven around, sitting between my two best friends in the world, feeling the sun beam through the windows. It was almost normal—or as close to normal as three geniuses, a cosmetics heiress-slash-senator's daughter, and a secret agent in a Ford Taurus can ever be.

Nestled in the backseat between Liz and Bex, I started thinking that it would have been way too much to ask for us to have a tour of the town before we were supposed to tail one of the most wanted men in the world through it. *Oh, yeah, that would have been a totally unfair advantage.* In the daylight, I could see thousands of hiding places where a girl could linger unseen. I recognized alleys and side streets that would have been great shortcuts. I started, despite everything, to want a rematch with Mr. Smith. But mostly, I wondered about the boy I'd seen. Was he real? Did he really walk these streets?

Then, I got my answer.

* * *

"What the bloody hell are you doing down there?" Bex asked.

"Looking for my contacts," I snapped back.

"You have twenty-twenty vision," Liz reminded me.

"It's just . . . I just . . . I can't look up right now."

I knew the car was stopped, probably at a traffic light—one of only two in the town, so Josh had to be getting close.

"What?" Bex asked in a whisper. "What's going on?" She shifted into spy-mode, sat up, and looked around. "There's nothing out there. Oh, well, you are missing a real hottie at three o'clock."

Liz craned her neck around to look. "Ooh, yeah, he's pretty skinny but worth checking out." Then she shrugged and said, "Oh. Never mind. He's giving us the *Gallagher Glare*."

I have no idea who came up with that name, but it's what we always call the look that people in town give us whenever they figure out where we go to school. It's the only time I ever hate our cover story—when people look at me as if I must be privileged, as if I must be spoiled. As if I must be like Macey McHenry. I want to tell them that I spent my summer cleaning fish and canning vegetables—but that's just one of a thousand things that the good people of Roseville will never know about me. Still, when people like Josh look at you like you're a cross between Charles Manson and Paris Hilton, it hurts a little—even for a spy.

"Yeah, but he's still a *boy*," Bex said longingly. "Hey, Cam, come take a peek."

"I am not going to look at some boy!" I snapped. "I don't care how wavy his hair is."

"Who said anything about wavy hair?"

Oh, Bex is good.

"I can't believe this!" Liz said, pacing. She hadn't sat down once since we got back to the mansion—she just kept going back and forth—trying to make sense of it all. I couldn't really blame her. Liz's belief system is pretty natural for scientific geniuses. She wants life to be something that can be tested in a lab or referenced in a book. She'd thought she'd known me. I'd thought I'd known myself. Now both of our hypotheses had been thrown out the window, and we hated to start from scratch.

I couldn't let her see how shaken I was, so I did the next best thing: I got angry.

"Exactly *what* is so unbelievable?" I asked. "That a boy looked at me?" Sure, I'd never be an exotic beauty like Bex or a pixyish waif like Liz, but I had yet to grow boils all over my body. Mirrors don't crack when I walk by them. My Grandfather calls me Angel. Was I that unworthy of being noticed?

"Cam!" Bex ordered. "Of course that's not it."

Liz threw her hands into the air and said, "I can't believe you didn't tell us! I can't believe you didn't tell someone."

Liz's definition of *someone* didn't mean *someone*. Liz's *someone* meant *a teacher*.

"So what?" I said, trying to brush the whole thing aside.

"*So what?*" Liz said. "So, he *saw* you! Cammie, no one sees you when you don't want to be seen." She eased onto the bed beside me. "When we were trailing Smith and I had to keep you in sight, it was almost impossible, and I could hear you through the comms unit. And I knew what you were wearing. And . . ." She threw her hands into the air. "*So what?*"

I turned to look at Bex, my eyebrows raised as if to ask *Are you freaked out, too?*

"You really are amazing, Cam," Bex said in a perfectly serious tone, so I knew it must be true.

"Something isn't right, here," Liz said as I went into the bathroom and started brushing my teeth. (It's hard to say things that will do lasting damage to a lifelong friendship when you're foaming at the mouth like a rabid dog.) "Mr. Solomon wants summaries of our mission, so we've got to include him. He could very well be trying to infiltrate the school through Cammie. He could be a honeypot!"

I nearly gagged on my own toothbrush. The technical definition of a honeypot is a female agent using romance to compromise a target. The practical definition is anyone with cleavage. (Rumor has it Gilly kind of inspired the term.) The thought that Josh could be the male equivalent made my stomach flip.

"No!" I cried. "No. No. No. He is *not* a honeypot."

"How do you know?" Bex asked, playing devil's advocate.

"I just do!" I replied.

But Liz was shrugging, saying, "We've got to include him in the reports, Cam."

But reports lead to reviews. Reviews lead to protocol. Protocol would lead to two weeks of the security department tailing him through town while they track down his birth certificate and find out if his mom drinks or his dad gambles—they've done far more for fewer reasons. After all, the Gallagher Academy hasn't remained a well-kept secret for more than a hundred years by taking chances.

I thought about Josh, how sweet and normal he had seemed. I didn't want strangers looking at him beneath a microscope. I didn't want there to be a file in Langley with his name on it. But mostly, I didn't want to sit in a room and explain why he'd approached *me*, when the town square had been full of far prettier girls.

I looked down at the floor, shaking off the thought. "No, Liz, I can't do it. That is way too high a price to pay for talking to a girl."

Then Bex crossed her arms and grinned deviously in my direction. "I think there's something more to this story," she said with her usual flair. The rush of blood to my cheeks must have been enough to betray me, because she leaned down and said, "Spill it."

So I told them about the trash can and the dropped Dr Pepper bottle and, finally, *Tell Suzie she's a lucky cat*, which, even if it hadn't been for the whole genius thing, I still would have been able to remember verbatim, because sentences like that are like peanut butter on a girl's mind. When I finished, Bex was staring at me as if she wondered whether or not I had been replaced by a genetically engineered clone, and Liz had a starry-eyed gaze very similar to the one Snow White wore while those birds fluttered above her head.

"What?" I asked, needing them to say something—anything.

"Sounds like I could snap his neck with one hand," Bex said, and she was probably right. "But if you go in for that sort of thing . . ."

". . . he's amazing," Liz finished for her.

"It doesn't matter what he is or isn't. He's . . ." I struggled.

Liz shot upright and finished for me. ". . . still got to go in the reports!"

"Liz!" I cried, but Bex's hand was on my arm.

"Why don't *we* do it?" Her most devious expression flashed across her face. "We'll check him out, and if he's an ordinary boy, we forget about it. If something's strange, we'll turn him in."

I knew instantly what the arguments against it should have been: we were too busy; it was against about a million rules; if we got caught, we could be risking our careers forever. But in the silence of the room, we looked at each other, our mutual agreement settling down upon us in the way of people who have known each other too well and too long.

"Okay," I said finally. "We'll do the basics, and no one has to know."

Bex smiled. "Agreed."

We both looked at Liz, who shrugged. "Let's face it—he's either an enemy agent trying to infiltrate the Gallagher Girls through Cammie . . ."

Liz stopped midsentence, prompting me to say, "Or . . . ?"

Her entire face lit up. "He's your soul mate."

Chapter ten

O kay, from this point on, if you are related to me or in a position to add things to my "permanent record" (which I'm assuming at the Gallagher Academy is a little more detailed than what they keep at Roseville High), you might want to stop reading. Seriously. Go ahead and skip the next hundred pages. It won't hurt my feelings *at all*.

In other words, I'm not proud of what comes next, but I'm not exactly ashamed of it either, if that makes any sense. Sometimes I think my whole life has been that kind of contradiction. I mean, all I've heard for the last three years has been *Don't hesitate, but be patient. Be logical—trust your instincts. Follow protocol—improvise. Never let your guard down—always look at ease.*

So, see, if you give a bunch of teenage girls those kinds of messages, then, yeah, eventually things are going to get interesting.

The rest of the week staggered on, our unspoken mission

looming in the back of our minds like a silent but ever-present charge that filled the air, so that every time one of us reached for the doorknob, I half expected to see sparks.

We were up at the crack of dawn on Saturday morning, which was definitely not my idea. Thanks to Tina Walters's annual *Dirty Dancing* extravaganza, where we watched the "nobody puts Baby in a corner" scene a dozen times, I was really needing a good "lie-in," as Bex calls it. But even though Liz might have been at the bottom of our class in P&E, she is the best person I've ever seen at getting me out of bed, which is saying something, considering the woman who raised me.

Macey was asleep in her headphones, so Liz felt free to yell, "We're doing this for you!" as she pulled on my left leg and Bex went in search of breakfast. Liz put her foot against the mattress for leverage as she tugged. "Come on, Cam. GET. UP."

"No!" I said, burrowing deeper into the covers. "Five more minutes."

Then she grabbed my hair, which is totally a low blow, since everyone knows I'm tender-headed. "*He's a honeypot.*"

"He'll still be one in an hour," I pleaded.

Then Liz dropped down beside me. She leaned close. She whispered, "*Tell Suzie she's a lucky cat.*"

I threw the covers aside. "I'm up!"

Ten minutes later Bex was falling into step beside me, handing me a Pop-Tart, as Liz led the way to the basement. The halls were empty; the mansion silent. It was almost like summer, except a chill had settled into the stone walls, and my best friends were beside me. When we reached the vending machines outside Dr. Fibs's office, I took a bite out of my breakfast and felt the sugar kick in.

"Ready, then?" Bex asked, and Liz nodded.

They both looked at me. I took another bite and figured that if we'd come this far (and since I *was* already out of bed), we might as well go all the way.

I pulled a quarter from my pocket and held it toward the slot, but Liz stopped me.

"Wait." She reached for the coin. "If anyone looks at the logs, my name will send up fewer red flags," she said, even though nothing we were doing was against school rules. (I know—I checked.) In fact, we are encouraged to do as many "special projects" for "independent study" as we'd like, and no one ever said we couldn't make a project out of studying special boys independently. Still, it seemed like a good idea to hand the quarter over to Liz and have her be the one to press her thumbprint onto George Washington's head, drop it into the vending machine, and order item A-19.

Two seconds later, the vending machine popped open, revealing a corridor to the most state-of-the-art forensics laboratory outside the CIA. (If Liz had ordered B-14, a ladder would have dropped down out of the mahogany paneling behind us.)

As we walked into the forensics lab, Liz was already pulling Mr. Smith's pop bottle from her bag and placing it in the center of a table. The broken shards were pieced together, and I could almost forget why I had dropped it—almost.

"We'll just run it through the system and see what we've got," Liz said, sounding very official and far too wide-awake for SEVEN A.M. on a SATURDAY MORNING! Besides, I could have told her what we were going to find— nothing. Nada. That Dr Pepper bottle was going to yield the fingerprints of a Gallagher Academy student (me), a nonexistent-as-far-as-technology-is-concerned-because-every-year-he-gets-new-fingerprints-to-go-with-his-face Gallagher Academy instructor (Smith), and a perfectly innocent bystander whose only crime was being concerned for teenage girls who are forced to pilfer from trash cans (Josh).

I started to share all this with Liz, but she'd already put on her white lab coat, and *nothing* gives Liz more joy than wearing a white lab coat, so I zipped my lips and tried to rest my head on the desk.

An hour later, Liz was shaking me awake, telling me that Josh's fingerprints were nowhere in the system (shocker, I know). This pretty much meant that he'd never been in prison or the army. He wasn't a practicing attorney or a member of the CIA. He'd never tried to buy a handgun or run for office (which, for some reason, came as kind of a relief).

"See?" I told Liz, thinking she'd abandon the hunt and allow me to go back to a proper bed, but she looked at me as if I were crazy.

"This is only Phase One," she said, sounding hurt.

"Do I want to know what Phase Two is?" I asked.

Liz just looked at me for a long moment and then said, "Go back to sleep."

"I can't believe I let you talk me into this," I said as we crouched in the bushes outside Josh's house. Another car drove by and the music got louder, and all I could say was, "I can't believe I let you talk me into this."

"*You* can't believe it?" Bex snapped then turned. "Liz, I thought you said that house was going to be empty at eight."

"Well, technically, the Abrams house *is* empty."

I couldn't blame Liz for being defensive. After all, it had taken her three hours of breaking through firewalls (*ours*, not *theirs*) and scrolling through the Roseville public schools' computer system to find out that "my" Josh was Josh Abrams of 601 North Bellis Street. It had taken another hour to access all the Abrams family accounts and intercept the e-mail in which Joan Abrams (aka Josh's mom) promised someone named Dorothy that "We wouldn't miss Keith's surprise party for the world! We'll be there at eight sharp!"

So imagine our surprise as we crouched in the azaleas and watched half the town of Roseville traipse in and out of a white house with blue shutters at the end of Josh's block. I pulled on a pair of glasses that only work if you're *really* nearsighted (they're actually binoculars) and zoomed in on the house where the party was in full swing.

"Keith who?" I asked, forcing Liz to think back on the e-mail we'd printed on Evapopaper and hidden under my bed.

"Jones," Liz said. "Why?"

I handed the glasses to her so that she too could look at the house at the end of the street and see the *Keeping Up with the Joneses* sign that hung over the front door.

"Oh," Liz mumbled, and we all knew that the Abrams family hadn't gone far.

I had imagined where Josh would live, but my dreams paled in comparison to what I actually saw. It wasn't a real neighborhood—it was a TV neighborhood, where lawns are manicured and porches are made for swings and lemonade. Before I came to the Gallagher Academy, we lived in a narrow town house in D.C. I spend my summers on a dusty ranch. I had never seen so much suburban perfection in one place as I looked through the dim streetlight toward the long rows of white picket fence.

Somehow, I knew a spy would never belong there.

Still, three *were* there—crouching in the dark—until Bex pulled out her lock-picking kit and rushed toward the back door. Liz was right behind her until she stubbed her toe on a garden gnome and landed flat on a holly bush with a quiet cry of "I'm okay!"

I helped Liz to her feet, and seconds later we were right behind Bex as she worked her magic on the lock of the back door.

"Almost got it," Bex said firmly, confidently.

I knew that tone. That tone was dangerous.

I heard the music from the party down the street, saw our picturesque surroundings, and a thought dawned on me.

"Um, guys, maybe we should try—" I reached for the knob. It turned effortlessly beneath my palm.

"Yeah," Bex said. "That works, too."

Stepping inside Josh's house was like stepping inside a magazine. There were fresh flowers on the table. An apple pie was cooling on a rack by the stove. Josh's sister's report cards were clipped beneath a magnet on the refrigerator—straight A's.

Bex and Liz darted through the living room and up the stairs, and I pulled my thoughts together long enough to say, "Five minutes!" But I couldn't follow. I couldn't move.

I knew at once that I wasn't supposed to be there—for a lot of reasons. I was trespassing not only on a house, but also a way of life. I found a sewing basket in a window seat, where someone was making a costume for Halloween. A book about do-it-yourself upholstery lay on the coffee table, and four fabric swatches hung on the arm of the sofa.

"Cam!" Bex called to me and threw a transmitter my way. "Liz says this has to go outside. Why don't you try that elm tree?"

I was glad to have a job. I was glad to get out of that house. Sure, doing basic reconnaissance was an essential part of honeypot detection. After all, if Josh was getting instructions from a terror cell or rogue government or something, planting a Trojan horse on his computer and digging through his underwear drawer was probably the best way to find out about it. Still, it was a relief to go outside and climb the tree.

I was on the third branch of the tree, tying off the

transmitter, when I looked down the street and saw a figure cutting through yards. He was tall. He was young. And he had his hands in his pockets, pushing down in a way I've only seen once before!

"Bookworm, do you read me?" I tried; but even though Liz had done her best to fix my shorted-out comms unit, the crackling static in my ear told me that her hasty repair job hadn't worked. I stayed crouched against the branch as summer's last remaining leaves swayed around me.

"Duchess," I whispered, praying Bex would answer—or better yet—tap me on the shoulder and scold me for not having a little faith. "Bex, I'll let you choose any code name you want, if you'll just answer me," I whispered through the dark.

Josh was crossing the porch.

Josh was opening the front door.

"Guys, if you can hear me, just hide, okay? The Subject is entering the house. I repeat. The Subject is entering the house."

The door closed behind him, so I jumped out of the tree and hurried to take cover in the bushes, constantly keeping an eye on the front door, which sounds great in theory except that meant I totally missed seeing Liz and Bex crawl out of a second-story window and take refuge on the roof.

"Chameleon!" Bex called through the dark, scaring me half to death as I dove headfirst into the bushes and then peeked up to see Bex peering over the eaves of the house.

They must have thought Josh was home for the night because they started attaching rappelling cables to the chimney, and they were about to jump off the roof, but then Josh stepped through the front door!

I watched from the bushes, frozen in terror, as I realized that my two best friends were about to land on top of the cutest boy I've ever seen—and the apple pie he was carrying.

They couldn't see him. He couldn't see them. But I could see everything.

He took a step. They took a step.

We were seconds away from disaster, and honestly, I didn't even know what I was doing until the words, "Oh, hi," were out of my mouth and I was standing in the middle of the Abrams family yard.

From the corner of my eye, I saw terror register on Bex's face above me as she grabbed Liz and tried to pull her away from the edge, but I wasn't really paying attention to them. How could I, when a boy as dreamy as Josh Abrams was walking toward me, looking totally surprised to see me— which was perfectly understandable.

"Hi. I didn't expect to find you here," he said, and immediately I freaked out. Did that mean he'd been thinking about me? Or was he simply trying to figure out how and why a strange girl dressed all in black appears in your front yard? (Thank goodness I'd dropped my hat and utility belt in the bushes.)

"Oh, you know the Joneses," I said, even though I *didn't*, but judging by the line of people going in and out of the house at the end of the block, it was probably a pretty safe thing to say.

Luckily, Josh smiled and added, "Yeah, these parties get wilder every year."

"Uh-huh," I said, all the while watching as Bex struggled to drag Liz across the roof—to the back of the house—but Liz slipped and started sliding down. She tried to hang on to a gutter, but slipped, and soon she was swinging off the side of the Abramses' house, and my heart was pounding harder and harder (for a lot of reasons).

Josh looked as embarrassed as I felt as he nodded toward the pie in his hand and said, "My mom forgot this." He paused, as if debating whether to say more. "Except she never just forgets her pies." He rolled his eyes. "See, she's kind of famous for her pies, so whenever she goes anywhere, she likes for people to ask about her pie about ten times before she unveils it, or something." His free hand was back in his pocket. He looked embarrassed that he'd shared that deep, dark family secret. "Lame, huh?"

Actually, the pie *did* look really good, but I totally couldn't tell him that.

"No," I said. "I think it's kinda nice." And I did. My mom isn't famous for her pies. No, she's famous for defusing a nuclear device in Brussels with only a pair of cuticle scissors and a ponytail holder. Somehow, at that moment, pies seemed cooler.

Josh started to turn, but Liz was still dangling off the roof, so I blurted out the first thing that came to my mind, "Was Keith surprised?"

Well, I didn't know who Keith was or why the Joneses

were throwing him a surprise party, but that was good enough to stop Josh and make him say, "No, he's never surprised. But he fakes it pretty good."

I was something of an expert at faking it myself—especially when I saw Bex lower herself to Liz's level—the two of them swinging in midair as Bex struggled to fix Liz's tangled cables—but Bex still managed to give me the big thumbs-up and mouth, *He's cute!*

"You wanna go get a Coke?" he asked, and I thought, Yes! There was nothing in the world I wanted more. But behind him, Bex was taking aim at the heel of his shoe, firing a tracking device into the back of his Nike.

I heard a subtle sound as the device buried itself into the rubber sole, but Josh didn't even bat an eye. Bex looked totally proud of herself, despite the fact that Liz was still spinning like an out-of-control piñata.

"So this is where you live?" I asked, as if I didn't know.

"Yeah. All my life," Josh said, but he didn't sound proud of it—not like Grandpa Morgan when he says he's lived on the ranch all his life—like he has roots. When Josh said it, he sounded like he had chains. I've spent enough time studying languages to know that almost any phrase can have two meanings.

Behind Josh, Bex must have fixed Liz's cable, because I heard the whizzing sound of two people in near free fall and then the clanging racket of someone landing in a pile of metal trash cans.

I was ready to knock Josh unconscious and run for it, but

he waved the noise away and said, "This neighborhood has all kinds of dogs."

"Oh." I sighed with relief. There was more clanging, so I said, "Big ones, I guess."

I didn't breathe again until I saw Bex clamp her hand over Liz's mouth and drag her into the bushes on the far side of the yard.

"Oh, um, I told my mom I'd go get her jacket out of the car," I said, stepping toward the dozens of vehicles that lined the street.

"I'll go with—" he started, but just then a boy appeared in the street and yelled, "Josh!"

Josh looked at the boy and waved at him.

"You go on," I said.

"No, that's—"

"Josh!" the boy called again, drawing nearer.

"Really," I said, "I'll catch up with you over there."

And then, for the second time, I found myself running away from him, trying to avoid the party.

I ducked behind an SUV, repositioned its side mirror, and watched as the boy met up with Josh in the middle of the street. He tried to take the pie from Josh, and said, "Did you bake that for me? You shouldn't have!" Josh punched him hard on the shoulder. "Ow," the boy said, rubbing his arm. Then he gestured toward where I had disappeared in the dark. "Who was that? She was kinda cute."

I held my breath as Josh followed his friend's gaze and then said, "Oh, nobody. Just some girl."

Chapter Eleven

Summary of Surveillance

Operatives: Cameron Morgan, Rebecca Baxter, and Elizabeth Sutton (hereafter referred to as "The Operatives")

After observing a Gallagher Academy operative (Cameron Morgan) on two routine assignments, The Operatives concluded that a young man (known at the time only as "Josh," aka Tell-Suzie-she's-a-lucky-cat boy) was a POI (Person of Interest).

The Operatives then began a series of recon operations during which they observed the following:

The Subject, Josh Adamson Abrams, resides at 601 North Bellis in Roseville, Virginia.

Known associates: a scan of The Subject's online activity revealed that he routinely e-mails Dillon Jones, screen name D'Man,(also of North Bellis Street)—typically in regard to "really awesome" video games, "lame" movies, "my stupid" dad, and school assignments.

Occupation: sophomore at Roseville High School—
home of the Fighting Pirates. (But evidently not fighting
too hard, since a further search revealed that their
record is 0–3.)

GPA: 3.75. The Subject exhibits difficulty in calculus
and woodworking. (Rules out career as NSA code breaker
and/or home improvement television "Sexy Carpenter
Guy." Does NOT eliminate possibility subject looks hot in a
tool belt.)

The Subject appears to excel at English, Geography,
and Civics (which is great because Cammie is English-
speaking and very civil!).

Family:

Mother, Joan Ellen Abrams, 46, housewife and very
experienced pie baker.

Father, Jacob Whitney Abrams, 47, pharmacist and
sole proprietor of Abrams and Son Pharmacy.

Sister, Joy Marjorie Abrams, 10, student.

Unusual financial activity: none, unless you count the
fact that someone in the family is way too into Civil War
biographies. (Can this be a possible indication of
Confederate insurgents still living and working in
Virginia? Must research further.)

Respectfully submitted, Cammie, Bex, and Liz

"I'm telling you it doesn't mean anything," Bex said as we
stood together in front of the mirror, waiting for the scanner

to slide across our faces and the light in the eyes of the painting to turn green. I hadn't mentioned Josh, but I knew what she was talking about. Bex read my reflection in the mirror, and I realized that the scanner wasn't the only thing that could see inside me.

The doors slid open, and we climbed in. "We've got the computer connection," Liz offered. "Financial records, for example, can illustrate many—"

"Liz!" I snapped. I looked up at the lights and watched our descent. "It's just not worth the risk, okay?" My voice cracked as I thought of how he'd said I was *just some girl*—I was *nobody*. It wasn't very spylike to be sad over such a silly thing, but mostly, I didn't want my friends to hear it. "Guys, it's okay. Josh isn't interested in me. That's fine. I'm not the kind of girl guys like. It's no biggie."

I wasn't searching for compliments, like when skinny girls say they look fat, or when girls with gorgeous curly hair say how they hate humidity. Sure, there are a few people who always tell me "Don't say you're not pretty" and "Of course you look like your mom," but I swear I wasn't silently begging Bex to roll her eyes and say, "Whatever! That guy should be so lucky." But she did, and I'd be lying if I said that didn't make it better.

"Come on, guys," I said, laughing. "What? Did you think he was going to ask me to the prom?" I teased. "Or, hey, Mom's burning macaroni and cheese for supper Sunday night; maybe he can come over and she can tell him about the time she jumped off a ninety-story balcony in Hong

Kong with a parachute she made out of pillowcases."

I looked at them. I tried to laugh, but Bex and Liz looked at each other. I recognized the expression that crossed their faces. For days, they had been passing it between them like a note under the desk.

"Come on." We walked past the dollhouse. "In case you've forgotten, we have better things to do."

That's when we turned the corner, and all three of us jolted to a stop. My jaw went slack, and my heart started to pound as we stared into Mr. Solomon's domain. The classroom in Sublevel One didn't look like a classroom—not anymore. Instead of desks there were three long tables. Instead of chalk and paper there were boxes of rubber gloves. With the frosted-glass partitions and gleaming white floors, it looked as if we'd been kidnapped by aliens and brought to the mother ship for invasive medical procedures. (Personally, I was hoping for a nose job.)

We all stood together, Gallagher Girls closing ranks, preparing for any challenge that might walk through that door.

Little did we know that the challenge was going to be Mr. Solomon carrying three seam-busting, black plastic bags. The sight of those bulging monstrosities made the whole extraterrestrial thing look pretty good. He dropped a bag onto each of the three tables with a sickening *thunk*. Then he tossed a box of gloves in our direction.

"Espionage is dirty business, ladies." He slapped his hands together as if brushing off the dust of his former life.

"Most of what people don't want you to know they send out with the weekly trash." He started working the knot at the top of one of the bags. "How do they spend their money? Where and what do they eat? What kind of pills do they take? How much do they love their pets?"

He grabbed the corners at the bottom of the plastic and then jerked, upturning the bag in one fluid motion that was part birthday-party magician and part executioner. Garbage went everywhere, bursting free, taking up every inch of the long table. The stench was overwhelming, and for the second time in two weeks, I thought I might throw up within that classroom, but not Joe Solomon—he leaned closer, fingering the filth.

"Is he the type of person who does crosswords with a pen?" He dropped the paper and picked up an old envelope that was covered with pieces of eggshell. "What does she doodle when she's on the phone?" Finally, he reached deep within the pile of garbage and found an old Band-Aid. He held it toward the light, studying the semicircle of dried blood that stained the square of gauze. "Everything a person touches tells us something—pieces of the puzzles of their lives." He dropped the bandage back onto the pile and slapped his hands together.

"Welcome to the science of Garbology," he said with a grin.

Thursday morning it was raining. All day, the stone walls seemed to seep moisture. The heavy tapestries and great stone fireplaces didn't seem up to the challenge of fighting the chill. Dr. Fibs had needed Liz, Bex, and me to help him after school on Monday, and we'd had to trade Driver's Ed days with Tina, Courtney, and Eva. So instead of a sunny Indian summer afternoon, we were going to go driving under a sky that matched my mood. I stood waiting for Bex and Liz downstairs by the French doors that lead to the portico. I traced my initials into the condensation, but the water only beaded and ran down the pane.

Not everyone felt as dreary as the day looked, though, because when Liz appeared beside me, she cried, "This is great! I can't believe we're going to get to use the wipers!" I guess when you get published in *Scientific American* at the age of nine, you have a slightly skewed idea of fun.

Our feet splashed down the soggy grass as we cut across the lawn toward where Madame Dabney sat waiting in the car, its headlights already slicing through the gray as the wipers sloshed back and forth.

Fifteen minutes later, Madame Dabney was saying, "Um, Rebecca dear, perhaps you should . . ." Her voice trailed off, though, as Bex made yet another turn and ended up on the wrong side of the road. One might have expected a spy to lay on the emergency brake and knock Bex unconscious with a well-placed blow to the back of her head, but Madame Dabney merely said, "Yes, a right up here, dear . . . Oh, my . . ." and gripped the dashboard as Bex turned across traffic.

"Sorry," Bex yelled, presumably to the truck driver she'd cut off. "Keep forgetting they're over there, don't I?"

The rain had stopped, but the wheels made a wet, slick sound as they threw water up into the undercarriage of the car. The windows were fogged, and I couldn't see where we were going, which was kind of a blessing, because every time I caught a glance at the world around us, I saw another year of my life flash before my eyes.

"Perhaps we should let one of your classmates take a turn?" Madame Dabney finally managed to say as Bex nearly ran into a cement truck, jerked the wheel, jumped the curb, and flew across the corner of a parking lot and onto another street.

But that's when I noticed something strange. Not only was Bex not paying attention to Madame Dabney's anguished cries and the laws which govern the operation of motor vehicles in this country, but—and here's the weird thing—Liz wasn't freaking out!

Liz, who hates spiders and refuses to go barefoot anywhere. Liz, who is a perfectly good swimmer and yet owns six different types of flotation devices. Liz, who once went to bed without flossing and couldn't sleep the entire night, was sitting calmly in the backseat while Bex nearly took out a trash can on the curb.

"Rebecca, that could have been a pedestrian," Madame Dabney warned, but she didn't use her emergency brake, so now I'll always wonder what Madame Dabney saw in France to make her definition of "emergency" so wildly skewed.

That's also when I noticed the street signs.

"Oh my gosh!" I muttered through clenched teeth. Liz

was grinning as a sign announcing we were on North Bellis whizzed by.

"Shhh," Liz said as she reached into the pocket of her bag and pulled out the remote control from the stereo she'd destroyed on her first day back.

"What are you doing with—"

"Shhh!" She cut a warning glance toward Madame Dabney. "It will only be a *little* explosion."

Explosion!

Seconds later a loud bang rocketed through the car. Bex fought for control of the wheel. I smelled smoke and heard the dull, lifeless flapping of rubber banging against the pavement.

"Oh, no, Madame Dabney," Bex exclaimed in her most theatrical voice. "*I think we've got a flat!*"

"Oh, do we now?" I said as I glared at Liz, who just shrugged. Maybe I should take back my ringing endorsement for having genius friends. Normal friends probably don't go around blowing up Driver's Ed cars—well, not intentionally, anyway.

When the car finally came to a stop—you guessed it—we were in front of Josh's house.

"Oh, girls," Madame Dabney soothed, turning around to make sure that Liz and I were still in our original one-piece bodies. "Is everyone okay?" We nodded. "Well," Madame Dabney said, composing herself, "I suppose we'll just learn how to change a tire."

Of course Bex and Liz had known that was coming. That

was the whole point. But Bex still sounded surprised as she shouted, "I'll get the spare!"

In a flash of blinding speed she was out of the car and popping the trunk, while Liz intercepted Madame Dabney.

"Tell me, ma'am, what causes the majority of flat tires, do you think?" As Liz dragged our instructor to inspect the damage at the front of the car, I met Bex around back.

"What are you doing?" I demanded.

But Bex only grinned and reached into the trunk, revealing a bulging trash bag just like the ones that lined the street. "Couldn't leave the curb bare, now, could we?"

And then I noticed it; all up and down Bellis Street, trash cans and plastic sacks covered the curb, waiting like soldiers standing at attention.

"You switched the days," I said, dismayed. "You blew the tire. You . . ." I trailed off, probably because the next words out of my mouth were either going to be "You care enough to do this?" or "You're destined for a life of crime." It was a toss-up either way.

"Can't give up now, can we?" Bex said, sounding very Bexish. Dramatically, she pulled the jack out of the trunk and cocked an eyebrow. "We owe it to your country."

No, they thought they owed it to me. I'm just really glad she didn't say so.

Within seconds, Bex and I had the spare tire out of the trunk, and Madame Dabney was illustrating the finer points of lug-nut-loosening, but all I could do was look up and down Bellis Street. What if he saw me and recognized the car and the uniforms? How would I ever explain? Would he *want* me to explain? Would he even see me at all, or would I simply be "some girl"? Would I just be "nobody"?

"School trip to D.C.," Liz whispered in my ear when she saw how tense I was. "He won't be back until after nine."

I felt myself exhale.

"Do you have any questions?" Madame Dabney asked as she eased the jack out from beneath the car and Bex went to put the ruined tire in the trunk. Liz and I shook our heads. "Well, that should do it, then," Madame Dabney said, slapping her hands together, obviously proud of her handiwork.

Yeah, I thought, as I stole one last look at the neighborhood around me and saw Bex flash me a quick thumbs-up. That should do it.

Summary of Surveillance

Operatives: Cameron Morgan, Rebecca Baxter, and Elizabeth Sutton

Report of trash taken from the home of Josh Abrams

Number of empty cardboard toilet paper rolls: 2

Preferred variety of canned soup: tomato (followed closely by Campbell's Cream of Mushroom).

Number of empty Ben & Jerry's containers: 3—two mint chocolate cookie, one plain vanilla. (Who buys plain vanilla ice cream from Ben & Jerry's, anyway? Is there a greater waste?)

Number of Pottery Barn catalogs: 14 (No items

marked or otherwise identified, even though the Windsor Washable Throw Pillows were on sale and appeared to be quite a bargain.)

"Where are we putting the paper towels again?" Bex asked, looking around our odd little circle of piles. "Are they household or food?"

"Depends," Liz said, leaning toward her. "What's on it?"

Bex took a whiff of the used paper towel in her hand and said, "Spaghetti sauce . . . I think. Or blood?"

"So, either they love pasta or are a family of axe murderers?" I quipped.

Bex turned and dropped the towels onto one of the half dozen piles that were growing around us while the original pile in the center began to slowly shrink. We'd opened all the windows in the suite, and a cool, damp breeze blew in, diluting the smell of garbage (a little) as we sat on a plastic tarp, examining everything from used tissues to empty cans of tuna.

If you ever wonder whether or not someone is too good for you, I'd advise going through their trash. Really. No one looks superior after that. Plus, if Mr. Solomon was right, there were answers here—answers I desperately wanted.

Why did he offer to walk with me to (supposedly) get my mom's jacket, and then turn around and tell his friend I was no one? Did he have a girlfriend? Had he struck up that conversation with me in the street so that he could win some horrendous bet with his friends, like they always do in teen movies? I mean, I know I spend my winters in a mansion with a bunch of girls, and my summers on a ranch in Nebraska, but both places have movies, and a lot of them involve wagers in which plain-looking girls (like me) are approached by really cute boys (like Josh).

But those boys aren't Josh-like, not really, or so I realized the deeper into his garbage we went. The boys in those movies wouldn't help their kid sisters with a fourth-grade ode to Amelia Earhart (Gallagher Academy, Class of 1915). Those boys wouldn't write notes like the one I have taken the liberty of pasting below:

Mom, Dillon says his mom can drop me off after the field trip, so don't wait up for my call. Love you, J.

He tells his mom he loves her. How great is that? I mean, the boys in the movies with the bets and the plain girls (who are never *really* plain, just poorly accessorized) and the big, dramatic prom scenes—those boys would *never* leave their mothers kind and courteous notes. Plus, boys who leave kind and courteous notes become men who leave kind and courteous notes. I couldn't help myself: I instantly imagined what it would be like to get a note like that myself someday.

Darling, I may have to work late, so I might not be here when you get back. I hope you had a great time in North Korea and disabled lots of nuclear weapons. With all my love, Josh.

(But that's just a draft.)

I stared at an empty pack of chewing gum—the teeth-whitening kind—and I tried to remember if his teeth had been extra white or just regular white. Regular white, I thought, so I chucked the pack into a stack beside Liz and dug back into the pile again, not knowing what I hoped to pull out.

I found an envelope, small and square, with beautiful calligraphy on the front. It was addressed to *The Abrams Family*. I'd never seen anything in my life addressed to *The Morgan Family*. We never got invited to parties. Sure, I remembered a time or two when Mom and Dad dressed up and left me with a sitter, but even then I knew she had a teeny tiny microfilm recorder in her rhinestone broach and his cuff links contained cables that could shoot out for fifty yards and let a person rappel down the side of a building if he really wanted to. (When you think about it, it's not that surprising we didn't get invited out much.)

I was just starting to imagine what it would be like to be the other kind of family, when I heard an ominous, "Uh-oh."

I turned to look at Liz, who was holding a piece of paper toward Bex.

She has to go through Bex first, I realized in terror. *Josh only has six months to live! He's taking drugs that will prepare him for a sex change operation! His entire family is moving to Alaska!*

It was worse.

"Cam," Bex said, her voice bracing me for the worst, "Liz found something you should probably see."

"It's probably nothing," Liz added, forcing a smile as Bex held out a folded piece of pink paper. Someone had written "JOSH" on it in blue ink with a flowery, ornate kind of penmanship that no one at the Gallagher Academy ever seemed able to master—after all, if you've got organic chemistry, advanced encryption, and conversational Swahili homework every night, you're not going to spend a lot of time learning how to dot your *i*'s with little hearts.

"Read it to me," I said.

"No. . . ." Liz started. "It's probably—"

"Liz!" I snapped.

But Bex had already started. "'Dear Josh. It was great seeing you at the carnival. I had fun, too. We should do it again sometime. Love, DeeDee.'"

Bex had done her best to make the note sound blah, adding lots of unnecessary pauses and dull inflections, but there wasn't any denying that this DeeDee person meant business. After all, *I* didn't write notes on pink paper with fancy writing. I didn't even own pink paper. Edible paper—yes, but pretty pink paper—no way! So there it was, proof in black-and-white (or . . . well . . . pink-and-blue, but you get what I mean), that I was officially out of my league. That I really was nobody.

Liz must have read my expression, because she jumped to say, "This doesn't mean anything, Cam. It's in the *trash*!"

She turned to Bex. "That's got to mean something, right?"

And that's when I couldn't ignore it anymore: the universal truth that, despite our elite education and genius IQs, we didn't know boys. DeeDee, with her pink paper and ability to make the big, puffy J's, might have known the significance of a boy like Josh putting her perfect pink note in the trash, but we sure didn't. The boy of my dreams may have been as close as the town of Roseville—just two miles, eighty security cameras, and a big honking stone fence away, but he and I would never speak the same language (which is totally ironic, since "boy" was the one language my school had never tried to teach me).

"That's okay, Liz," I said softly. "We knew it was a long shot. It's—"

"Wait!" I felt Bex's hand lash out and grab my wrist. "Tell me what you told him again." She read my blank expression. "That night?" she prompted. "When you told him you were homeschooled."

"*He* asked if I was homeschooled, and I said yes."

"And what reason did you give?"

"For . . ." I started, but my voice trailed off as I looked at the stack of papers that she had laid out between us. "Religious reasons."

There was a program for the Roseville Free Will Baptist Assembly, a flyer for the United Methodist Church of Roseville, and a handful of others. Either Josh was collecting church bulletins for some kind of bizarre scavenger hunt, or he'd been busy traipsing to Sunday schools and

Tuesday-night teen socials for an entirely different reason.

"He's looking for you, Cam," Bex said, beaming as if she'd just made the first step in cracking the ultimate code.

Silence washed over us. My heart pounded in my chest. Bex and Liz were staring at me, but I couldn't pull my gaze away from what we'd found—from the hope that was spread out across our floor.

I guess that's why none of us noticed the door opening. I guess that's why we jumped when we heard Macey McHenry say, "So, what's his name?"

Chapter twelve

"I don't know what you're talking about," I shot back, way too quickly for the lie to be any good. Here's the thing about lying: a part of you has to mean it—even if it is a tiny, sinister shred that only lives in the blackest, darkest parts of your mind. You have to want it to be true.

I guess I didn't.

"Oh, come on," Macey said with a roll of her eyes. "It's been, what? Two weeks?" I was shocked. Macey cocked her head and asked, "You been to second base yet?"

There are entire books in the Gallagher Academy library about female independence and how we shouldn't let men distract us from our missions, but all I could do was look at Macey McHenry and say, "You think I could get to second base?"

I hate to admit it, but it was probably one of the greatest compliments I had received in my whole, entire life.

But Macey only rolled her eyes and said, "Forget I asked," as she strolled to the pile of garbage and, unsurprisingly, turned up her perfect nose and said, "This is disgusting!" Then she looked at me. "You must have it bad."

Leave it to Bex to keep her cool and say, "We've got CoveOps homework, Macey."

Even I almost believed that what we were doing was perfectly innocent.

Macey looked down at our piles, examining the scene as if this were the most exciting thing she'd seen in months, which absolutely, positively could not have been true, since I know for a fact that her class had been in the physics labs when Mr. Fibs got attacked by the bees he thought he'd genetically modified to obey commands from a whistle. (Turns out they only respond to the voice of James Earl Jones.)

"His name is Josh," I said finally.

"Cammie!" Liz cried, as if she couldn't believe I was giving such sensitive intel to the enemy.

But Macey only repeated, "Josh," as if trying it on for size.

"Yeah," I said. "I met him when we had a mission in town, and . . . well . . ."

"Now you can't stop thinking about him. . . . You always want to know what he's doing. . . . You'd kill to know if he's thinking about you. . . ." Macey said, like a doctor reeling off symptoms.

"Yes!" I cried. "That's sooooo it!"

She shrugged. "That's too bad, kid."

She was only three months older than me, so I totally could have gotten mad about the "kid" thing, but I couldn't get mad at her—not then. I wasn't exactly sure what was happening, but one thing was becoming obvious: Macey McHenry had intel I desperately needed.

"He told me I had a lucky cat," I said. "What does that mean?"

"You don't have a cat."

"Technicality." I waved that fact away. "So, what does it mean?"

"It sounds like he wants to play it cool. . . . That he *might* like you, and he wants to keep his options open in case you decide *you* don't like *him*, or if he decides *he* doesn't like *you*."

"But then I saw him on the street, and I overheard him telling a friend that I was 'nobody.' But he'd been really nice and—"

"Oh, you have been busy."

"He acts really nice, but based on what he told his friend—"

"Wait." Macey stopped me. "He said that to a friend? Another guy?"

"Yes."

"And you believed him?" She rolled her eyes. "Total hearsay. Could be posturing, could be territory marking, could be shame over liking the new weird chick—I'm assuming he thinks you're a weird chick?"

"He thinks I'm homeschooled for religious reasons."

"Yeah," she said, nodding as if that were answer enough. "I'd say you've still got a shot."

OH. MY. GOSH. It was as if the gray storm clouds had parted and Macey McHenry was the sun, bringing wisdom and truth into the eternal darkness. (Or something a lot less melodramatic.)

Just in case you missed my point: Macey McHenry knows about boys!! Of course, this shouldn't have come as a huge, colossal surprise, but I couldn't help myself; I was groveling at her feet, worshipping at the altar of eyeliner, push-up bras, and coed parties without parental supervision.

Even Liz said, "That's amazing."

"You've got to help me," I pleaded.

"Oooh, sorry. Not my department."

Of course it wasn't. It was clear that Macey McHenry was the *lurkee*, not the *lurker*. She couldn't possibly understand life on the outside, looking through the window at a place she'd never know. Then I thought about the hours she'd spent locked away in the silence of those headphones and wondered, Or could she?

Before me stood a person who was capable of cracking the Y chromosome code, and I wasn't going to let her get away that easily.

"*Come on!*" I said.

"Yeah, well tell it to someone who isn't the *freaking* mascot of the seventh-*freaking*-grade!" She eased onto her bed and crossed her legs. "So there is only one way that I am going to care about your boy problems."

Work brain, work, I urged my mind, but it was like a car stuck in the mud.

"I'm getting out of the newbie classes," Macey said. "And you're going to help me."

I really didn't like the sound of this, but I still managed to ask, "What's in it for me?"

"For starters, I don't have a conversation with our friend Jessica Boden about an early morning trip to the labs with an old Dr Pepper bottle, or a late-night trip outside the grounds, where someone came home with leaves in her hair." She smirked at Liz. "Or a certain Driver's Ed incident."

For the first time, I didn't doubt that Macey was a Gallagher Girl, too. The looks Liz and Bex were giving me said that they agreed.

"Did you know Jessica's mother is a trustee?" Macey said, her voice dripping with sarcastic irony. "See, Jessica's mentioned that fact to me about a hundred and fifty times now and—"

"Okay, already," I said, stopping her. "What else do I get?"

"A *soul mate.*"

"Ladies, this is a business of alliances," Mr. Solomon said as he stood in front of our class the next morning. "You may not like these people. You may hate these people. These people may represent everything you hate, but all it takes is *one* thing, ladies—one thread of commonality to form a bond in our lives." He strolled back to his desk. "To make an ally."

So that's what I had with Macey—an alliance. We weren't friends; we weren't enemies. I wasn't exactly blocking off Fourth of July weekend to spend at her place in the Hamptons, but I planned on playing nice just the same.

When lunchtime rolled around, Macey strolled over to our table, and I braced myself for what was going to happen. *If the Communists and the Capitalists could fight together to take down the Nazis . . .* I told myself. *If Spike could fight alongside Buffy to rid the world of demons . . . If lemon could join forces with lime to create something as delicious and refreshing as Sprite, then surely I can work alongside Macey McHenry for the cause of true love!*

She was sitting beside me. She was eating pie. I had to look again. *Macey's eating pie?!* And then she actually spoke, but I couldn't hear her over the roar of a nearby debate (in Korean) about whether Jason Bourne could take James Bond, and if it mattered whether it was *Sean-Connery-Bond* or *Pierce-Brosnan-Bond*.

"Did you say something, Macey?" I asked, but she cut me a look that could kill. She reached into her bag, ripped off a sliver of Evapopaper, and scribbled:

Can we study tonight? (Tell anyone, and I'll kill you in your sleep!)

"Seven o'clock?" I asked her. She nodded. We had a date.

136

The pie had looked pretty good, so I got up to go get some, and when I did, I glanced at the *Vogue* Macey had been reading, but I couldn't learn much about fashion, because Macey's organic chemistry notes were taped inside, covering that month's salute to silk.

Sitting on the floor of our suite that night with Macey's homework scattered around us, I wasn't really sure how this alliance business was supposed to work. Luckily, Liz had been giving it some thought

"You can start by explaining what this means." She held DeeDee's note up to Macey's face.

"Ew!" Macey cried, turning her head and holding her nose as she pushed the paper away.

But what Liz lacked in strength, she made up for in tenacity. She shoved the note back in Macey's direction despite Macey's complaint of, "I thought you got rid of all that trash!"

"Well, not this. This is evidence," Liz said, stating what, in her mind, was the obvious.

"Ugh! Gross."

I saw Bex shift. She'd been doing a better than average job of ignoring us, but I knew all of her sensors were on full alert. Her eyes never left her notebook, but she saw everything. (Bex is super sleuthy that way.)

"*What does it mean?*" Liz asked again, inching closer and closer to Macey McHenry, our new professor of boys.

Macey looked back at her notebook, and must have come to the conclusion that she'd studied enough for one night, because she tossed her notes aside. She marched to her bed, glanced at the scrap of paper once more, then dropped it to the floor.

"It means he's in demand." She nodded at me. "Good choosing."

"But does he like her back?" Liz wanted to know. "This DeeDee person?"

Macey shrugged and stretched out on her bed. "Hard to say."

That's when Liz pulled out a notebook I'd seen her carrying around for the past week. I'd thought it was for an extra project—little did I know it was *our* extra project. She threw the binder open with a *thunk*, and a hundred pieces of paper ruffled with the sudden waft of air. I looked at the headers of each piece as Liz rifled through them. "See . . ." She pointed to a highlighted portion of one page. ". . . in this e-mail he used the word 'bro' in reference to his friend Dillon. As in, and I quote, 'chill out, bro. It will be okay.' He doesn't have a brother. What is it about boys that makes them refer to each other in that way? I don't call Cam or Bex *sis*. Why?" she demanded, as if her life depended upon her understanding this fact. "WHY?"

Yeah, that's when *Macey McHenry* looked at *Liz* as if she were stupid. Of all the crazy things I've seen in this business, that was one of the craziest.

Macey cocked her head and said, "*You're* the uber-genius?"

Just like that, Bex was up off the bed and moving toward

Macey. Things were about to get bad—really bad. But poor Liz wasn't hurt by what Macey said. In fact, she just looked at her and said, "I know—*right?*" as if she too were outraged.

Bex stopped. I exhaled. And eventually Liz shook her head in amazement, scattering the unanswered questions from her mind—something I must have seen her do a thousand times. That's when I knew that boys were just another subject to Liz—another code she had to crack. Eventually, she dropped to the floor and said, "I've got to make a chart."

"Look." Macey seemed to give up as she straightened herself on the bed. "If he's the sentimental type, then it means he doesn't care about her. If he's not, then he might like her—or might not." She leaned closer, needing us to understand. "You can analyze or theorize—or whatever—but seriously, what good do you think it will do? You're in here. He's out there. And there's nothing I can do about that."

"Oh," Bex said, speaking for the first time. "That's not your area of expertise anyway." I saw her mind churning. She looked like a girl on a mission as she stepped forward. "It's ours."

Chapter Thirteen

S pies are wise. Spies are strong. But, most of all, spies are patient.

We waited two weeks. TWO WEEKS! Do you know how long that is in fifteen-year-old-girl time? A lot. A LOT, a lot. I was really starting to empathize with all those women who talk about biological clocks. I mean, I know mine's still got a lot of ticks left in it, but I still managed to think and worry about Operation Josh every spare minute—and *that* was at genius spy school, where spare minutes aren't exactly common. I can only imagine the misery of a girl going to a normal school, since she probably isn't going to spend her Saturday nights helping her best friend crack the codes that protect U.S. spy satellites. (Liz even split the extra credit she earned from Mr. Mosckowitz with me—the cash prize offered by the NSA, she kept.)

We were in the classic holding pattern, gathering info, building his profile and my legend, biding our time until we had what we needed to go in.

Two weeks of this. TWO WEEKS! (Just in case you missed it before.)

Then, as with all good covert operatives, we caught a break.

Tuesday, October 1. Subject received an e-mail from Dillon, screen name "D'Man," asking if The Subject would like a ride home from play practice. The Subject responded by saying that he would be walking home—that he needs to return some videos at "AJ's" (local establishment located on town square that specializes in movie and video game rentals).

I looked at the e-mail as Bex slid it onto the breakfast table in front of me.

"Tonight," she whispered. "We're on."

During CoveOps class I honestly couldn't write fast enough. Joe Solomon is a genius, I thought, wondering why I'd never realized it before.

"Learn your legends early. Learn them well," he warned as he leaned over, gripping the back of the teacher's chair I'd never seen him sit in. "The split second it takes you to recall something your cover identity would know is the split second in which very bad people can do very bad things."

My hand was shaking. Pencil marks were going everywhere on the page—kind of like the time I picked up a pencil to use in Dr. Fibs's class, only it turned out it wasn't an ordinary pencil, but rather a prototype for a new Morse code auto-translator. (Needless to say, I still haven't fully recovered from the guilt of sharpening it.)

"Most of all, remember that going into deep cover does not mean approaching subjects." Mr. Solomon eyed us. "It means putting yourself in a position where *the subject* approaches *you*."

I don't know about regular girls, but when you're a spy, getting dressed to go out can be something of a production. (Can I just say thank goodness for Velcro—seriously—no wonder the Gallagher Academy invented the stuff.)

"I still think we should have put her hair up," Liz said. "It looks *glamorous*."

"Yeah," Macey scoffed, "because so many girls go for glamour when they hang out at the Roseville town square."

She had a point.

Personally, I didn't care, which was kind of ironic since it was *my* hair and all, but I had plenty of other things on my mind—not the least of which was the arsenal of items that Bex was spreading out on the bed in front of me—not that I could really see all that well, because Macey was doing my makeup and she kept telling me to "look up" or "look down" or "hold perfectly still."

When she wasn't barking demands, she was saying things like, "Talk, but not too much. Laugh, but not too loud." And, my personal favorite, "If he's shorter than you, slouch."

Then Bex took over. "Let's talk pocket litter." (Not a sentence you hear every day unless you're . . . well . . . *us*.) "You're not sixteen, so IDs aren't a problem, but we still have to support your cover identity." She turned and began scanning the items on the bed. "Take this," she said, tossing a pack of gum in my direction. It was the same brand we'd pulled from Josh's garbage. "To display common likes and help with the whole breath thing." Bex scanned the bed again. "What did we say, handbag or no handbag?" she asked, turning back to the group.

"She should definitely carry a purse," Macey said, and Bex agreed. I couldn't believe it! Macey and Bex were bonding . . . over accessories! Would wonders never cease?

Bex pulled a bag off the bed and opened it. "Movie ticket stub—if he asks you how you liked it, just say you did, but you didn't buy the ending." She dropped the tiny scrap of paper into the bag and picked up another item. "Binocuglasses. You shouldn't need them tonight, of course, but it won't hurt to have them." She dropped yet another item inside our pack of lies then topped everything off with a *What Would Jesus Do?* ink pen, then snapped the bag shut with a very self-satisfied smirk.

I had no idea how Bex had found all that stuff, and to tell you the truth, I didn't want to know. But as I looked at everything I was supposed to carry and thought about all the things I was supposed to know, I had to wonder: Do all girls go through this? Is every girl on a date really in deep cover?

"And, don't forget . . ."

I looked up to see the silver cross swinging back and forth on its chain.

"It's broken," I told Bex. "It hasn't worked right since the water from the tank shorted it out; and you still wouldn't have been able to pick up the signal because of the jammers."

"Cammie," Bex said, sighing. "*Cammie, Cammie, Cammie* . . . this is your legend." The cross kept swinging. "*This* is how it's accessorized."

I knew she was right. As soon as I crossed that fence, I had to stop being me and start being that other person—the homeschooled girl who wore that necklace and . . .

"You have got to be kidding me!" I snapped, but it was too late, Liz had appeared in the doorway, holding Onyx.

And I thought this boy business was hard *before* I had to rub a cat all over my body to give the hair-covered illusion of a feline-lover.

All these years I'd thought being a spy was challenging. Turns out, being a girl is the tricky part.

They walked with me downstairs to the most remote of the secret passageways.

"Did you check your flashlight?" Liz asked, the way Grandma Morgan always says "Do you have your ticket?" whenever they take me to the airport. It was sweet. I wished they could go with me, but that's something every spy learns early in the game—it doesn't matter how skilled your team is, there will come a time when you have to go on alone.

As we walked along, Macey said, "I still don't understand how you're going to get out and back in without getting caught."

She sounded genuinely confused, but I wasn't. Someday, I really ought to write a book about the mansion. I could probably make a fortune selling copies to the newbies, sharing tricks like how you can jiggle the door of the janitor's closet in the west stairwell, then slide down a pipe all the way to the butler's pantry. (How you get back up is up to you.) Another good one is the wooden panel on the landing of the stone staircase in the old chapel. If you press it three times, it will pop open, and from there, you have ceiling access to every room in the North Hall. (I just wouldn't recommend this one if you are in any way afraid of spiders.)

"You'll see, Macey," I told her as we turned to walk down a long stone corridor toward the old ruby-colored tapestry that hung alone on the cold stone wall. I looked at the Gallagher family tree, and then at Macey. She didn't study the generations, didn't find her own name there or ask questions; she just said, "You look good," and I nearly passed out from the shock of such high praise.

I pulled the tapestry aside and started to slip in, just as Bex said, "Knock 'em dead!"

I was already inside when Liz yelled after me, *"But not literally!"*

Chapter fourteen

I don't know how I let them talk me into it. Well, I do, but you'll never hear me admit it out loud. Sneaking outside the campus grounds was one thing—that was merely a matter of memorizing the sweeping grids of the cameras, knowing the blind spots of the guards, and circumventing the motion detectors along the south wall. But wearing shoes that made the sneaking infinitely more difficult was something I will never be proud of. Sure, Macey's black boots elongated my legs and gave me an aura of Charlie's Angels-ness, but by the time I was in position on a park bench at the corner of the town square, my feet were sore, my ankle was twisted, and my nerves were shot.

Lucky for me, I had some time to collect myself. So. Much. Time.

Here's the thing you need to know about surveillance: it's boring. Sure, sometimes we blow stuff up and jump off buildings and/or moving trains, but most of the time we just hang around waiting for something to happen (a fact that almost never makes it into the movies), so I might have felt pretty silly if I were a normal girl and not a highly trained secret-agent-type person as I sat on that park bench, trying to act normal when, by definition, I'm anything but.

17:35 hours (that's five thirty-five P.M.): The Operative moved into position.

18:00 hours: The Operative was wishing she'd brought something to eat because she couldn't leave her post to go buy a candy bar, much less use the bathroom.

18:30 hours: The Operative realized it's almost impossible to look pretty and/or seductive if you SERIOUSLY have to go pee.

My homework for that night consisted of fifty pages of *The Art of War*, which needed translating into Arabic, a credit card–slash–fingerprint modifier that need perfecting for Dr. Fibs, and Madame Dabney had been dropping big pop-quiz hints at the end of C&A. Yet, there I was, rubbing my swelling ankle and thinking that I really should be getting CoveOps extra credit for this.

I looked at my watch again: seven forty-five. Okay, I thought, I'll give him until eight and then . . .

"Hi," I heard from behind me.

Oh, jeez. Oh, jeez. I couldn't turn around. Oh heck, I had to turn around.

"Cammie?" he said again as if it were a question.

I could have said hi back in fourteen different languages (and that's not including pig Latin). And yet I was speechless as he came to stand in front of me.

"Um . . . Oh . . . Um . . ."

"Josh," he said, pointing to himself as if he thought I'd forgotten.

How sweet is that? I know I'm no boy expert, but I have heard entire lectures on reading body language, and I have to say that assuming that a person will have forgotten your name is *way* high on my "indicators of humbleness" list (not that I have one, but I totally have a starting point now).

"Hi."

I said that in English, didn't I? It wasn't Arabic or French? Oh, please, God in Heaven, don't let him think I'm an exchange student . . . or worse, a girl who knows, like, three words of a foreign language and goes around using them all the time just to prove how smart/cultured/generally better than everyone else she is.

"I saw you sitting over here," he said. *Okay, looks like we're good on the English thing.* "I haven't seen you around at all lately."

"Oh." I shot upright. "I was in Mongolia."

Note to self: learn to be a less extreme liar.

"With the Peace Corps," I said slowly. "My parents are big into that. That's when they started the homeschooling thing," I said, remembering my legend, feeling the momentum.

"Wow. That's so cool," he said.

"It is?" I asked, wondering if he was serious. But he was smiling, so I said, "Oh, yeah. It is."

He slid onto the seat beside me. "So, have you lived, like, a lot of places?"

I've traveled quite a bit, but I've actually only lived three places: a Nebraska ranch, a school for geniuses, and a D.C. town house. Luckily, I'm an excellent liar with a very thorough legend. Four years' worth of COW lessons swam in my head, and I went for some of the highlights. "Thailand's really beautiful."

"Wow."

Then I remembered Macey's *don't be cooler than he is* advice. "It was long time ago," I said. "It wasn't a big thing."

"But you live here now?"

The Subject likes to state the obvious, which may signify a defect in observation skills and/or short-term memory?

"Yeah." I nodded. And then things got quiet—painfully quiet. "I'm waiting on my mom," I blurted, finally remembering my cover story. "She takes a class at night . . . at the library." I gestured to the red brick building across the square. "And I like to come into town with her because I don't get out much, thanks to my nontraditional education."

The Subject has really blue eyes that twinkle when he looks at someone like she's maybe a little bit insane.

After a long stretch of really awkward silence, he stood up and said, "I gotta go." I wanted to beg him not to leave, but even *I* knew that might come off as a tad bit desperate. He stepped away, and I didn't know how to stop him (well, I did, but several of the moves I had in mind are really only legal during times of war).

"Hey," he said, "what's your last name?"

"Solomon," I blurted.

Ew! A large portion of my future government salary will someday be spent trying to understand why I chose *that* name at *this* moment, but it was out there and I couldn't take it back.

"Are you, like, in the book?"

The book? What book?

He laughed and stepped closer. "Can I *call* you?" he asked, reading the confusion on my face.

Josh was asking if he could call me! He wanted my phone number! What it meant—truly and irrevocably meant—I didn't know. But I felt very safe in ruling out the possibility that he thought I was "nobody." Still, that didn't change the fact that the last phone I used doubles as a stun gun (so for obvious reasons I probably shouldn't give him the number of that one).

I said, "No." But then the most amazing thing happened: Josh looked totally sad! It was as if I'd run over his puppy (though no actual puppies were harmed in the formation of that metaphor).

I was shocked. I was amazed. I was drunk on power!

"No!" I said again. "Not, 'no *you* can't call me.' I meant, 'no, you *can't* call me.'" Then, seeing his confusion, I added, "There are strict rules at my house." Not a lie.

He nodded, faking understanding, then asked, "What about e-mail?"

I shook my head.

"I see."

"I'll be back here tomorrow," I blurted, stopping him in his tracks. "My mom, she has class again. I'll . . ."

"Okay." He nodded, then turned to go. "Maybe I'll see you around."

"What the heck is that supposed to mean?" I yelled at Macey, though it wasn't her fault. I mean, if a boy gets all gooey and disappointed because you won't give him your phone number and then you tell him you will be at a designated place at a designated time—therein eliminating the need for a phone number—and he says "maybe" he'll see you there? That's cause to yell—isn't it?

"Maybe?" I yelled again, which might have been overkill since I'd had the whole walk back to school to simmer in his words, and my roommates were hearing them for the first time.

Liz was wearing the same expression she gets whenever Dr. Fibs tells us we'll be needing our gas masks for class—equal parts fear and euphoria. Macey was doing her nails, and Bex was doing yoga in the corner of the room.

Most people are supposed to get calmer with deep

breathing and inner reflection—not Bex. "I could take him out," she offered, and if she hadn't been twisted up like a pretzel at the time, I might have worried more about it. After all, she knew where he lived.

"Well . . ." Liz stammered. "I supposed you'll just have to go, and then if he shows, it means he likes you."

"Wrong," Macey said, making a buzzer sound as she flipped through a textbook. "If he comes, it means he's curious—or bored—but probably curious."

"But when will we know if he likes her?" Liz pleaded.

Macey rolled her big, blue, beautiful eyes. "That's not the question," she said, as if it were the most obvious thing in the world. "The question is—how much?"

Is there no end to the things we have to learn?

Chapter Fifteen

Spy training isn't something you can turn off and on. We eat, sleep, and breathe this stuff. It has become as much a part of my DNA as lackluster hair and a weakness for peanut M&M's. I know that probably goes without saying, but before I tell you what came next, I thought I'd better point it out.

After all, imagine if *you* were a fifteen-year-old girl standing alone on a deserted street on a dark night, preparing for a clandestine meeting, when, all of a sudden you can't see anything because a pair of hands are covering your eyes. One second you're standing there, being grateful that you'd remembered to pack a candy bar, and then . . . POW . . . everything goes black.

Well, that's what happened. But did I panic? No way. I did what I was trained to do—I grabbed the offending arm, shifted my weight, and used the force of my would-be attacker's momentum against him.

It was fast. Really fast. Scary, these-hands-are-lethal-weapons fast.

I am so good, I thought, right up until the point when I looked down and saw Josh lying at my feet, the wind knocked out of him.

"Oh my gosh! I'm so sorry!" I cried and reached down for him. "I'm *so* sorry. Are you all right? Please be all right."

"Cammie?" he croaked. His voice sounded so weak, and I thought, This is it. I've killed the only man I could ever love, and now I'm about to hear his deathbed (deathstreet?) confession. I leaned close to him. My hair fell into his open mouth. He gagged.

So . . . yeah . . . on my first psuedo-date, I not only physically assaulted my potential soul mate, I also made him gag—literally.

I pushed my hair behind my ear and crouched beside him. (Incidentally, if you ever want to feel a boy's abs, this is a pretty good technique—because it seemed perfectly natural for me to put my hands on his stomach and chest.) "Ooh. What is it?"

"Do something for me?"

"Anything!" I crouched lower, not wanting to miss a single, precious word.

"Please don't ever tell any of my friends about this."

He smiled, and relief flooded my body.

He thinks I'll meet his friends! I thought—then wondered, What does that mean?

The Subject demonstrates amazing physical fortitude, as was exhibited by his ability to recover quickly after a very hard fall onto asphalt.

The Subject is also surprisingly heavy.

I helped Josh get up and brush himself off.

"Wow!" he said. "Where did you learn to do that?"

I shrugged, trying to guess how Cammie the home-schooled girl who had a cat named Suzie would reply. "My mom says a girl needs to know how to take care of herself." *Not a lie.*

He rubbed the back of his head. "I feel sorry for your dad."

Bullets couldn't have hit me any harder. But then I realized that he wasn't taking it back, slinking away, trying to pull his foot out of his mouth. He just looked at me and smiled. For the first time in a long time, when thinking about my father, I felt like smiling, too.

"He says he's pretty tough, but I think she could take him."

"Like mother like daughter, huh?"

He had no idea what an amazing compliment he'd just given me—and the thing was: he'd never know.

"Can you . . . like . . ." He was gesturing to the town around us. ". . . walk around or something?"

"Sure."

We set off down the street. For a girl who has been described as a pavement artist, I was a little surprised at how hard it is to walk when you're actually trying to be seen.

After a few minutes of listening to our feet on the street, I realized something. *Talking. Shouldn't there be talking?* I searched my mind for something—anything—to say, but kept coming up with things like "*So, how 'bout those new satellite-controlled detonators with the twelve-mile range?*" Or, "*Have you read the new translation of* Art of War? *Because I prefer it in the original dialect. . . .*" I half wished he'd charge at me again or draw a knife or start speaking in Japanese or something . . . but he didn't, and so I didn't know what to do. He walked. So I walked. He smiled, so I smiled back. He turned a corner (without using the Strembesky technique of detecting a tail, which was really sloppy of him), and I followed.

We turned another corner, and I knew from my Driver's Ed recon that there was a playground up ahead.

"I broke my arm there," he said, pointing to the monkey bars. Then he blushed. "It was a real rumble—bodies everywhere—you should have seen the other guy."

I smiled. "Oh, sounds wild."

"As wild as anything in Roseville ever gets." He laughed, and then kicked a stone with the toe of his shoe. It skidded across the vacant street and into an empty gutter. "My mom totally freaked out. She was screaming and trying to drag me into the car." He chuckled, then ran a hand through his wavy hair. "She's a little high maintenance."

"Yeah," I said, smiling. "I know the type."

"No," he said. "Your mom must be cool. I mean, I can't

imagine getting to see the places you've seen. All my mom does is cook all the time, you know? Like one kind of pie isn't enough. No. She's got to have three different kinds, and . . ." His voice trailed off as he looked at me. "I bet your mom doesn't do that."

"Oh, yes she does!" I said quickly. "She's really big on all that stuff."

"You mean, I'm not the only kid who has to sit through eight-course dinners?"

"Oh, are you kidding?" I said. "We do that all the time!" (If eight courses could be defined as five Diet Cokes and three Twinkies.)

"Really? I thought that with the Peace Corps and . . ."

"Oh, no, are you kidding? They're big on family time and"—I thought back to the huge stack of Pottery Barn catalogs—"decorating."

"Yes!" he said. "I know. You know how they decide, overnight, that you need new curtains in your bedroom. . . . Like plain curtains aren't really getting it done, and now you need striped curtains?"

Plain curtains? Striped curtains? What kind of society had I stumbled into? *I should be getting COW extra credit for this!* We walked farther, down a winding street with manicured lawns and perfect flower beds that couldn't possibly have been mere miles from the Gallagher walls. I was getting an insider's tour behind the picket fence. I was going where no Gallagher Girl (well, at least *this* Gallagher Girl) had ever gone before—into a normal American family.

"This *is* nice. It's a nice . . . night." And it was. The air was chilly but not cold, and only a light dusting of clouds blew across the starry sky.

"So what was it like?" he pried. *What was* what *like?* "Mongolia? Thailand? It must be like . . ."

"Another world," I said. And it was true—I *was* from another world—just one that was surprisingly near his own.

Then he did the coolest thing. We were stopped under this streetlight, and he said, "Hold it. You've got a . . ." And then he reached up and brushed my cheek with his finger. "Eyelash." He held it out in front of me. "Make a wish."

But right then, there was nothing else I wanted.

I don't know how long we wandered the streets of Roseville, because, for the first time in years, I lost track of time.

"But I guess you don't have crazy teachers," he said, teasing after he'd finished a story about his psycho track coach.

"Oh, you'd be surprised."

"Tell me something about you," Josh was prompting me. "I've told you all about my crazy Martha Stewart–wannabe mom and my hyper kid sister and my dad."

"Like what?" I asked, freaking out, as was probably evident by the mind-numbing silence.

"Anything. What's your favorite color? Your favorite band?" He pointed at me as he jumped off the curb and turned in the street. "What's your favorite thing to eat when you're sick?"

How great a question is that? I mean, my whole life I've

been answering questions—hard ones, too—but that one seemed especially telling.

"Waffles," I said, suddenly amazed when I realized it was true.

"Me too!" Josh said. "They're so much better than pancakes, which my mom says is crazy because it's the same batter, but I tell her that it's a—"

"Texture thing," we said at the exact same time.

OH MY GOSH! He gets the pancakes versus waffles thing! He gets it!

He was smiling. I was melting.

"When's your birthday?" He shot the question at me like a dart.

"Um . . ." *The second it takes for you to recall something your cover should know, is the second it takes for bad people to do bad things.* "November nineteenth," I blurted for no apparent reason; the date just landed in my head like a stone.

"What's your favorite ice cream?"

"Mint chocolate cookie," I said, remembering that was what we'd found in his garbage.

His face lit up. "Me too!" *Fancy that.* "Do you have brothers and sisters?"

"Sisters," I replied instinctively. "I have sisters."

"What does your dad do? When he isn't off saving the world?"

"He's an engineer. He's wonderful."

I didn't even pause before I said it. The words were out, and I didn't want to shove them back in. Of all the lies I'd told that night, that was the only one I knew I wouldn't have to try to remember. *My dad's strict, but he loves me. He takes care of me and my mom. When I get home—he'll be there.*

And he did save the world—a lot.

I looked at Josh, who didn't doubt me. And I knew that right then, right there, that in a way, all of it was true. I knew that from that point on, the legend would live.

"It's not a family business, though. Right?" Josh asked.

I shook my head, knowing it was a lie.

"Good," Josh said. "Be glad you don't have someone breathing down your neck to follow in your old man's shoes." He kicked a stone. "What's that they call it—you know, in the Bible—about how we can do whatever we want?"

"Free will," I said.

"Yeah." Josh nodded. "Be glad you've got free will."

"Why? What do you have?"

We'd reached a corner of the square I'd never paid much attention to before. Josh pointed to the sign above a row of dark windows—ABRAMS AND SON PHARMACY, FAMILY OWNED SINCE 1938.

And then I knew why we do fieldwork. Of course I knew that Josh's dad was the town pharmacist. But computer files and tax records hadn't told us how Josh would react to that place. They hadn't prepared me for the look in his eye when he said, "I don't really like running track. I just . . . It keeps me away from here after school."

Something in the way he said it told me that it was something he hadn't told anyone else, but I was no one his friends knew. I was no one who'd let it slip to his parents. I was no one.

"I guess there's some pressure to follow in my dad's footsteps, too," I admitted.

"Really?"

I nodded, unable to say any more, because the truth was, I didn't know where those footsteps led. I didn't have that kind of clearance.

The clock in the tower over the library chimed ten, and I knew it may as well have been midnight, and I may as well have been Cinderella.

"I've got to . . ." I motioned toward the library (and, far beyond it, the towering walls of my home). "I can't get . . . I've got . . . I'm sorry."

"Wait." He grabbed my arm (but in a nice way). "You've got a secret identity, don't you?" He grinned. "Come on. You can tell me. You're Wonder Woman's illegitimate daughter? Really, it's okay. I am fine with it—just as long as your father isn't Aquaman, because, to tell you the truth, I always got a really superior vibe off of him."

"This is serious," I said through my laughter. "I've got to go."

"But who's going to make sure I get home safely? These are dark and dangerous streets." Across the square, a group of older women was leaving the movie theater. "See, I'm not safe out here by myself."

"Oh, I think you'll survive."

"Will I see you tomorrow?" Gone was the silly tone, the

flirting cadence. If he hadn't been holding me I might have fainted—seriously. It was just that sweet and strong and sexy.

Yes, my heart cried, but my brain spoke of a biochemistry midterm, seven chapters of COW reading, and two weeks' worth of lab reports for Dr. Fibs.

Sometimes I really hate my brain.

But most of all, I heard Mr. Solomon's voice, and it was telling me that a good spy always varies her routines. The people at the Gallagher Academy might not notice one stray girl two nights in a row—but three would be pushing my luck, and I knew it.

"I'm sorry." I pulled away from him. "I never know when my mom has classes or when I'll get to come. We live out in the country, and I can't drive yet, so . . . I'm sorry."

"Will I just see you around, then? You know, for self-defense tips and stuff?"

"I . . ." I stumbled, knowing I'd finally made it to the edge of the cliff, and I had to decide if it was worth the fall.

I attend the best school in the country. I can speak fourteen languages, but I can't talk to this boy? What good is a genius IQ? Why bother teaching us the things we know? What's the use in . . .

And then I saw it.

I turned to Josh. "Do you like spy movies?"

He looked at me, then muttered, "Um . . . sure."

"Well . . ." I inched closer to the gazebo, which was very Americana. Very *Sound of Music.* Very *Gilmore Girls.* But the really important thing about the Roseville gazebo wasn't that it had awesome twinkle lights. No, it was better—it was the loose stone jutting out from its base.

(FYI, for the most part, spies love loose stones.)

"I saw this movie," I said, pacing myself. "It was an old movie . . . in black-and-white . . . and this girl wanted to communicate with this boy, but they couldn't, because it was too dangerous."

"Why? Because he was a spy?"

He? Sometimes the sexism in this country amazes me, but then I remembered that society's tendency to underestimate women is a Gallagher Girl's greatest weapon, and I consoled myself by remembering how it had taken less than two seconds for me to level Josh flat and hard onto the pavement.

"Yes," I said. "*He* was a spy."

"Cool." He nodded.

"You can leave me notes in there." I removed the stone, revealing the small hole in the mortar. "And just replace the stone backward, so I'll know there's a note." I slid the stone in so that the painted face was on the inside. The effect was of one gray piece of slate in a snow-colored field. "And when I leave a note, I'll turn it around the other way. See?" I said, feeling perhaps a little too proud of myself. "We used to do this all the time . . . in Mongolia."

Doesn't she know there's such a thing as e-mail? I imagined him wondering. Instant Messenger? Cell phones? Even tin cans tied together with string probably seemed high-tech compared to what I was proposing. He either thought I was crazy or from some really bizarre experiment where they freeze people for decades, even though I know for a fact that technology isn't to a prototype phase yet.

He looked at me like I was crazy, so I said, "You're right. It's stupid." I turned. "I've got to go. It was . . ."

"Cammie." The word stopped me. "You're not a normal girl, are you?"

Okay, so maybe Josh was pretty smart, too.

Chapter Sixteen

Summary of Communication

On October 18, during a routine Driver's Ed assignment,
The Operatives noticed that the "fill sign" was marked (in
other words, the stone was turned) at the designated
dead letter drop, so Agent Morgan faked a stomachache
when everyone else was engaged in a Gilmore Girls
marathon and went to retrieve the following:

Okay, so if your dad's not Aquaman, is he The Flash?

Translation: Please think I'm funny, because my self-
esteem is fairly low, and humor may be all I have going
for me. (Translation done by Macey McHenry.)

After a brief reply from The Operative, The Subject
wrote back the following week:

Today my shop teacher gave me detention for not properly sanding a birdhouse. Then my dad told me I should start helping him at the pharmacy two nights a week. When I got home, I found out that my mom made 18 different kinds of banana bread, and I had to taste-test each one. It was torture.
How was your day?

Translation: I feel very comfortable sharing things with you because you are separate from my ordinary, mundane life. Leaving these notes and having clandestine meetings is exciting. Having a relationship with you is new and unique, and I'm enjoying it. (Translation done by Macey McHenry, with assistance from Elizabeth Sutton.)

The Operatives took this message as a positive sign and fully expected The Subject to continue communication. A level of trust seemed to be building, and The Operatives felt as if The Subject may soon be ready to be called on to act. The Subject was making excellent progress.

Then they received the following:

This is crazy. You know that, right?

Translation: While I enjoy the temporary release from normalcy this relationship provides, I can see that it is impractical in the long run. However, I am willing to see where it goes. (Translation done by Macey McHenry.)

Following this communication, The Operatives knew that it was important to proceed slowly in order to bring The Subject along at a manageable pace. They agreed that any mention of dates, making out, and any sort of formal events should be postponed indefinitely.

Another week passed before The Operatives received their most significant piece of communication to date:

Is there any chance you can come to the movies this Friday? I know you may not be able to, but I'll be here (at our place) at seven if you can.

Translation: WE'RE IN!! (Translation done by Cameron Morgan and verified by Macey McHenry.)

We had a *place*! We had a date—to the movies!

My euphoria lasted from the time I picked up the note and all the way through our customary debrief up in the suite. By the next morning, however, I wasn't thinking like a girl—I was thinking like a spy.

What if movies were the favorite pastime of the guys in the Gallagher Maintenance Department? Or, what if the movie was gross and I got nauseous and puked Milk Duds everywhere?

MILK DUDS! What if I got caramel in my teeth and had to go digging around in a molar or something to get it out? There is simply no attractive way of doing that! What was I going to do—only eat popcorn? But then the same thing could happen with the little kernel pieces!

Oh my gosh! I had an Organic Chemistry test and a Conversational Swahili exam, but both of those things seemed like child's play compared to the dilemma at hand— right up until Macey joined us at our lunch table and said, "Junior Mints."

Junior Mints—of course! Minty chocolate fun with none of the dangerous side effects. I take back everything I ever said about her ever in my life. MACEY McHENRY IS A GENIUS!

Liz was looking at the note, comparing it against the others she'd already run through the lab to see if the chemical composition of the paper or the ink could tell us anything. (It did—he shops at Wal-Mart.)

"Notice how he tilts the M in movie," Liz said, holding the note toward us. "I think I remember reading that this shows a tendency to . . ."

But a tendency *to what*, we'd never find out, because just then the sophomore lunch tables went quiet in a way that could only mean one thing.

"Hello, ladies," Joe Solomon said, but not before I snatched the piece of paper and crammed it in my mouth, which ordinarily would have been really great spy maneuvering except that Josh doesn't use Evapopaper.

"How's the lasagna?" Mr. Solomon asked, and I started to say something before I remembered that my mouth was . . . well . . . otherwise engaged.

"The Gallagher Academy career fair is this Friday evening," Mr. Solomon said. My roommates and I all looked at each other—the exact same thing crossing our minds—*this Friday evening!* "Here's a list of agencies and firms that will be represented." He tossed a stack of flyers onto the long table. "Great chance to see what's out there—especially for those of you who won't be joining me in Sublevel Two."

Okay, I admit it. That part made me swallow a little paper.

After Mr. Solomon left, I spat out what was left of Josh's note (which luckily included all of the writing) and stared at it and the shiny flyer, which announced a chance for me to chart the course of the rest of my life. I wasn't hungry anymore.

Career day at spy school is probably like career days at regular schools except . . . well . . . we probably have a lot more guests who arrive by rappeling out of black helicopters. (The guys from Alcohol Tobacco and Firearms have always been kinda show-offy.)

The hallways were full of folding tables and cheesy banners. (GO ALL THE WAY WITH THE NSA—who thinks of this stuff?) Every classroom had a scout perched at a back table, watching in amazement as we went through our routines. Even P&E was crawling with spies—literally—as we spread out in the barn and showed off our overall lethal-ness for the recruiters.

"Don't take my head off!" Liz cried.

I wasn't sure if she was talking about the roundhouse kick that had just passed inches from her nose or the fact that Bex was refusing to consider postponing my big date. In any case, I was fairly certain we probably shouldn't be having that conversation in a hayloft full of current and future government agents.

Light cascaded through the skylights. Barn swallows nested in the rafters up above. And ten feet away, Tina Walters was showing an agent from the FBI how we'd learned to kill a man with a piece of uncooked spaghetti.

"Guys!" I snapped.

A whistle blew, telling us it was time to shift positions, so Bex came to stand behind me. As she wrapped her arms around my neck, she whispered in my ear, "Crowded corridors. Tons of people. No one will miss you—not The Chameleon."

I flipped her over my back and glared at her as she lay sprawled on the mat beneath me.

"I think you have to cancel," Liz said as she charged at me. I slid aside and dropped her neatly to the mat next to Bex. She pushed up on her elbows and whispered, "This is an opportunity for the Gallagher Girls of today to decide how they will become the Gallagher Women of tomorrow." (Or so we'd read on the flyer.)

I was just starting to feel in control of the situation,

when Bex's leg swung swiftly around, catching me off guard, dropping me to the top of the pile. "Yeah, like Cammie doesn't know what she's going to be when she grows up."

Before I could reply, we saw a man walking toward us, so we scrambled to our feet. He wasn't tall or short; he wasn't handsome or ugly. He was the kind of person you could see a dozen times and never quite remember, and with just one glance I knew he was a pavement artist—I knew he was like me.

"Very nice," the man said. There was no telling how long he'd been in that crowded loft, watching. "You girls are sophomores, is that right?"

There was an extra bounce in Bex's step as she inched toward him. "Yes, sir," she said, her voice full of swagger.

"And you're all studying Covert Operations?" he asked with a sideways glance at Liz, who had somehow gotten her hair tangled in the laces of my shoe.

"Just for this semester," Liz said, sounding totally relieved.

"Next semester we can specialize if we want to," Bex clarified. "But a lot of us continue training for fieldwork."

I'm pretty sure she was getting ready to slip into the conversation how she got to be lookout for her dad once while he took out an arms dealer at an outdoor market in Cairo, but the man didn't give her a chance.

"Well," he said. "I'll let you get back to your practice." He placed his hands in his pockets and smiled. When he turned to walk away, I didn't think he'd seen me at all, until he glanced in my direction and nodded. "Ms. Morgan." If he'd had a hat he would have tipped it.

On the other side of the room, Ms. Hancock blew her whistle again and yelled, "Circle up, girls. Let's show our guests how we play rock-paper-scissors."

Bex winked at me and rolled up a copy of the October *Vogue* that she'd borrowed from Macey.

I felt sorry for whoever drew rock and scissors.

Operation Divide and Conquer

The operation, which took place on Friday night, October 29, was a basic four-man op with three agents holding in secure sweeping patterns throughout the Gallagher Academy for Exceptional Young Women. The Reserve Operatives were assigned a portion of the main campus, and when asked where Agent Morgan was, The Operatives were to reply "I don't know" or "I just saw her heading that way" while pointing in a very general direction.

If asked more directly about the location of Agent Morgan, The Operatives were to exclaim, "You just missed her!" and then walk very quickly away.

I followed Bex and Macey through the corridors. Sounds bounced off the hardwood floors and stone walls as newbies drooled over the Mr. Solomon-like recruiters from the CIA, and a flock of seventh graders oohed and aahed over the latest satellite feeds from Homeland Security. (So *that's* what Brad Pitt's bedroom looks like. . . .)

Bex was totally right. I've seen the Gallagher Academy in states of organized chaos before, but never have I seen it so alive. The air was full of something (and not just the gases that had escaped from the labs when someone from Interpol got a little too close to one of Dr. Fibs's classified projects).

"Okay," Bex said to me beneath her breath. "Knock 'em dead."

I glanced at Macey. "You'll be fine," she said, and I started to feel really good. Then she finished. "Just don't be an idiot."

I turned down an empty corridor, leaving the sounds of our future behind me, and sensed something else drawing closer. I reached out for the tapestry and the crest-slash-trigger behind it, when I stopped frozen at the sound of my name.

"You must be Cameron Morgan."

The man strolling toward me had a dark suit, dark hair, and eyes so black they could get completely lost in the night.

"And where are you running off to?" the man asked.

"Oh, they needed more napkins at the refreshments table." (Whether you agree or disagree with my actions, you've got to admit that my fibbing ability was totally getting better.)

He laughed. "Oh, child, don't you know that anyone with your pedigree should never have to fetch the napkins?" I stared blankly at him, unable to smile, until he extended his hand. "I'm Max Edwards. I knew your father."

Of course he did. I'd met a half dozen men like Max

Edwards already that day—men with stories, men with secrets—all wanting to pull me aside and return a little piece of my father to me. Even without Josh waiting for me at the end of the tunnel, I think I might have felt like running the other way.

"I'm with Interpol now." Max Edwards said, eyeing me. "I know you're a CIA legacy and all, but that's no reason not to give the rest of us a shot, eh?"

"No, sir."

"Started the CoveOps training yet?"

"Yes, sir, with the intro class."

"Good. Good. I'm sure Joe Solomon is finding plenty to teach *you*," he said, patting me on the shoulder, emphasizing the word in a way I didn't understand. Then he leaned closer and whispered, "I'm going to give you some advice, Cammie. Not everyone can live this life, you know. Not everyone has it in their blood—the stress, the risk, the sacrifice." He reached into his pocket and pulled out a business card with a phone number centered and alone on the plain white background. "Call me anytime. You'll always have a place with us."

He patted me on the shoulder again and walked away, his footsteps echoing down the empty stone corridor. I watched him turn the corner; then I counted to ten and slipped behind the tapestry. Halfway down the tunnel, I stopped and changed my clothes. I never saw that card again.

Chapter SEVenteEn

I know in spy movies it always looks really cool when the operative goes from a maid's uniform to a slinky, sexy ballgown in the amount of time it takes an elevator to climb three floors. Well, I don't know how it is for TV spies, but I can tell you that even with Velcro, the art of the quick change is one that must take a lot of practice (not to mention better lighting than one is likely to find in a tunnel that was once a part of the Underground Railroad).

That's probably why I panicked when I saw the strange look on Josh's face when he first saw me outside the gazebo. Either my blouse was open, or my skirt was stuck in my underwear, or something even more mortifying. I froze.

"You look . . ."

I have lipstick on my teeth. My hair is full of cobwebs. I'm wearing two different kinds of shoes and my backup is two whole miles away!

". . . amazing."

I'd never felt less invisible in my life. I forgot about Bex and Macey and their great bodies, Liz and her gorgeous blond hair. Even my mother faded from my mind as I saw myself through Josh's eyes. For the first time in a long time I didn't want to disappear.

Then I remembered that it was my turn to say something. He was wearing a leather jacket and khaki pants that had the kind of crisp creases that made me think of the Navy SEALs, who were probably doing a demonstration in the Gallagher Academy pond at that very moment, so I said, "You look very . . . clean."

"Yeah." He tugged at his collar. "My mom found out and . . . well . . . let's just say you were this close to having to wear a wrist corsage." He held two fingers inches apart, and I remembered one time when my dad got my mom a corsage— of course it came equipped with a retinal scanner and comms unit, but still, the thought was nice.

I started to say so, but just then Josh said, "I'm sorry, but we kind of missed the movie. I should have looked up the times before I asked you. It started at six."

The mission was compromised at 19:00 hours when The Operative and The Subject realized they had missed their window of opportunity—which in The Operative's opinion was a waste of her best outfit.

"Oh," I said, trying not to sound too heartbroken. I'd let Liz do my hair. I'd jogged two miles in the dark. I had been looking forward to this all week, but all I could do was put on my best spy face and say, "That's okay. I guess I'll just . . ."

"Do you want to grab a burger?" Josh blurted before I could finish my thought.

Grab a burger? I'd just eaten filet mignon with the Deputy Director of the CIA, but I found myself saying, "I'd love to!"

Across the square, bright lights beamed through one set of windows. We walked toward the light, and Josh held the door open for me and gestured for me to walk in (how sweet is that!). The diner had a black-and-white checkerboard floor with red vinyl booths and lots of old records and pictures of Elvis nailed to the walls. The whole place was a little too doo-woppy for my personal taste, but that didn't stop me from crawling into a booth—unfortunately on the side facing away from the windows since Josh had already nabbed the best position for himself. (Mr. Smith would have been very disappointed in me.) But at least across the booth he probably couldn't feel my leg shaking.

The Operative tried to implement the Purusey breathing technique, which has been proven effective at fooling polygraphs. There is no conclusive evidence as to whether it is effective at masking the internal lie detectors of fifteen-year-old boys.

The waitress came and took our orders, and Josh leaned way back in his seat. I knew from Liz's notes on body language that this meant he was feeling pretty confident (either that or I smelled like the tunnel and he wanted to get as far away from me as possible). "I'm sorry we missed the movie," Josh said as he rearranged his pickles.

"That's okay," I said. "This is fun, too."

Then the strangest thing happened—we both stopped talking. It was like that episode of *Buffy the Vampire Slayer* where everyone in town got their voices stolen. I was beginning to wonder if that had actually happened—like maybe, back at school, the CIA had been fiddling around with one of Dr. Fibs's experiments and something had gone *horribly* wrong. I started to open my mouth and test my theory, when I heard a muffled cry of "Josh!" and some banging on the diner windows, and I realized that the muteness hadn't affected anyone but us.

When I heard the ding of the diner door, I spun to see a mob of teenagers heading our way, and let me tell you, for a girl who's gone to a private all-girls school since the seventh grade, that's a pretty scary sight.

I have never been so behind enemy lines in my life! I thought, scrolling back through our P&E training on how to handle multiple attackers. Normally, I might have counted on Josh—my guide in that strange and foreign land—but he was panicking, too. I could tell by the way his jaw had gone all slack and a french fry was poised, midair, en route to his mouth.

I mentally reeled through the things in my favor: no one knew me. I wasn't wearing my uniform. And if push came to shove I could . . . well . . . push and shove. (Two of the boys looked pretty football player-ish, but I did an entire project once on the "the bigger they are the harder they fall" philosophy of hand-to-hand combat, and there is *totally* something to it.) I was safe, for the meantime.

My cover might not have been blown, but I couldn't say the same for my confidence—especially when one of the girls, a very pretty blond, said, "Hi, Josh," and he said, "Hi, DeeDee."

The Operative realized that the band of insurgents was led by the suspect known as DeeDee (even though she did not appear to have any pink paper in her possession).

Most of the mob walked by with just the occasional "Hey, Josh" as they passed, but DeeDee and another boy crawled into the booth with us, and oh yeah, guess who ended up being pressed up against Josh? DEE DEE! (*Soooo* not an accident!) Can I just say that it is such a good thing that there was an entire diner full of witnesses, because I'm fairly certain I could have killed her with a bottle of ketchup.

"Hi, I'm DeeDee," she said as she helped herself to one of Josh's fries (rude!). "Have we met?"

I'm the daughter of two secret agents who has a genius IQ and the ability to kill you in your sleep and make it look like an accident, you silly, vapid, two-bit . . .

"Cammie's new in town."

Okay, this is why it's always best to have backup. Josh

totally saved me, because I was seriously starting to finger the ketchup bottle about then.

"Oh," she said. Even though Macey McHenry herself had done my makeup, I felt completely covered with boils as I sat there. She helped herself to another fry, but didn't look at me when she said, "Hi."

"DeeDee and I have known each other for forever," Josh said, and DeeDee blushed.

Two of the girls from the mob put some money in the jukebox and soon a song I'd never heard was echoing throughout the diner, causing the boy who was sliding into the booth next to me to yell when he said, "Yeah, she's just one of the boys." He thrust a hand in my direction.

"Hey, I'm Dillon."

THIS is Dillon? My superspy instincts were taken aback as I studied the small boy who was supposedly "D'Man." (Note to self: don't believe everything you read when hacking into the DMV, because short boys will totally lie about their height when applying for their learners' permits.) It took a second for me to recognize him and realize he'd been the boy with Josh in the street—the one who'd been told I was nobody.

Somehow I managed to say, "Hi. I'm Cammie."

Dillon was nodding his head slowly as he eyed me and said, "So this is the mystery woman." DeeDee instantly stopped chewing on her fry. "So she exists!" Dillon exclaimed. "You have to forgive my friend here," Dillon said as he slid one arm around my shoulders. "He's not the most outgoing of hosts, so if *I* can do anything to help you feel at home here, consider me at your disposal."

Dillon's arm was still around me, so I was feeling pretty grateful for all those P&E classes when Josh reached across the table and punched Dillon in the shoulder.

"*What?*" Dillon cried. "I'm just being hospitable."

If *that* was hospitable then Madame Dabney really needed to update her curriculum.

"Well, Cammie," Dillon went on, unfazed, "please allow me to say that I can see why doofus here's been keeping you to himself."

Dillon reached for a fry, but this time Josh moved the plate away and said, "Well, thanks for stopping by. Don't let us keep you." And then Josh tried to kick Dillon under the table, but he missed and hit me, but it's not like I screamed or anything. (I've totally been kicked harder.)

"Are you kidding?" Dillon asked, elbows-on-table as he lowered his voice, forcing us all to huddle around his conspiracy. "We're gonna go climb the wall and moon some rich girls later. Wanna come?"

The wall? OUR wall? I wondered in disbelief. Is it possible I've been routinely mooned for the past three years and didn't know it? Has Josh's very own backside been exposed (and possibly photographed by the security department) without my knowledge?

(Note to self: find those photographs.)

I must have looked as confused as I felt, because Josh leaned closer and said, "The Gallagher Academy?" as if wondering whether or not I'd heard of the place. "It's a really snooty boarding school. The girls there are all rich delinquents or something."

I wanted to jump to our defense. I wanted to proclaim that you shouldn't judge someone until you've walked a mile through an underground tunnel in her uncomfortable shoes. I wanted to tell them everything they owed to the Gallagher Girls who had gone before me, but I couldn't. Sometimes spies can only nod and say, "Oh, really?"

"What?" Dillon said. "You don't, like, *go* there?" he asked, then laughed so loudly that everyone in the restaurant turned to stare.

I studied Dillon and wondered how long it would take me to hack into the IRS—I bet, by December, Uncle Sam could be repossessing everything his family owned. "I'm homeschooled," I said, while silently chanting, *And I have a cat named Suzie, and my dad's an engineer, and I love mint chocolate cookie ice cream.*

"Yeah," Dillon said. "I forgot. You know that's kinda weird, don't you?"

But before I could defend myself, DeeDee said, "I think that's really nice." Making it infinitely more difficult to hate her.

"So, what do you say?" Dillon asked, turning back to Josh. He sounded almost giddy, and can I just say, giddy is *not* an expression that most boys wear well. "Wanna TP the grounds or something?"

But Josh didn't answer. Instead, he was pushing DeeDee

out of the booth and pulling money out of his wallet. He dropped the bills on the table, then reached for my hand. "You wanna leave, too. Right?" he asked.

Yes! I wanted to cry. I read his face. I knew what he was feeling, and I was feeling it, too. I took his hand, and it was as if he were helping me into another world instead of out of a red-vinyl booth. The two hamburgers lay, barely touched, on the table behind us, but I didn't care.

Dillon got up and let me out, but Josh didn't drop my hand.

WE WERE HOLDING HANDS!

He started pulling me toward the door, but a girl doesn't forget three years of culture training just like that, so I turned to Dillon and DeeDee and muttered, "Bye. It was nice meeting you." Total lie, but one even non-spies tell in polite society, so it probably doesn't count.

Dillon yelled, "Whoa," in the manner of someone who's seen way too many Keanu Reeves movies. "You're missing out, bro. We're gonna mess with some rich chicks!"

Yeah, D'Man, I thought, as Josh opened the door. Why don't you go ahead and try it?

Now, normally, I'm not a huge fan of hand-holding, but that's really just in movies when the hero and the heroine have to run from the bad guys, and they do it while holding hands, which is just crazy. No one can run as fast when they're holding someone else's hand. (A fact I once verified in a P&E experiment.)

But Josh and I weren't running. Oh, no. We were strolling. Our joined hands kind of swayed back and forth as if we were about to ask Red Rover to send someone on over.

After a long time, he looked down at the street and said, "I'm sorry."

"For what?" I honestly couldn't think of one thing he'd done wrong. Not one thing.

He jerked his head back toward the diner. "Dillon. He's really not that bad," he said. "We've been having that same conversation since kindergarten. He's big on the talk—not so much on the action."

"So we don't need to go warn the Gallagher Academy, then?" I teased.

"No," he said, smiling. "I think they're safe."

"Yeah," I said, "they probably are." I thought about our walls—our world. "And DeeDee?" I asked and felt my breath catch. "She seems sweet." *Sadly, not a lie.*

"She is, but"—his hand tightened around mine—"I don't want to talk about DeeDee."

Maybe it was the twinkle lights of the gazebo or the way Josh's hand felt in mine, or perhaps it was the exposure to Dr. Fibs's purple sneezing gas I'd had earlier in the day, but when we stopped walking, everything got really, really whirly, like the whole world was a merry-go-round and Josh and I were standing in the center. There must have been all kinds of centripetal force, because we were getting closer and closer together, and before I knew it, something I'd been dreaming about my whole life was happening. But I'm

184

not going to write about it here, because—seriously—my mother is going to read this! Plus, all kinds of VIPs are probably going to commission this report, and *they* seriously don't need to hear about my first kiss.

(Oh, jeez! I didn't mean to say that. . . .)

So, okay, Josh kissed me. I know some of you might want details—like how soft his lips were, and how, as I breathed out, he breathed in and vice versa so that it seemed we were permanently joined at the soul or something. . . . But I'm not going to tell you those parts. No way. They're private.

But I will say that it was everything it was supposed to be—warm and sweet and very much the beginning of . . . well . . . just the beginning.

Chapter Eighteen

Pros and cons of being a girl-genius-slash-spy-in-training-slash-girlfriend of cutest-slash-nicest-slash-sweetest boy in the world:

PRO: ability to tell the boy how you feel in any of fourteen different languages.

CON: boy cannot understand any of the languages (well, except English, of course, but even then he speaks with the highly specialized and often untranslatable "boy" dialect).

PRO: when boy is having trouble with his chemistry project, you can meet him at the library and help him study.

CON: you can't help him too much because it's kind of hard to explain how you're doing PhD-level chemistry in the tenth grade.

PRO: the look on your boyfriend's face when he surprises you with an assortment of cat toys and asks, "Do you think Suzie will like them?"

CON: knowing there is no Suzie, and you can never tell him that.

Three weeks later I was sitting in the Grand Hall, listening to my classmates talk about how they were going to use their Saturday night to catch up on movies (or homework . . . but mostly movies), when Liz came in and dropped about a dozen textbooks on the table so hard my fork jumped off my plate.

"Are you ready for this?" she said, her voice reverberating with glee. "We've got a little Chang, a little Mulvaney, a lot of Strendesky, some—"

"Liz," I said, really hating what had to come next. "Oh, gee, Liz, I thought you knew . . . I've got plans with—"

"Josh," she finished for me. She picked up a copy of *A Mayan's Guide to Molecular Regeneration* that had fallen to the floor and added it to the top of the stack. "This project's due on Wednesday, Cam."

"I know."

"It's thirty percent of our midterm grade."

"I know. I'm gonna work on it. . . ." But I didn't know when. I hadn't thought about it once since Dr. Fibs assigned it three weeks ago—the Monday after my first date with Josh. I was taking life one day, one outfit, one date at a time.

The Grand Hall was starting to empty as some girls went to grab dessert and others headed upstairs or outside. I glanced at my watch and got up. "Look, Josh has got something planned, okay? It's this whole surprise thing he's been talking about and . . . I think it's a big deal. It'll be okay. I'll do the project tomorrow." That was what I'd said yesterday.

But Liz didn't remind me of that. She just nodded and told me to be careful as I dashed out of the Grand Hall and toward the library, where, if you push against the D–F shelf while pulling on a copy of Downing's *Modern Uses for Ancient Weapons*, you can slip into my second favorite passageway.

That is, unless Mr. Solomon is in the library.

"Hello, Ms. Morgan," Mr. Solomon said, stopping me in my tracks. I'm pretty sure he doesn't know about any of the secret passageways—especially that one, since it took me two full years to find it—but still it totally freaked me out to turn around and see him standing there.

"And what are you up to this fine evening?" He shoved both hands into his pockets, then leaned forward. "Hot date?"

I'm pretty sure that was Joe Solomon's attempt at male-role-model humor, but it still didn't stop me from making a noise that sounded like *hahahahahaha*. Yeah. I know. How covert am I?

"Oh, I was just . . . Um . . ."

"Hey, kiddo," I heard from behind me. "Were you looking for me?"

The library is probably my favorite room in the mansion. It has a huge stone fireplace in the middle of a two-story circular space that's filled with study tables and big comfy armchairs. Overhead, a second-story balcony over-

188

looks everything, and that's where I saw my mother.

She started down the stairs, a book of poetry in her hands, and I thought she looked like the most beautiful thing I'd ever seen. She reached the main floor and slipped her arm around me. "I was just coming to find you."

"Uh, you were?"

And then I remembered Joe Solomon who was standing there, looking on.

"Well then," he said, taking a step toward the door. "I'll leave you two girls alone."

Okay, I'm not sure, but I think my mom could totally take Joe Solomon, and as soon as he called her a "girl" I thought for sure I'd see the proof. But Mom didn't say anything. She didn't pin his arm behind his back or jump into the air and slash him across the face with one of her high-heeled black boots (a move I totally want to perfect someday—just as soon as I can borrow those boots). Oh, no, she just smiled at him. Like a *Thanks, I can take it from here* smile.

I felt sick. She pulled me into the hall and walked with me toward the chapel. Behind me, I heard the scrape of forks on plates and dinner chatter (in Farsi) as we passed the Great Hall. She looped her arm through mine and said, "I was wondering if you wanted to do something tonight."

Okay, so I know I have lots of different languages at my disposal and everything, but I honestly didn't understand what my mother was asking. It was weird— not like Nazi-submarine-in-the-lake weird, but someone's-been-watching-too-many-made-for-TV-movies weird.

"Or not," she jumped to say when she read my bewildered expression. "I just thought you might want to go into town or something."

Well, actually, I *did* want to go to town—just not with her. In fact, I was already wearing lipstick, and an outfit was stashed in the tunnel. Josh had sounded so excited when he'd said, "Now, you're coming Saturday night, right? You don't have to do something with your parents, do you?"

I'd said no, but now my mother was asking me to do just that. I looked into her eyes—her beautiful eyes that have seen horrors and miracles and all things in between, and then I said, "I'm pretty tired." Technically not a lie.

"Something low-key, then," she said with all her super-spy persistence. "Maybe a movie?"

"I . . ." *I am a terrible person.* "I . . . See, I've got to . . ."

Then I heard a voice behind me. "Cammie promised to help me with my organic chemistry paper."

I turned to see Macey McHenry strolling my way. Her face was blank, her tone perfectly normal. Macey might have been behind the curve academically, but when it came to the lyin' side of spyin', the girl was a natural. (And the fact that Tina Walters swears she hijacked a sheik's yacht in the Mediterranean probably played into that a little bit.)

Mom looked at Macey and then back at me. "Oh," she said, but her smile seemed a little forced and her tone a little sad as she lowered her voice and rubbed my arms. "Okay. I just didn't want you to be alone tonight."

Alone? When am I ever alone? I live in a mansion with about a hundred girls, and except for when I'm in my secret room or one of the window seats or by myself in the loft of the P&E barn or . . . Okay, so *sometimes* I'm alone.

Macey slipped away, and Mom watched her go. "I know it hasn't been easy . . . with her. But I'm proud of you, kiddo." She hugged me again. It was a hug that lingered, like there might not be another one for a long, long time, and I wished for a second that I didn't have to pull away so soon. Or ever. But I did anyway. Josh was waiting.

"Supper?" I asked. "Tomorrow night?"

"Sure thing, kiddo," Mom said as she tucked a stray strand of hair behind my ear. I turned and headed down the corridor, my footsteps thankfully louder than my thoughts. That is, until I turned the corner in the long stone corridor and ran right into Macey.

She was leaning against the wall, hands on hips as she looked at me. "I don't like lying to your mom," she said. "I'll lie to mine, but not yours. That's messed up." Then Macey let out a low, soft laugh, pushed off from the wall and studied me. "I hope he's worth it."

"He is," I whispered.

She stopped just before she passed me. "Really? He is? 'Cause I don't see what's so special about him that you'd risk losing what you've got."

It was a good question. A great question, especially if you're Macey McHenry and everything in life has been given to you but nothing has been earned. If the world looks at your slick, plastic shell and expects there to be nothing but candy inside. If this is your one and only shot at being part of a family—despite your famous last name. Yeah. Then that's a really good question.

"He's just . . ." I tried, wanting to say "sweet" or "caring" or "funny"—because they're all totally true. But instead, I said, "He's just a normal boy."

"Hmph," Macey scoffed. "I know lots of normal boys."

I looked at her. "I don't."

Chapter nineteen

Josh was supposed to meet me at the gazebo, but he wasn't in sight. In fact, *no one* was in sight. I glanced toward the movie theater—nothing. The lights were off in all the stores, and as a scrap of orange paper blew across the deserted town square, I was reminded of a scene from just about every apocalypse movie ever made (and at least three episodes of *Buffy*).

I was a little freaked out.

The Operative surveyed the area, assessing possible threats and exit routes and whether or not that really cute purse in the Anderson's Accessories store window ever would go on sale.

Then a minivan turned onto the street. I guess I was too busy staring at its MY CHILD IS AN HONOR STUDENT AT ROSEVILLE ELEMENTARY SCHOOL bumper sticker to notice who was driving, because I didn't realize it was Josh until he parked and got out and stood there in the middle of the empty street, holding a wrist corsage.

That's right. You read that correctly—flowers on a stick (or, well, flowers on a stretchy band thingy).

He walked toward me slowly, as I said, "That's a wrist corsage."

"Yeah," he said, blushing. "Well, it's a special occasion."

"So, is this an inside joke thing or a your-mom-made-you-buy-it thing?"

He leaned down to kiss me but stopped halfway. "You wanna know the truth?" he whispered.

"Yes."

I felt a quick peck on my check, then he said, "Both."

At approximately 18:07 hours The Subject presented The Operative with a vital piece of (floral) evidence. Macey McHenry later determined this to be an eight on the overall "lameness scale." The Operative, however, thought it was sweet and kind of funny, and decided to wear it with pride.

"You look great," he said, but I totally didn't. I mean, I looked movie okay or bowling okay. I *soooo* didn't look wrist-corsage okay.

I tugged at my skirt. "So what is this special occasion?"

And then he laughed. "You didn't think I'd remember, did you?" he teased.

Remember what? the girl in me wanted to scream, but the

spy in me just smiled and said, "Of course I knew you'd remember." *Total lie.*

"So"—Josh went to open the door—"shall we?"

According to protocol, an operative should never allow herself to be transported to a secondary location. However, because of her history with The Subject and the fact that she once tossed him to the street like a sack of potatoes, The Operative thought it was probably safe.

I'd never been in a minivan before. It was like the road-trip portion of my great small-town experiment—with cup holders. Take it from someone who is highly interested in gadgetry on both a personal and professional level—the modern-day espionage world has nothing on the good folks at General Motors when it comes to cup holder design.

"I like your van."

"I'm saving for a car, you know?" he said, like he'd thought I was being sarcastic.

"No, really," I hurried to say. "It's . . . roomy, and it's got these great . . . I just like it."

Maybe wrist corsages cut off circulation to the brain? I mean, is that why so many girls do stupid things on prom night? I was really going to have to investigate this further, I decided. Then I caught a glimpse of Josh in the dashboard lights, and he was, in a word, beautiful. His hair was longer now, and I could see the shadow of his long eyelashes on his cheekbones. The more I was around him the more I saw the little things—like his hands or the small scar at the edge of his jaw where (he says) he got cut in a knife fight, but where (according to his medical files) he fell off his bike when he was seven.

I have scars, too, of course. But Josh can never hear the stories.

"Josh?" I said, and he glanced at me. We were almost out of town, and the trees were growing heavier overhead as the road curved.

"What?" he asked softly, as if secretly fearing something was wrong. He turned off of the highway and onto a winding bit of blacktop.

"Thanks."

"For what?"

"For everything."

Okay, so there are two basic things I know for a fact about the good citizens of Roseville. One: they honestly have no clue about what really goes on at the Gallagher Academy. None. You'd think there would be a few government conspiracy theories floating around about what takes place behind our ivy-covered walls, but I never heard a single one (and I had reason to listen).

The second thing about Roseville is that it takes its small-town-ness seriously. As if the gazebo and town carnival hadn't been enough to tip me off, I saw a man with a reflector vest and a flashlight directing traffic as soon as Josh pulled into a pasture. Yeah, that's right, crowd control in pastures is key to small-town life.

We parked at the end of a line of cars, and I looked at Josh. "What's going—"

"You'll see." Then he walked around to open my door. (I know—totally sweet!)

We followed the gentle strains of music that floated out toward us, riding on a wave of light that filtered between the slats and through the sliding doors of a huge old barn.

"Hey," I cried, "that looks just like our barn—" He looked at me quizzically. "—in Mongolia."

"It's the fall harvest dance," Josh explained. "It's a Roseville tradition from back when almost everyone farmed. But now it's just an excuse for everyone to get drunk and dance with people they're not married to." He stopped and looked at me. "We can do whatever you want to do, but when I heard this was tonight I kinda thought you might want to come," he said. "I mean . . . it's okay if you want to go do something else. We could . . ."

I shut him up with a kiss (a basic technique that, I've been told, even non-spy girls have used with great success). "Let's dance."

Can I just say that doing the tango with Madame Dabney had totally not prepared me for what actual dances are like? Sure, if I ever have to infiltrate an embassy party, I'll probably be glad I've had C&A, but I could tell as soon as we walked into the barn that I didn't have the training for this.

Streamers hung from the rafters above us. Twinkling

lights formed a tentlike dome. A flatbed trailer sat along the south wall, and a band was playing an old country song while what looked like the entire population of Roseville danced around in circles. I saw a hayloft above us at the far end of the barn, but where we stood there was nothing above us but rafters and lights. Old women sat on bales of straw, clapping, keeping rhythm as the deputy chief of police (I recognized him from the dunk tank) picked up a fiddle and started to play.

Little girls danced by, standing on their fathers' feet, and Josh led me to a folding table that was draped with crepe paper. "Well, hi there, honey," said the woman sitting behind it.

"Hi, Shirley," Josh replied as he reached for his wallet. "Two, please," he said.

"Oh, honey," she said, "your momma already took care of that."

Josh looked at me, panic in his eyes, as every ounce of blood in my body turned cold.

"They're here already?" Josh asked, but before Shirley could answer, I heard someone cry, "Josh! Cammie!"

The deputy chief of police put down his fiddle, and everyone clapped as the kid who works the ticket booth at the movie theater picked up a saxophone. Everyone on the floor picked up their tempo—especially the thin, immaculate woman who was rushing toward us with her arms outstretched.

"Josh! Cammie!" Her ivory sweater set and light-colored trousers were just begging for a stain in the dusty barn, but she didn't act like she cared as she pushed her way through the tide of dancing couples—a tall, thin man trailing dutifully behind her.

"I'm sorry," Josh whispered as he pulled me away from Shirley and toward the stampeding couple. "I'm so sorry. I'm so sorry. We only have to say hi to them. I thought I'd have time to warn—"

"Cammie, darling!" the woman cried. "Well, if you aren't just the cutest thing?" And then she hugged me. Oh, yeah, a complete stranger actually hugged me—something the Gallagher Academy had *totally* not prepared me for. She gripped me by the shoulders and stared into my eyes. "I'm Mrs. Abrams. It is so nice to finally meet you!"

And then she hugged me *again*!

Once deep inside enemy territory, The Operative met with high-ranking officials in the organization. She was NOT prepared for this development, but any diversionary tactics would SERIOUSLY compromise the entire operation!

"Oh," Mrs. Abrams said, "I see you're wearing your corsage." And then she fingered the flowers. "Isn't that lovely?"

I looked at Josh in his neatly pressed khakis and his button-down shirt, and I suddenly understood why he always dressed less like a high school boy and more like a . . . pharmacist.

"Hello, young lady," the man said, once his wife released

me. "I'm Joshua's father, Mr. Abrams. And how are you finding our fair town?"

This isn't good, I thought, realizing I was surrounded. I didn't belong here, and it wasn't going to take Josh's parents long to realize it.

I thought about my options: A) fake a medical condition and rush outside, B) pick up the pen with which Shirley was writing receipts and do some damage before getting gang tackled by some well-meaning townspeople, or C) think of this as my most deep-cover assignment yet and milk it for all it was worth.

"It's a very nice town," I said, extending my hand to the man. "Mr. Abrams, so nice to meet you."

He was tall and had wavy hair like Josh's. He wore wire-rimmed glasses and relished in waving at the people who passed by. "Hi, Carl, Betty," he said to one couple. "Got those new bunion-removing pads you like, Pat."

"Our family's run this town's pharmacy since 1938," Mrs. Abrams told me proudly.

Then Mr. Abrams asked, "Has Josh told you about our little business?"

"Yes," I said. "He has."

"There's not a person in this room I haven't medicated," Mr. Abrams said, and beside me, I felt Josh choke on the punch his mother had handed him.

"That's . . ." I struggled for words. ". . . impressive."

He clamped a hand onto his son's shoulder. "And some day, it's all going to belong to this guy."

"Oh, Jacob," Mrs. Abrams said, "give the poor kid a break." An air of perfection floated all around her even in that dusty barn, and I knew that she'd never been stained, wrinkled, or unaccessorized in her life.

I tugged at the hem of my skirt and fingered my corsage, feeling naked since I hadn't known to wear my mother's pearls. (Even the ones without the microfilm reader could have come in handy.) There were a lot of things I wanted to ask, like *How do you stay so clean?* and *Does that tooth-whitening gum really work?* but I couldn't say any of that, so I just stood there like an idiot, smiling at her, clinging to my cover.

"Are your parents here, darling?" she asked, and then started scanning the crowd.

"No," I said, "they're . . . *busy*."

"Oh, what a shame," she said, with a tilt of her head. But she didn't give me time to reply before blurting, "Cammie, I want you to feel as welcome in our house as you do your own."

Immediately, I started fantasizing about the recon we could set up with that kind of access, but all I could manage to say was, "Oh . . . Um . . . Thanks."

The band changed songs, and Mrs. Abrams leaned close to yell through the noise, "What's your favorite kind of pie?"

I barely heard her, and was on the verge of shouting, "I'm not a spy!" when I saw Dillon standing on a bale of straw, waving wildly in our direction.

Josh glanced at his mother but didn't have to say a word

before she said, "Okay, darling. You kids go have fun." And then she gave me another hug. THREE HUGS! This was seriously freaking me out.

"Cammie, darling, you just come over any time, okay? And when you get a chance, give our number to your parents. Maybe they'd be interested in joining our bridge club."

The last bridge my parents had anything to do with involved the Gansu Province, dynamite, and a really ticked-off yak, but I just smiled and said, "Thanks."

As Josh pulled me away, I risked a glance back. Mr. Abrams had his arm around his wife's shoulders, and Mrs. Abrams raised her hand in a sad half-wave, as if she were freezing that bit of Josh in space and time. *So those are normal parents.* I studied the boy beside me who longed for a life in Mongolia and wasn't allowed to leave the house in anything wrinkled or stained, and another piece of his code fell into place—he was a little less encrypted.

I started walking toward Dillon and the crowd of kids our age (if you're going to do the deep-cover thing you might as well do it all the way), but Josh tugged at my hand, stopping me.

"Come on, let's dance."

"But"—I pointed to the teenage mob—"aren't those your friends?"

Josh looked at them. "Yeah, those are the kids from my school."

"If you want to go say hi or something . . ."

"Let me think," he said, teasing. "I could dance with the

prettiest girl at the party or go hang out with a bunch of idiots I see all day every day. What do you think?"

I thought he was getting some serious bonus points for the *prettiest girl at the party* line, was what I thought, but that didn't stop me from looking at him in a new way as he steered us to the opposite side of the barn, away from his friends, away from his parents. For the first time, I realized I might not be the only one in deep cover.

We danced for a long time before Josh said, "Thanks for meeting my parents. They're big on that."

"Yeah," I said. "They're really nice."

"They're psycho," he corrected me. "Did you hear what he said? About the store? He seriously thinks everyone in this town would die if it weren't for him." He shook his head. "You're so lucky no one cares what you do. I mean, you can be anything you want to be. No one's waiting on you to be some kind of chosen one."

"No," I said. "I guess no one is." *Lie*—absolute, total, and complete lie.

He pulled me tighter, which was a good thing for two reasons, because A) it kept him from seeing the tears that were forming at the corners of my eyes, threatening to test the waterproofness of Macey's new mascara, and B) it gave me pretty good cover, which I was about to totally need. In fact, no spy in the history of the known universe has ever needed cover more.

"Oh my gosh!" I gasped and ducked, hiding my head behind Josh's shoulder.

"What?" he said.

"Oh, um, I just stubbed my toe," I lied, because that was hardly the time to say, *Hey Josh, speaking of parents,* MY MOM JUST WALKED IN WITH MY COVEOPS TEACHER!

Across the dance floor, Mom was in Mr. Solomon's arms. They were both totally laughing, and he was twirling her, and her hair was flying around like she was in a shampoo commercial. Seriously. She could have sold conditioner to a bald man the way she looked out there.

I started easing toward the shadows, far away from the main doors, cursing myself for not marking all the exits earlier. I was stupid. STUPID. STUPID. STUPID.

"I think I want to sit down for a while." I found a stretch of shadowy space at the back of the barn, beneath the hayloft, far away from Mom and Mr. Solomon.

"Do you want some punch?" he asked.

"YES! Punch sounds great!"

I watched Josh disappear into the crowd, and for a second the panic stopped and I felt another feeling in my gut, like the ground had been swept out from under me. But it wasn't just nerves. I was flying, hurtling through the sky. Literally.

Chapter Twenty

Oh my gosh! I thought but didn't scream—partly because all the air had been jerked out of my lungs, and partly because Bex had one hand clamped over my mouth. Liz was looking at me through the pale light that floated into the hayloft from the party below, the noise muffled by bales of last year's straw.

"Cammie," Liz said patiently, as if trying to wake me from a deep sleep. "We had to get you out of there. Your mom and Solomon—they're here!"

That's when I looked around the hayloft and saw the series of pulleys the girls had constructed—the wires that were tied to Bex and to me—and I suddenly understood why I felt like a fish Grandpa Morgan had just jerked out of the water.

Even Macey was there, lying on her stomach, peering over the edge of the loft. "We're good." She rolled onto her side to face us. "The shadows are so thick back there; I don't think anyone saw."

"Oh my gosh," I finally said.

For someone who was technically involved in her first act of espionage, Macey was acting pretty calm about it—like maybe Tina's theory that she had once blackmailed the editor of *Vogue* into bringing back gaucho pants was actually true.

Liz, on the other hand, was freaking out. "Cammie, did you hear me?" she nearly shouted. "Your mom and Solomon are here! They're here! They could have seen you! Do you know what would happen if they saw you?"

"I know," I said as I sank to the floor of the loft. I breathed in the sweet smell of the hay and waited for my heart to stop pounding. Then I realized something. "They didn't see me," I said.

"But how can you be sure?"

This time, Bex answered. "Because she isn't dead yet."

The hayloft was dark and at least thirty feet above the heart of the party, so Bex and Liz sank to the floor and together we crawled toward Macey and the edge. Dim lights twinkled below us, and the band played a slow song. I watched my mom dance with Mr. Solomon. She rested her head on his shoulder, and suddenly, having them skin me alive seemed like a totally better option than watching *that*.

"Wow," Macey muttered. "Killer couple." But I don't know if she meant it literally.

"Oh, Cammie," Liz said, "I'm sure they're just here as friends. Right, Bex?"

Bex was speechless.

Oh my gosh!

"I mean, I'm sure they're just—" Liz tried to make things better, but it was Macey who said, "Don't worry, they aren't dating or in love or anything."

She sounded so decisive—so sure. I looked at her, wondering *How can she possibly know such a thing?* Then I remembered—she was Macey McHenry! Of course she knew! I was totally starting to feel better until she added a fateful, "*Yet*," and I thought I was going to be sick.

I couldn't watch any more, so I turned away and asked, "How did this happen?"

"After you turned your mom down, I saw her talking to double-O-hottie down there," Macey said. "And they decided to go do something."

"And we knew something like this could happen, so we slipped a tracker into your mom's purse," Bex said smugly, loving the situation a little too much, if you ask me.

"And we activated the tracker in Josh's shoe." Liz held her wrist toward me, and suddenly I saw two red dots blinking side by side, as beneath us, Josh carried two cups of punch through the party, passing inches away from my mother.

"And then we decided you might need an emergency operative extraction," Liz said, reveling in the chance to quote one of her flash cards.

I threw my arms over my head, burying my face in the sweet-smelling hay, willing it all to be a dream, and I had almost succeeded when I heard, "Nice corsage." I looked up and glared at Macey, who shrugged and said, "What? Like you didn't think it?"

But that was hardly the time to explain. Oh, no, we totally had better things to do, as Bex was no doubt aware, because she was backing farther into the shadows, saying, "Come on. One operative extraction coming up."

Before I knew what was happening, Bex was pulling me to my feet and hooking me to the cable, and Macey was pushing open the loft door to the chilly autumn night, getting ready to lower me outside like a great big bale of hay.

"No," I said, but Liz pushed me out the door.

"I can't," I cried, but I was spinning around and around in midair. Before I knew it, Liz was joining me on the ground, followed by Macey, who bolted for the trees that lined the edges of the pasture.

"Liz, I can't do this," I said as I gripped my friend's skinny shoulders. "I've got to get back inside, somehow."

"Have you gone completely bonkers?" Bex said as she joined us on the ground.

"But Josh is in there," I protested.

"So are your mother and Mr. Solomon," Bex pointed out. She jerked the stretch of cable I was holding, and it burned through my hands.

"Bex, I can't just leave him! He'll worry. He'll start looking and asking around and . . ."

"She's right," I heard Liz saying. "It's a direct violation of CoveOps rule number—"

But I was never going to know which CoveOps rule that violated, because just then a big ruby-colored flash came zooming out of the forest.

"Get in!" Macey cried from the driver's seat. For a moment, I didn't know which was more surprising, the fact that my classmates had come to rescue me in a Gallagher Academy golf cart or that Bex had let Macey drive (although, when you think about it, Macey probably did have way more golf-cart experience than the rest of us).

When Liz saw the dazed look on my face, she blushed and said, "Let's just say Bubblegum Guard is going to wake up in a few hours, amazed that his sinus medicine made him so drowsy."

I heard the music stop and wild applause, but it felt like we were a mile from the party. Josh was in there. Of course, so were two people who could punish me in ways that have been illegal since the Geneva Convention. But still, I looked at Bex and said, "I can't go."

Liz was already climbing into the golf cart, leaving Bex and me alone in the dark.

"I'll be okay," I told Bex. "I'll get Josh and we'll leave." She didn't say anything. We were on the dark side of the party, but I could read her face in the light of the full moon. I didn't see fear; I saw disappointment. It seemed a whole lot worse.

"They could catch you, you know?" Bex asked.

"Hey," I tried, forcing a laugh, trusting my smile to thaw her, "I'm The Chameleon, right?"

But Bex was already sliding into the backseat. "See you at home."

The Operative decided to go into a holding pattern in hopes of extracting The Subject and salvaging the mission. At least two hostile agents were inside (and they were going to get a lot more hostile if things didn't go well), so it was a risky move, but one she was willing to make, even as she watched her backup drive away.

Mom and Mr. Solomon might have had the advantage when it came to training and experience, but I had a superior position and far more information. As I crouched behind the hood of a big, black Buick, watching the doors, I went through my options: A) cause a diversion and hope to pull Josh away in the chaos, B) wait for either Josh or Mom and Mr. Solomon to leave, and pray they didn't decide to leave at the exact same time, or C) think of more options.

After all, I did have access to gasoline, rocks, and aluminum cans, but that old barn seemed really, really flammable, and I wasn't exactly in the mood to take chances.

I was just starting to wonder if one of the pickup trucks parked beside me would have a rope, when I heard someone say, "Cammie?" I spun around to see DeeDee heading my way. "Hi. I thought that was you."

She was wearing a really pretty pink dress that matched her stationery. Her blond hair was pulled away from her face.

She looked almost doll-like as she floated toward me through the dark.

"Hi, DeeDee," I said. "You look really nice."

"Thanks," she said, but didn't sound like she believed me. "You, too."

Nervously, I fingered the corsage. The orchid petals felt like silk against my hand.

"I see he went ahead and got you one."

I looked down at my wrist. "Yeah." I didn't know how to feel about the fact that Josh had discussed his corsage plans with another girl, but then I looked at her and realized I didn't feel nearly as weirded-out about it as she did.

DeeDee pointed toward the lights and swaying couples in the distance and said, "I figured if I came late then I wouldn't have to be a wallflower for too long."

I imagined her blending in with the wooden slats and bales of hay, disappearing among the sea of couples until no one noticed one girl standing alone, not quite a part of the party. That's when I knew that DeeDee was a chameleon, too.

"So, what are you doing out here by yourself?" DeeDee asked.

It was a pretty good question. Thankfully, one I was ready for.

I rubbed my temples and said, "It's so loud in there, my head is killing me. I had to get some air."

"Oh," she said, and started digging in her tiny pink purse. "Do you want some aspirin or something?"

"No. Thanks, though."

DeeDee stopped digging, but she still didn't look at me when she said, "He really likes you, you know? I've known him for forever, and I can tell he really likes you."

Even if I hadn't read her note, I would have known how much she liked Josh, how deeply she wished that he would someday buy *her* a wrist corsage. And she'd wear it—not because it was part of some silly inside joke but because Josh had given it to her.

"I really like him, too," I said, not knowing what else to say.

She smiled. "I know."

And then I thought she'd walk away. I really *needed* her to walk away, because I absolutely had to come up with a way of getting Josh out of there! "Well, don't let me keep you, DeeDee," I said, running through possible distractions in my mind: small explosion, easily contained forest fire, the possibility that there might be some pregnant woman inside who could go into labor in the next half hour . . .

"Cammie?" DeeDee asked, and I couldn't help myself, I snapped, "What?"

"Do you want me to tell Josh you need to go home?"

Or that could work, too.

As DeeDee walked toward the party, I found myself envying her. She saw Josh at school. She knew what he ate in the cafeteria and where he sat in class. There was no part of her life she couldn't share with him—nothing he didn't already know from a lifetime of dances and carnivals and ordinary days. And then I found myself thinking: if all things were equal, would he still like me then?

But I would never know, because things would never be equal. DeeDee would always be flesh and blood to him, and I'd always be a legend.

"Are you sure I can't drive you home?" Josh asked as he turned the van onto Main Street and we headed for the square. "Come on. I know you're not feeling well. Let me—"

"No, that's okay," I said. "My head doesn't hurt now." Not a lie.

"Are you sure?"

"Yeah."

He parked along the square, and we got out and walked to the gazebo. He held my hand, and it was a very *Dear Diary* moment, if you know what I mean, because the lights in the gazebo were on but the town was deserted and his hand was soft and warm, and then . . . *he handed me a present!*

The box was small and blue (but not *Tiffany* blue as Macey would later point out) and circled by a pink ribbon.

He said, "I hope you like it."

I was stunned. Completely. I'd gotten presents before, sure, but usually they were things like new running shoes or a signed first edition of *A Spy's Guide to Underground Russia.* Never had the presents come with pretty pink ribbons.

"My mom helped me wrap it," Josh admitted, then motioned to the gift in my hands. "Go ahead," he told me, but I didn't want to open it. How sad is that—that the idea of a present was more precious to me than the gift itself?

"Go on!" Josh said, growing impatient. "I wasn't sure what you wanted, but . . . oh, well . . ." He started tearing at the paper. "Happy birthday!"

Yeah, in case you haven't figured it out already: it totally wasn't my birthday.

The present in my hands felt foreign and heavy then. Doesn't it usually take 365 days to earn a birthday present? I wondered. I mean, I know I've had a pretty sheltered life and all, but I'm pretty sure that's the standard way in which these things work.

"I bet you thought I'd forgotten," he teased, pulling me into a bone-crushing hug.

"Oh, um . . . yeah?" I tried.

"DeeDee helped me pick them out." He had taken the lid off the box and was pulling out the most delicate pair of silver earrings I'd ever seen. (Note to self: get ears pierced.) "I thought they'd go with your necklace—you know, the silver one, with the cross?"

"Yeah," I said, dismayed. "I know the one."

The earrings glistened in the night, and all I could do was stare at them, hypnotized, thinking that no girl has ever had a nicer boyfriend, and no girl has ever been less deserving of him.

I felt like I was outside myself looking down. Who is that girl, I wondered. Doesn't she know how lucky she is? Doesn't she realize that she has really pretty earrings that match her necklace and a boy who would think of such a thing? Who is she to worry about quantum physics or chemical agents or NSA codes? Doesn't she know this is one of those rare moments in life where everything is right and good and wonderful?

Doesn't she know these moments always end?

Chapter twenty-one

As I inched through the secret passageways, my thoughts seemed to echo in the narrow space: *But it isn't my birthday.*

I wished the nagging doubt would just go away. I had earrings, didn't I? Does it really matter why he'd given them to me? After all, normal girls get mad when their boyfriends forget their birthdays, so shouldn't remembering a wrong birthday be worth bonus points or something? I should have been crediting Josh's account in case he ever forgot something else—like twenty years from now he could forget our wedding anniversary and I could say, *Don't worry, darling; remember when you gave me earrings when it wasn't my birthday? Now we're even.*

But it wasn't my birthday.

I thought about the date: November nineteenth. I remembered telling Josh that was my birthday during his rapid-fire interrogation by the park, and I wasn't sure which was more sobering—that he'd remembered or I'd forgotten.

The empty corridors seemed to spiral out in front of me. I was tired. I was hungry. I wanted to take a shower and talk to my friends, and so I was already half asleep as I leaned against the back side of the ancient stone that framed the huge fireplace in the second-floor student lounge. In just a couple of weeks the fireplace was going to be useless to me as a passageway unless I wanted to wear one of Dr. Fibs's fire-proof bodysuits on my dates with Josh (but they make even Bex look fat), so I pulled the lever one last time, expecting the stones to part, but when I did, I accidentally knocked an old torch holder that slid down, opening yet another hidden door, and revealing a branch in the passageway that I don't think I'd ever seen before.

I don't know why I followed it—spy genetics or teenage curiosity—but soon I was wandering down the corridor, not knowing where I was until I walked through thin slivers of light and stopped to peer through cracks into the Hall of History, where Gilly's sword stood gleaming beneath its perpetual spotlight.

That's also when I heard the crying.

Farther down the passageway I found my mother's office and the bookshelves I had watched spin around to reveal the memorabilia of a headmaster of an elite boarding school. I leaned against them, peered through a crack in the plaster, and watched my mother cry. Someone could have thrown a switch, and the bookcase would have spun around, taking me with it, but as I stood in the cramped and musty space I couldn't turn away.

She was alone in her office, curled up in her chair. The last time I'd seen her she'd been dancing and laughing, but now she sat alone, and tears ran down her face. I wanted to hold her so that we could cry together. I wanted to feel her salty tears on my cheek. I wanted to smooth her hair and tell her that I was tired, too. But I stayed where I was—watching, knowing the reasons I didn't go comfort her: I couldn't explain what I was wearing; I couldn't tell her why I was there; but mostly, I knew that it was something she didn't want me to see.

When she reached for a tissue on the shelf behind her desk, her eyes were closed, and yet she found the box with the sure, steady motion of someone who had known it would be there. It was a practiced gesture, a habit. And I knew that my mother's grief, like her life, was full of secrets. Then I felt the earrings in my pocket, and I knew why the tears had picked that night to come.

"Oh my gosh," I said, once more that night—this time for a very different reason.

I slipped farther down the passageway and eventually slid to a window seat in an abandoned classroom. I didn't cry. Something told me the universe couldn't handle both Morgan women weeping at the same time, so I sat there stoically, letting my mother be the weak one for a little while, taking my turn on duty.

I didn't move; I just waited out the night. The school was quiet around me, and I let the silence calm my heartbreak, lull me into a sleepless trance as I stared past my reflection in the dark glass, and whispered, "Happy birthday, Daddy."

I stayed away as long as I could that Sunday morning, but by noon, I had to see my mother; I had to know that she was okay and apologize somehow for forgetting my father in that small way. I had to know if that was the beginning of the end of my memories.

I burst through her office door, armed with a dozen excuses, but they all flew from my mind when I saw Mom, Mr. Solomon, and Buckingham staring at me as if I'd just been beamed down from outer space. They shut up too quickly—something you'd think spies would know better than to do. I didn't know what was more disturbing—the fact that something was obviously wrong, or that three faculty members of the world's premiere spy school had forgotten to lock the door.

After what seemed like forever, Buckingham said, "Cameron, I'm glad you're here. You have firsthand experience in a matter we've been discussing." At that moment it didn't matter that Patricia Buckingham had two bad hips and arthritic fingers, I still would have sworn she was made of steel. "Of course, Rachel, you are Cameron's mother, not to mention headmistress of this school, so I would respect your opinion if you chose to ask Cameron to leave."

"No," my mom said. "She's in now. She'll want to help."

The whole vibe of the room was starting to seriously creep me out, so I said, "What is it? What's—"

"Close the door, Cameron," Buckingham instructed. I did as I was told.

"Abe Baxter missed a call-in," Mr. Solomon said, crossing his arms as he leaned on the corner of Mom's desk, just like I'd seen him do a hundred times during CoveOps class. And yet, it didn't feel like a lecture. "Actually, he's missed *three* call-ins."

I didn't realize his words had knocked me off my feet until I felt my backpack pressing against my spine as I tried to lean back on the sofa. Does Bex know, I wondered for a split second before the obvious answer dawned on me: of course not.

"He may just be delayed, of course," Buckingham offered. "These things happen—communications difficulties, changes in cell operation . . . This doesn't necessarily mean that his cover has been compromised. Still, three missed calls is . . . troubling."

"Is Bex's mom . . ." I stumbled over my words. "Is she with him?"

Mr. Solomon looked at Buckingham, who shook her head. "Our friends at Six say no."

And then I realized why Buckingham was in charge of that discussion—she had been MI6, just like Bex's parents. She had been the one to get the call. She was the one who was going to have to decide what, if anything, to tell Bex.

"It doesn't mean anything," my mom soothed, but I heard traces of the woman I'd seen the night before—traces I probably wouldn't have heard twenty-four hours earlier, but I knew they were there now, and I'd be listening for them for the rest of my life.

"Bex . . ." I muttered.

"We were just talking about her, Cam," Mom said. "We don't know what to do."

Say what you will about spies, but they don't do anything halfway. Our lies come complete with Social Security numbers and fake IDs, and our truths cut like Spanish steel. I knew what my mom was saying. I knew why she risked saying it to me. The Gallagher Academy was made of stone, but news like that could burn it to the ground as quickly as if it were built out of newspapers and painted with gasoline.

"Cam"—Mom sat on the edge of the coffee table in front of me—"this has happened before, of course, but each case is different, and you know Bex better than anyone—"

"Don't tell her." The words surprised even me. I know we're supposed to be tough and hardened and in the process of being prepared for anything, but I didn't want her to know just because we were too weak to carry the secret on our own. I looked at my mother again, remembered how long it takes some wounds to heal, and realized there would be plenty of time for grieving.

Bex's father was thousands of miles away, but she still had the promise of him. Who was I to take that away too soon? What would I have given for a few extra hours of it myself?

* * *

"Hey," Macey McHenry said behind me, and I instantly regretted showing her the small, ancient corridor and telling her it was a great place to study. "That had better not be because of a boy."

She dropped her stack of books beside me, but I couldn't look at her. Instead, I just sat there wiping away the tears I was crying quietly for Bex's father—swallowing the tears I was crying for my own. A long time passed. I don't know—maybe like a millennium or something—before Macey nudged me with her knee and said, "Spill."

Say what you will about Macey McHenry, but she really doesn't beat around the bush. A superspy would have lied to her—good lies, too. But I couldn't. Maybe it was stress. Maybe it was grief. Maybe it was PMS, but something made me look up at Macey and say, "Bex's dad is missing. He might be dead."

Macey slid to sit beside me. "You can't tell her."

"I know," I said, and then I blew my nose.

"When will they know for sure?"

"I don't know." And I didn't. "Could be days. Could be months. He hasn't called his handler. If he calls, then . . ."

"We can't tell her."

Of course we couldn't, but something about that statement made me stop and look at her. I thought back on it, and for the first time, I heard the *we*. There were things I couldn't tell my mother, things I couldn't tell my boyfriend, and things I couldn't tell my friends. But sitting there with Macey McHenry, I realized for the first time that someone knew all my secrets—that I wasn't entirely alone.

Macey stood and started to walk away. "Cammie, no offense . . ." When someone like Macey McHenry says "no offense" it's almost impossible for someone like me *not* to be offended by what she says next, but I tried. ". . . but don't go up there now. You look like hell, and she'll see it."

I wasn't offended. I was actually glad she'd said it, because it was true and I might not have realized it if Macey hadn't said so.

Macey walked away, and I sat there for a long time—thinking. I remembered the time my dad took me to the circus. For two hours we sat side by side, watching the clowns and cheering for the lion tamer. But the part I remember most was when a man stepped out onto the high wire, fifty feet above the ground. By the time he reached the other side, five other people had climbed onto his shoulders, but I wasn't watching him—I was too busy staring at my father, who looked on as if he knew what it felt like, up there without a net.

Sitting there that day, I knew that the only thing I could do was keep putting one foot in front of the other, hoping none of the secrets on my shoulders would make me lose my balance.

Chapter Twenty-two

"**E**yes closed," Mr. Solomon commanded again, and we followed his instructions.

The projector purred behind me. I felt its white light slicing through the room as we cinched our eyes together and trained our minds to recall even the most minute details of the things we had just seen. I thought about the photo of a supermarket parking lot as Mr. Solomon said, "Ms. Alvarez, what's wrong with this picture?"

"The blue van has handicapped plates," Eva said. "But it's parked at the back of the lot."

"Correct. Next picture." The projector clicked, the image changed, and we had two seconds to study the photo that flashed before our eyes.

"Ms. Baxter?" Mr. Solomon asked. "What's wrong here?"

"The umbrella," Bex said. "There's rain on the window and the coat on the hook is damp, but the umbrella is bundled up. Most people leave them open to dry."

"Very good."

When we opened our eyes, I didn't look at the screen, I looked at our teacher and wondered yet again how he could talk to Bex, challenge her as if nothing in the world was wrong. I didn't know whether to envy him or hate him, but I didn't have time for either, because he was saying, "Eyes closed." I heard him take a step, and I wanted to know how he could stand there when all I wanted to do was run away. "Ms. Morgan, what's wrong with this picture?"

"Um . . . I didn't . . . I mean, I'm . . ."

What was wrong was that I hadn't been able to look my best friend in the eye for days. What was wrong was that people like Abe Baxter live and die, and the whole world goes on—never knowing what they've sacrificed. There was so much wrong that I didn't know where to start.

"Okay. How about you, Ms. Bauer?"

"The teacup at the head of the table," Courtney said.

"What about it?"

"Its handle is facing the wrong way."

"So it is," Mr. Solomon said as the lights in the class-room flickered to life and we all squinted against the glare.

Our internal clocks were telling us the same thing—class wasn't over.

"I've got something for you today, ladies," Mr. Solomon said as he handed a stack of papers to each girl in the front row.

Liz's hand was instantly in the air.

"No, Ms. Sutton," Mr. Solomon said before Liz could

even ask the question. "This isn't a test, and it's not for a grade. Your school just needs you to say in black and white whether you are going to keep studying covert operations next semester."

All around me, my classmates started filling out the form—a check mark here, a signature there, until Mr. Solomon stepped forward and snapped, "Ladies"—he paused as everyone looked up—"my colleague Mr. Smith is fond of saying, 'It is a big world full of dark corners and long memories.' Do not"—he paused, surveying us, and I could have sworn his stare lingered on me—"take this decision lightly."

Bex poked me in the shoulder. When I turned around, she flashed a big thumbs-up and mouthed the words "This is awesome!"

I looked back down at the form in my hands, rubbed it between my fingers, and tried to smell if there was poison in the ink.

It's just paper, I told myself. Ordinary paper. But then that very fact sent chills down my spine as I realized the form wasn't on Evapopaper. It wasn't meant to dissolve and wash away. I caught Joe Solomon's eye, and I'm pretty sure he saw me notice that—the permanence of what it meant. And even though it wasn't meant to be eaten, I still got a bad taste in my mouth.

Chapter twenty-three

Now, you may think that if you're a Gallagher Girl dating a boy from Roseville that the best thing in the world would be having Tina Walters come running up to you at breakfast, exclaiming, "Cammie, I talked to your mom, and she said we can all walk into town on Saturday!"

You may think that—but you'd be wrong.

Every moment I spent in town while it was swarming with Gallagher Girls was a moment they could see me with Josh, or Josh could see me with them. Still, I looked at Bex across the breakfast table, felt the sadness that I'd been carrying for days, and even though Liz whispered, "Cam, it's a *big* risk," I knew I had to go. I needed a few hours of forgetting.

Saturday morning, the suites were buzzing as girls collected their Christmas shopping lists and checked what movies were playing. (I'd already seen them both with Josh, of course.) Some of us rode into town in Gallagher Academy vans, but I chose to walk with the rest of the sophomores—amazed at how that familiar terrain looked by the light of day.

When we reached the edge of town, I started rubbing my temples. "Oh," I said, "my head is killing me. Does anybody have any aspirin?" My classmates checked their pockets and purses, but no one could find any little bottles of pills (probably because I'd stolen them all the night before).

"You guys go on without me," I said, when we reached the square. "I'm gonna run to the pharmacy." Not a lie.

"The movie's gonna start in ten minutes," Bex reminded me, but I was already walking away, calling after them, "I'll meet you in there."

As plans go, it was a pretty good one. I could spend two hours with Josh, then sneak into the back of the theater, say something about the movie on the way home, and they'd never know I hadn't been there all along.

The door dinged when I pushed inside. I'd never been to the pharmacy with Josh. It had always seemed better not to see him there. But he'd told me his dad was making him work on Saturdays, and having permission to be in town was too good an opportunity to pass up.

I walked to the counter and spoke to the woman behind it. "Hi. Is Josh here?"

"Well, hello, Cammie," a man said behind me. I turned to see Mr. Abrams walking my way. He was wearing a white smock with his name embroidered above the pocket. I felt like I was getting ready to have my teeth cleaned. "This is a nice surprise."

"Oh, hello, Mr. Abrams."

"Is this your first trip to our little store?"

"Yes, it is. It's . . ." I looked around at the long rows of cough syrups and greeting cards and bandages for every occasion. ". . . nice."

Mr. Abrams beamed. "Well, Josh just ran out to make a delivery. Ought to be right back, though. In the meantime, I want you to go over to the counter and order up any kind of ice cream you want—on the house. How's that sound?"

I glanced behind me to see an old-fashioned soda fountain stretching across the far wall. "That sounds great!" Totally not a lie.

Mr. Abrams smiled at me and started toward a set of narrow stairs, but before climbing, he turned and said, "Cammie, you come back any time."

He disappeared around a corner. I was almost sad to watch him go.

The ice-cream counter was smooth against my hands as I walked in front of the huge mirror that hung behind the bar. The woman from the counter followed me over and slipped on an apron as I climbed onto one of the old metal stools.

A sign above the bar read "Proudly serving Coca-Cola since 1942." There was a tall glass jar full of straws. The woman didn't bat an eye when I ordered a double chocolate sundae, and for the first time in weeks I felt almost normal.

Outside it was November and cold, but the sun was beaming through the glass storefront, warming my skin as I ate my ice cream and fell into a dreamy, sugar-induced trance.

Then, I heard the jingling of the little brass bells above the door.

I didn't turn around. I didn't have to. The woman who'd been helping me pulled off her apron and headed toward the counter as I paused with a spoon halfway to my mouth and saw Anna Fetterman's reflection in the mirror behind the bar.

"Can you help me?" Anna said, once the clerk drew near. "I need to have my inhaler refilled."

"Sure, honey." The woman took the slip of paper from Anna's hand. "Let me go check on this. It'll just be a minute."

I was already off my stool and crouching behind an adult diapers display, when I realized that all I was really guilty of was eating a hot fudge sundae so soon after lunch, and let me tell you—Anna has seen me eat way more than that (a certain incident involving Doritos, squirty cheese, and the winter Olympics comes to mind), so I was just getting ready to go say hi, when I heard something that made me freeze.

The bells rang again, and I glanced through the shelves to see Dillon and a bunch of boys from the barn dance walk in. But they didn't walk down the aisles. No. They'd already found what they were looking for.

"Hey, don't I know you?" Dillon asked, but he wasn't talking to me. It was worse. He was talking to Anna, and he wasn't simply asking a question. His words were too sharp. His tone too predatory as he stepped closer to little Anna Fetterman and said, "No, wait, you don't go to *my* school." In the mirror above the bar I saw him crowd Anna against the shelves. "I bet *you* go to the Gallagher Academy."

Anna drew her purse to her chest as if he were going to grab it and run away. "What a nice purse," Dillon said. "Did your daddy buy you that purse?"

Anna's daddy is an eighth-grade biology teacher in Dayton, Ohio, but Dillon didn't know that and Anna couldn't tell him. She was clinging to her cover just as ardently as I was clinging to mine.

The boys around Dillon started to laugh. And just like that I remembered why Gallagher Girls and town boys aren't supposed to mix.

Anna stumbled backward, because, despite nearly three and a half years of P&E training, she could hardly swat a fly. The town was swarming with Gallagher Girls that afternoon, but Dillon and his friends had found Anna. It wasn't an accident. Anna was alone and weak, so obviously someone like Dillon would be there to try to thin her from the herd.

"I'm just here to . . ." Anna tried to speak, but her voice was barely more than a whisper.

"What's that?" Dillon asked. "I didn't hear you."

"I . . ." Anna stuttered.

I wanted to go to her, but I was frozen somehow—halfway between being her friend and being a homeschooled girl with a cat named Suzie. If I were one and not the other,

I could have stopped it, but instead I told myself over and over, She'll be okay; she'll be okay; she'll be—

"What's the matter? Don't they teach you how to speak at the Gallagher Academy?" Dillon said, and I would have given anything for Anna to bite back in Arabic, or Japanese, or Farsi, but she just took another backward step. Her elbow knocked a box of Band-Aids, and it teetered on the edge of the shelf.

Anna inched toward the door and mumbled, "I'll come back for—"

But a couple of Dillon's friends stepped in front of her, surrounding her with a wall of crimson lettermen's jackets, and I couldn't see her anymore.

She'll be fine, I said again, willing it to be true. Which in a way it was, because just then the doorbells chimed, and in walked Macey McHenry.

"Hey, Anna." To my knowledge, Macey had never said more than two words to Anna Fetterman, but as she strolled through the door, her voice was light and free, and she sounded like the tiny girl's best friend in the world. "What's going on?"

The four boys parted around Anna, backing away; maybe because of the way Macey chomped her gum then blew a bubble that popped in Dillon's face; maybe because they'd never seen a girl so beautiful in person before. But Dillon didn't stray.

"Oh," he said smugly, looking Macey's amazing figure up and down. "She has a friend."

Anna looked at Macey as if she half suspected her classmate to say, *Who me? I'm not* her *friend.* But Macey only fingered the bottles on the shelves, handing Anna a bottle of vitamin C. "You should really take these."

Macey walked down the aisle, examining the shelves, ignoring Dillon and the gang, who kept looking at their leader for directions.

"I should have known the Gallagher Academy wouldn't let its precious darlings out on their own," Dillon mocked. But Macey only smiled one of her patently beautiful smiles.

"Yeah," she said, eyeing his buddies. "We're not brave like you."

"Is there a problem here?" I knew the voice, but the accent was one Bex only used on rare occasions. To this day, I don't know how she got through the front door without setting off the chimes, but there she was, strolling past the Cold and Flu section, coming to stand on Anna's other side. I didn't know why she wasn't at the movie. I didn't care.

It was three against four now, and Dillon didn't like those odds. Still, he managed to look at Bex and say, "What's the matter? Is your yacht broken or something?"

Dillon snickered. The friends snickered. It was an idiot snicker-a-thon until Macey said, "Not that I've heard."

"Did you boys come over here to flirt with Anna?" Bex said, laying on her faux charm. She pushed a petrified Anna toward the clan. "Anna, tell the boys a little something about yourself."

"I have a boyfriend!" she blurted in a way that told me

it totally wasn't a lie. I was stunned. Bex was stunned. Even Macey took a second to recover. *Anna has a boyfriend?*

In all this time, I'd never thought that one of my classmates might have a boyfriend—especially not Anna. "His name is Carl," she added.

"Sorry, boys," Bex said, sliding her arm around Anna's shoulder. "Carl beat you to it."

"Oh, so they have boyfriends. Tell me, is Carl a townie?" Dillon asked, as if he wanted to be let in on a secret. "Do you girls like to go slumming?"

"It's probably Carl Rockefeller," Macey added, and Bex squeezed Anna harder until she said, "Yes. Carl Rockefeller. We know each other from the physics"—another hard squeeze—this time with fingernails—"um, yacht," Anna corrected, "club."

Two pats on Anna's shoulder told her she'd done well.

"Hey," Dillon said, stepping forward as if he were tired of beating around the bush. "I was wondering if you know someone I know. . . ." His voice trailed off. He leaned forward, and I just knew—I mean KNEW—that he was on to me, but then he said, "The Queen of England."

Well, Bex actually has met the queen, but obviously she wasn't about to say so. She just stood quietly as Dillon and his buddies laughed far too hard at the joke, making it even less funny.

"Honey, I got your—" The woman behind the counter stopped abruptly when she saw four boys closing in on three girls. The only sound in the room was the white paper bag that held Anna's prescription as it crinkled in her hands.

"Thanks," Bex said, snatching the package. "Is this all you needed?" she asked Anna, who nodded, and the color slowly returned to her cheeks.

"How 'bout you?" Macey asked Dillon. "You get what you came for?"

But they didn't wait for his response. Instead, they walked together past a long shelf of magazines, where Macey's face stared out from the cover of *Newsweek*, along with the rest of the McHenry family, beneath a caption that read *The Most Powerful Family in America?*

Dillon looked at it, then at her. Macey cocked a hip. "We appreciate your vote."

A long time after they'd gone, I still couldn't turn away from the bells that were still ringing. I watched Anna stroll down the street with her saviors—with her friends. A hand circled my wrist, and Josh said, "Hey." I saw his reflection in the mirror from the corner of my eye, but there was something through that window I couldn't turn away from.

Liz was standing on the sidewalk, staring at me through the glass as if she didn't know me. As if she didn't want to.

"Hey, what's wrong?" Josh asked, finally turning me to face him. "What are you doing with those?" He gestured to the half dozen bottles of aspirin I must have subconsciously gathered in my arms to throw like snowballs at Dillon and his cronies if help hadn't come.

"Oh." I looked down. "I knocked them off and was picking them up."

"That's okay," he said, and pushed the bottles back onto the shelf.

I turned back toward the window, but Liz was already gone.

Chapter twenty-four

A cold front blew in that night—in a lot of ways.

Fires burned in all the lounges. We traded our knee-socks for tights. Every window we passed was covered with frost, blocking our view of the world outside. But nothing made me shiver quite as much as the look on Liz's face. For days, it was as if we were still separated by the pharmacy windows. It was as if she hardly knew me.

When I went to the chem lab after supper Tuesday night, Liz was already there.

"Well, fancy seeing you here," I said, trying to sound chipper as I gathered my things and moved to the lab table across from her.

Her eyes were shielded behind her protective goggles. She didn't even look up.

"Earth to Liz," I tried again, but she turned away.

"I don't have time to help you with your homework, Cammie," she said, and it might have been my imagination, but I could have sworn all the beakers frosted over.

"That's okay," I said. "I think I've got it under control."

We worked in silence for a long time before Liz said, "He was Josh's friend—wasn't he?"

I didn't have to ask who she was talking about. "Yeah, they're neighbors. I'd met him before, that's why I couldn't compromise—"

"Nice friend," Liz snapped.

"He's all talk," I said, repeating Josh's words to me. "He's harmless."

But Liz's voice was shaking when she said, "Go ask Anna how harmless he is." Of course, word of Anna's encounter in the pharmacy had spread like crazy, and Anna was now something of a hero—thanks to the fact that Bex and Macey insisted that Anna had the situation well under control when they got there.

But I couldn't share this with Liz. We both knew the truth. "If things had gotten out of hand I could have—"

"*Could* have or *would* have?" Liz asked.

The difference between those two words had never seemed so huge. "Would," I said. "I would have stopped it."

"Even if it meant losing Josh?" Liz said, not asking what she really wanted to know—that if it had been her instead of Anna in Dillon's sights, would I have saved her; if it came down to a fight between the real me and my legend, which one would I choose?

The glass doors at the back of the lab slid open, and Macey walked in. "Hey, I thought I might find you two—"

"It's gone too far, Cammie," Liz said, shaking ingredients wildly into the mix until the whole thing started to bubble and change colors like something in a witch's caldron. "You've gone too far."

"*I've* gone too far?" I said. "I wasn't the one blowing up Driver's Ed cars!"

"Hey," Liz snapped. "We thought he was a honeypot!"

"No." I shook my head. "We thought he was a boy." I gathered my things. "We thought he was worth it. And, you know what? He was."

"Yeah," Liz called after me. "Well, I never thought you were someone who'd choose a boy over her friends!"

"Hey, cool it," Macey said.

"Well, I never thought I had friends who'd make me choose!"

As I neared the door, I heard Liz start to speak, but Macey cut her off, saying, "Hey, genius girl, you don't have any idea what kinds of sacrifices she's willing to make for her friends."

"What are you—" Liz started, then her voice softened slightly as she asked, "Why? What do you know?"

When Macey spoke, she left no room for doubt. "Enough to say, back off."

The glass doors slid open and I darted through them just as Liz said, "Okay," but I couldn't stop moving, didn't dare break my pace until I reached the supply closet in the east corridor, where I slid aside a stack of long fluorescent lightbulbs, grabbed a flashlight from the top shelf, and found the loose stone that I had discovered one day during my seventh-grade year while looking for Onyx, Buckingham's cat.

The stone was cold beneath my hand when I pushed against it and felt the rush of air as the wall slid aside. A small sliver of light slipped beneath the door behind me, but it faded into nothing in the deep expanse of black.

An hour later I was standing in the shadows of Bellis Street, shivering in the dark.

What did I intend to accomplish by sneaking through a secret tunnel, climbing over a fence, and literally staking out Josh's house in the dark? I didn't have a clue. Instead, I just stood there like an idiot (and even an idiot who is very good at not being seen while standing around can feel pretty silly while doing it).

This is probably a pretty good time to point out that while it may appear that I was lurking—I wasn't. Lurking is what creepy guys with random facial hair and stains on their shirts do. Geniuses with three years of top secret spy training don't *lurk*—we *surveil*.

(Okay, I might have been lurking—a little.)

White eyelet curtains were pushed back from a kitchen window where Josh's mother was washing dishes. When Josh walked through the kitchen, his mother blew soapsuds at him, and he laughed. I thought about Bex, who was probably laughing right then, too. I thought about my mother, whose tears only came in secret. I thought about my life—the one I had and the one I wanted, so all I did was stand shivering in the cold, watching Josh laugh, as I started to cry.

But that's a girl's right—isn't it? To cry sometimes for no reason? Really, when you think about it, that ought to be in the Constitution. Maybe I'll break into the National Archives sometime and write that in. Bex would totally help me. Somehow, I don't think the Founding Fathers would mind.

Chapter twenty-five

With finals and the stress that comes with them, I didn't really see Liz again until supper the following night when she brought her slice of pizza and came to sit beside me. "So, where did you go last night?" she asked. But before I could answer, she said, "To see Josh?"

I nodded.

"You didn't break up with him, did you?" She sounded genuinely concerned.

"No," I said, shocked.

"Good." Then she must have sensed my confusion because she said, "He's good to you, and you deserve that." She looked around the Grand Hall at the hundred other girls who were like us. "We all deserve that."

Yeah, I realized, I think we do.

I stole a glance at Bex who sat beside me, laughing. We all deserve laughter and love and the kinds of friends I had beside me, but as I watched her, I couldn't help but wonder if she'd still find life so funny if she knew all I knew. I wondered if our fathers' fates had been reversed, would our personalities have switched, too? Would I be the one standing in the Grand Hall allowing Anna Fetterman to demonstrate how she'd defended herself against a mob of twenty angry townspeople (because, by that time, the mob had grown considerably)? Would Bex, beautiful Bex, be a chameleon, then?

"Ms. Baxter!" I turned to see Professor Buckingham starting toward us. I felt my heart stop—literally. (It can do that—I know, I asked Liz.) She was walking toward us, bearing down like the force of nature she was.

Macey was across the table from me, and we glanced at each other—an unspoken dread lingering between us like the smell of olive oil and melting cheese, but beside me, Bex was unfazed, and I remembered the power of a secret.

As she drew near, I tried to read something in Buckingham's eyes, but they were as cold and blank as stone.

"Miss Baxter, I just had a phone call . . ." Buckingham started and then, ever so slightly, turned her gaze toward me. ". . . *from your father*." Air returned to my lungs. Blood started moving in my veins, and I'm pretty sure Buckingham gave something that resembled a wink in my direction. "He said to tell you hello."

My elbows fell to the table, and across from me, Macey mirrored my relief. It was over.

"Oh," Bex said, but she hadn't even stopped chewing. "That's nice."

She would never know *how nice*.

I glanced toward the head table, and Mom raised a glass in my direction. Beside me, Bex didn't breathe a sigh of relief. She didn't say a prayer. She didn't do any of the things I felt like doing, but that's okay, I guess. Her father was still on his high wire. It was just as well she'd never looked up.

Almost everyone had gone upstairs twenty minutes later when Bex and I started to leave.

"So, what do you want to do now?" Bex asked.

"I guess we could do anything," I said, and it was true. We were leaving the hall, and it didn't matter where we were going. We were trained and we were young and we had the rest of our lives to carry the worry of grown-ups. Right then, I just wanted to celebrate with my best friend—even if she didn't know why.

"Let's get all the ice cream we can carry and . . ."

But then I saw Liz running down the spiral staircase, crying, "Cammie!" as if I hadn't already stopped. And then Liz whispered, or at least she tried to whisper, but I swear everyone in the entire mansion must have heard her when she said, "It's Josh!"

Wars have been won and lost, assassination attempts have been thwarted, and women have avoided showing up at the same event in the same dress—all because of really good intel. That's why we have entire classes devoted to this stuff. But as Liz dragged me into our suite, I didn't really appreciate its importance until I saw the screen.

"These were here when I got back from supper."

Poor Liz. She'd done this amazing job of getting us patched into Josh's system, and I could tell by looking at her that she would have given just about anything to undo it all right then. Ignorance is bliss, after all. But the problem is, for spies, ignorance is usually pretty short-lived.

From D'Man
To JAbrams
Have you come to your senses yet? I'm telling you—I saw her WITH MY OWN EYES. You've got to believe me now. SHE GOES TO THE GALLAGHER ACADEMY!! She's been lying to you!! How can you take HER word over MINE?

From JAbrams
To D'Man
I trust Cammie. I believe her. You probably just thought you saw her walking with a bunch of those girls on Saturday. She doesn't even know them. Trust me. Give it a break.

Dillon's response was a single line.

From D'Man
To JAbrams
Tonight. 9:00. WE'LL GET PROOF!

Now, at this point I was starting to panic, which isn't very spylike, but is pretty girl-like, so I figured I was well within my feminine rights. The "proof" to which I'd seen teenage boys refer in movies usually involved video equipment and/or feminine undergarments, so I yelled, "Oh my gosh!" and started looking around for Liz's flash cards. Surely somewhere in all that vat of knowledge there had to be instructions on what to do when your cover is completely and irrevocably blown.

Faced with the knowledge that the operation had been severely compromised, The Operatives formed a list of alternatives, which included (but were not limited to) the following:

A. Misdirection: in a variation of the "you must have seen someone who looks like me" approach, one of The Operatives could impersonate Cammie and climb the wall while Cammie looks on with Josh and Dillon and says, "Is that who you saw?" (Which is especially effective when The Subject is nearsighted.)

B. Sympathy: this technique has not only been used successfully by spies for many centuries, but it is also a staple of teenage girls. The conversation would likely resemble the following:

JOSH: Cammie, is it true you attend the Gallagher Academy, home of filthy rotten heiresses, and are not homeschooled, as you initially told me?

CAMMIE: (instantly bursts into tears—note: tears are very important!) Yes. It's true. I do go to the Gallagher

Academy, but no one there understands me. It's not a school; (dramatic pause) it's a prison. I'll understand if you never want to see me again.

JOSH: How could I ever hate you, Cammie? I love you. And, if possible, now I love you even more.

C. Elimination: Dillon, aka D'Man, could be "taken out." (This alternative failed to achieve universal support.)

These were all pretty good options (well, not C, but I felt as if I owed it to Bex to at least include it), but as I weighed them in my mind, and nine o'clock drew closer, I knew there was another option. One we hadn't put on paper.

Josh and Dillon were coming to get proof, and even though the rumor that the security division had recently invested in poisonous darts probably wasn't true, I still didn't want to think about what would happen if Josh came looking for me—now or ever. And when I thought about it that way, I really only had one choice.

"I'll be back soon," I said as I shoved Josh's earrings in my pocket and reached for my silver cross, clinging to my legend till the end.

I walked toward the door as Bex called, "What are you gonna tell him?"

I didn't stop as I said, "The truth."

Chapter twenty-six

Well, obviously I didn't mean "The truth, the whole truth, and nothing but the truth" truth. More like Code Red truth—the abridged kind. Spy truth.

Yes, I go to the Gallagher Academy.

Yes, I have been lying to you.

Yes, you can't believe a single thing I've said or done.

But here's the thing about spy truth: sometimes it isn't enough to achieve your mission objectives. Sometimes you need more, and even though I didn't want to do it, maybe it's only fitting that a relationship that started with a lie would end with one.

No, I never really loved you.

No, I don't care that you're hurt.

No, I never want to see you again.

The mansion seemed especially silent and empty for so early on a Monday night. My footsteps echoed in the dim halls, but I didn't fear the noise. The tunnels were awaiting me, and Josh, and the end of something I had cherished.

Still, before I climbed the wall one last time, there was something I couldn't stand to carry over it.

Mr. Solomon's office wasn't exactly on my way—but it was close enough. I reached into the back pocket of my jeans for the folded form that Mr. Solomon had given us—that everyone but me had long since turned in. It was creased and mangled, and I realized that I'd carried it with me almost everywhere I'd gone for weeks—unsigned, unfinished.

Twenty-four hours before, I had been afraid to even look at it, but so much can happen in a spy's life in that amount of time—a father can get reborn, a friendship can live and die, a true love can dissolve like the paper its love notes are written on. Twenty-four hours before, I had been sitting on top of our walls, but now I knew on which side I belonged.

The two boxes lay at the bottom of the page, like a fork in the road that I had grown tired of straddling. Beyond our walls was a boy I could only hurt, and inside them were people I could help. It was probably the hardest decision of my life, and I made it by drawing an X. That's one of the golden rules of CoveOps: don't make anything more difficult than it has to be.

It was true; things were hard enough already.

"Hi, Josh. Hello, Dillon, so nice seeing you again," I practiced as I paced the shadows of the sidewalk—waiting, not really thinking about what I had to do, but instead trying to figure out a way to accidentally-on-purpose kick Dillon in the head—hard.

Beep. Beep beep. Beepbeepbeep.

I glanced down at my watch and saw the red dot on the screen moving closer to my position as the tracker became a constant *Beep-beep-beep-beep-beeeeeeeeeeeeeep.*

I temporarily deactivated it just as I heard Dillon's echoing, "I'm telling you, this is gonna be off the—"

"Hi, guys." Okay, so my chameleon-ness wasn't entirely gone, because it was pretty obvious they hadn't had a clue I was there. Dillon even dropped his rope. (By the way, what kind of wuss needs a rope to climb a twelve-foot stone wall? I'd totally been doing that since second grade!)

But the fact that I'd caught him off guard didn't stop Dillon from being super cocky (once he'd managed to round up his rope and all). "Well, well, well." He strolled toward me. "There she is. How was *school* today?" he asked, as if he was going to be really clever and trip me up.

"Fine." I swallowed. I didn't want to look at Josh. If I did, I feared my nerve would crumble. More than anything, I wanted Dillon to pick a fight. I could yell at Dillon; I could scream; I could earn my Gallagher glare from him. Josh was another story.

"We were just coming to see you," Dillon said, inching closer.

"Really?" I said, adding an artificial nervousness to my voice. "But . . ." I glanced between the two of them. "You don't know where I live."

"Oh, sure we do," Dillon said. "I saw you Saturday. Walking back to *school*. With your *friends*."

"But . . . I'm homeschooled." *And the Academy Award for Best Actress in a Teenage Drama goes to—Cammie Morgan!* "I don't know what you're talking about."

The streetlight above us flickered off and on, and in that half second of darkness, Dillon stepped closer.

"Give it up, rich girl. I SAW you!"

Behind him, Josh whispered, "Dillon . . ."

"Yeah, you don't own this town, you know. I don't care what your daddy—"

"Dillon," Josh said again, growing louder.

Now I couldn't help looking at Josh. I couldn't stop looking at him.

"I'm so sorry," I whispered. It was the admission of guilt Dillon had been waiting for. He just didn't know it was for the wrong crime. "I'm so sorry. I'm so . . ."

"Cammie?" Josh asked, as if trying to recognize me. "Cammie, is it—"

I nodded, unable to meet his gaze through my tear-blurred vision.

"See!" Dillon said, mocking me. "I told you—"

"Dillon!" Josh cut him off. "Just . . . get out of here."

"But—" Dillon started, and Josh stepped in front of me. He was trying to shield me from Dillon, but really he'd just taken away the best chance I'd ever have to claw the little jerk's eyes out. (Literally, eye-clawing was going to be on the P&E final.)

"Dillon, just go," Josh said, forcing his friend to back away. But that didn't stop D'Man from smugly saying, "See you around."

I wanted to punch and kick and make him feel as much pain as possible, but I remembered that no amount of P&E training would help me make him hurt the way that I hurt. Even at the Gallagher Academy they don't teach you how to break somebody's heart.

As Dillon walked away, I thought of the lies I had planned to tell Josh, and for a second I thought I couldn't do it. I couldn't hurt him—then or ever. But just as soon as Dillon disappeared, Josh spun and shouted, "Is it true?"

"Josh, I—"

He stepped closer. His voice was harder. "You're one of them?"

One of them?

"Josh—"

"A *Gallagher Girl*." All my life, that term had been revered, almost worshipped, but on Josh's lips it was an insult, and in that instant he stopped being the boy of my dreams and started being one of Dillon's hoodlums at the pharmacy; he was ganging up on Anna; he was judging me, so I snapped, "So what if I am?"

"Humph!" Josh said then shook his head, staring into the dark night. "I should have known it." He kicked at the ground like I'd seen him do a thousand times, and when he spoke, it was almost to himself. "Homeschooled." Then he looked at me. "So what was I? Some kind of joke? Was it like, hey, who can make a fool out of a townie? Was that—"

"Josh—"

"No, I really want to know. Was it charity case week? Or date your local delivery boy month? Or—"

"Josh!"

"Or were you just bored?"

"YES!" I yelled at last, wanting it to stop. "Yes, okay. I was bored, and I wanted to see if I could get away with it, okay?"

Mr. Solomon was right—the worst kind of torture is watching someone you love get hurt.

Josh backed down, and his voice was almost a whisper as he said, "Okay." We'd both gone too far—said too much—but we both knew then that there are reasons Gallagher Girls don't date boys from Roseville. He just didn't know that the reasons are classified.

"Look, I'm leaving tomorrow," I said, knowing that I couldn't have Josh climbing the fence that night or any other. "I had to say good-bye." I reached into my pocket for the earrings. They glistened in my hand like fallen stars. "You should probably take these back."

"No," he said, waving them away. "They're yours."

"No." I forced them into his hand. "You take them. Give them to DeeDee." He looked shocked. "I think she'd really like them."

"Yeah, okay." He shoved the earrings into his pocket as I forced a smile.

"Hey, take care, okay?" I took a step, then remembered

how he'd felt chained to one kind of life while I felt bound to another. "And you know free will?"

"Yeah?" he said, sounding surprised that I'd remembered.

"Good luck with that."

Free will. I used mine to walk away—back to the life I'd been bound to, the life I'd chosen—and away from the boy who had shown me exactly what I was giving up. I hoped he wasn't watching me go. In my mind, he had already turned a corner—hating me a little, allowing that to bridge the gap over his grief. I walked on through the darkness, but I didn't look back.

If I had, I probably would have seen the van.

Chapter Twenty-Seven

Tires squealed across the pavement. I smelled burning rubber and heard shouting and the sound of metal against metal—a door, I think. Hands were around my eyes, covering my mouth, just like on another night, on another street, when another set of hands came from out of nowhere. Autopilot kicked on, and seconds later my attacker lay at my feet—but it wasn't Josh—not that time.

Another set of hands were on me. Fists were everywhere. I kicked—made contact—heard a familiar, "Oh, jeez that hurt."

But before I could process what I had heard, I was on my stomach in the van, and someone was commanding, "Drive!"

I lay there, motionless, really ticked off, because, even though Mr. Solomon had been hinting for weeks that our CoveOps semester final was going to be a practical exam, I hadn't realized how literally he'd meant it until Mr. Smith blindfolded me and bound my hands.

"Sorry, Mr. Mosckowitz," I muttered, feeling guilty about kicking him so hard. After all, it was only the second mission he'd ever been on, and I kicked him in the gut. Plus, I'm pretty sure he's a bruiser.

He wheezed a little before saying, "That's okay. I'll be . . . fine."

"Harvey . . ." Mr. Solomon warned.

"Right. Be quiet," Mr. Mosckowitz said, jabbing me softly in the ribs, sounding like he was having the time of his life.

Since it was a test and everything, I knew I'd better do as I was trained. I lay on the floor of the van, counting seconds (nine hundred eighty-seven, by the way), noting how we made a right-hand turn, two lefts, one U, and eased over some speed bumps that left me with the distinct impression that we'd detoured through the Piggly Wiggly parking lot.

As the van veered south, I was willing to bet my semester grade in CoveOps (which, technically, was exactly what I *was* betting) that we were heading to the industrial complex on the south edge of town.

Doors opened and slammed. People got out. Someone pulled me to my feet on a gravel parking lot, then two strong sets of hands dragged me onto a concrete floor and then into the artificial light and empty echo of a large, hollow space.

"Sit her down. Tie her up," Mr. Solomon commanded.

Do I fight now? Do I fight later? I wondered, then took a chance—I kicked and I made contact.

"You know, Ms. Morgan, that was your mother you just hammered," Mr. Solomon said.

"Oh, I'm so sorry!" I cried, spinning around, as if I could see my mom through my blindfold.

"Good one, kiddo."

Someone pushed me into a chair, and I heard Mr. Solomon say, "Okay, Ms. Morgan, you know the drill: there are no rules. You can hit as hard as you want to hit. You can run as fast as you want to run." His breath smelled like peppermint gum.

"Yes, sir."

"Your team was tasked with retrieving a disk with pertinent information. You were captured and are being held for interrogation. The retrieval team will be after two packages. Care to guess what they are?"

"The disk and me?"

"Bingo."

"You can't be certain that they can track you to this location." I heard him step away, his feet scraping across the concrete floor.

"Are they Gallagher Girls?" I asked.

"Yes."

"Then they'll be here."

Fifteen minutes later, I was locked in a room. I was blindfolded and tied to a chair and thanking my lucky stars that they'd made it so easy on me.

They'd left me with Mr. Mosckowitz.

"I really do feel bad, Mr. M," I said. "Really."

"Um, Cammie, I'm pretty sure we're not supposed to be talking."

"Oh, right. Sorry." I shut up for about twelve seconds. "It's just that if I'd known it was a test, I never would have used one of the forbidden moves—I swear!"

"Oh." A heavy silence filled the room as I waited for Mr. Mosckowitz's inevitable, "Forbidden?"

"Don't worry. I'm sure you're okay. It's not like you're light-headed or seeing spots or anything."

"Oh, dear."

For the world's foremost authority on data encryption, Harvey Mosckowitz was pretty much an open book.

"Hey, Mr. M, don't worry," I said, trying to sound all fake-calm. "It's only a problem if the red splotches appear on the small of your back. You don't have red splotches. Do you?"

That's when I heard the sounds of a certified genius spinning around in circles like a dog chasing its tail.

"I can't . . . Oh, the light-headedness is getting worse." (I didn't doubt it—he'd been spinning pretty fast.) "Here." He ripped the blindfold off. "You look."

Sadly, it was just that easy, and it would have been a lot easier if I hadn't been afraid to use any of the actual forbidden moves (mainly because I like Mr. Mosckowitz, and I didn't have written permission from the Secretary of Defense and all). Still, Mr. Mosckowitz was a pretty good sport about it.

"Oh, you girls," he said in a very *aw-shucks* way, once I had him tied to the chair.

"Just sit tight, Mr. M. It'll be over soon."

"Um, Cammie?" he asked as I headed for the door. "I wasn't too bad, was I?"

"You were awesome."

The first thing I had to do was get out of that room. The disk wasn't there—if it was, no way would Mr. Solomon have left only Mr. Mosckowitz to guard it, so I darted through the empty warehouse to an exit door, checked it for sensors and alarms, then rushed out into the shadows of the complex.

Outside, I felt my eyes adjust to the black. A little light escaped from the building I'd just left, but otherwise I was surrounded by nothing but old rusty steel, and dark, cracked windows. A cold wind blew through the maze, whistling between the buildings, blowing dead leaves and plumes of dust along the gravel lot. I squinted through the night, trying to sense movement of any kind, but if it hadn't been for the glistening new wire of a tall chain fence and some very well-hidden surveillance cameras, I would have sworn the place was a ghost town.

Then I heard crackling static and a familiar voice.

"Bookworm to Chameleon. Chameleon, do you read me?"

"Liz?" I spun around.

"Chameleon, it's Bookworm, remember? We use code names when on comms?"

But I wasn't on comms! I was on a mission to break up with my secret boyfriend. I wasn't exactly prepared for active duty. But then I remembered the silver cross that dangled from my neck.

Before I could even ask, Liz explained. "I got bored one weekend and decided to fix your necklace. And upgrade it. What do you think?"

I think my friends are both brilliant and a little scary, is what I think. But of course I couldn't tell her that.

"So, how'd it go with your *project?*" Liz asked, and I remembered that half the school was probably listening. "I mean, were there complications or—"

"Liz," I snapped, not wanting to think about Josh or what I'd just done. The time for crying with your girlfriends about a broken heart is over chocolate ice cream and chick flicks—not stun guns and bulletproof vests. "Where's the disk?" I asked.

This time, it was Bex's voice that answered, "We think they're in the big building on the north side of the complex. Tina and Mick went to recon, and we're holding here."

"Where's *here?*"

"Look up."

Two days after my dad's funeral, my mom went on a mission. I never understood it until then—that sometimes a spy doesn't need a cover so much as she needs a shield. Crouched on the roof between Bex and Liz, I wasn't a girl who had just broken up with her boyfriend;

I looked at my watch and checked my gear instead of crying. I had a mission objective and not a broken heart.

"Okay," Liz said, as the majority of the sophomore class circled around her. "My guess is the school actually owns this place, because someone has sunk some serious cash into it." She pointed to a crude diagram, which my superspy instincts were telling me was made out of Evapopaper and eyeliner. "There are motion triggers on the perimeter. The windows are rigged to an alarm." Bex lit up at the sound of this, but Liz stopped her enthusiasm cold. "A Doctor Fibs original. No way we're cracking it in the middle of the night with minimal equipment."

"Oh." Bex deflated as if they weren't going to let her have any fun.

Eva pointed a device that looks like an ordinary radar gun but is really a body-heat detector toward the building across from us and swept it side to side before saying, "Bingo. We have a hot spot."

At least a dozen red images walked back and forth across the screen, but the majority of the red figures were huddled in the center.

"That's our package," Bex said.

"Doors are problematic," Liz said, reeling off options. "Windows are out. You'd better believe they're watching the heating ducts and—"

"You know what that leaves," Bex said, her voice like a dare.

Liz looked at us one by one, realizing what we were all

thinking—what our only mission option was—and that we had twenty pounds on her.

"No!" Liz snapped. "I'll get tangled or decapitated or—"

"I'll do it." And that's when I turned to look at Anna Fetterman—Anna, who had clutched her class assignment slip just months before as if CoveOps was going to be the death of her, was stepping forward, saying, "I'm the right size, am I not?"

And that's when I knew that Dillon was going to see Anna again someday, and then he'd be the one who would need saving.

Beep.

What was that? I wondered.

Beep-beep.

"Is it a missile?" Anna snapped, looking to the sky.

Beep-beep-beep-beep-beep.

"We're locked in as targets of a heat-seeking tranquil-lizer dart!" Eva yelled.

Beeeeeeeeeeeeep

"Okay, everybody, freeze!" a male voice behind us cried out.

Some of my classmates did as they were told. I did too, but for an entirely different reason. I'd never thought I'd hear that voice again, but there it was, saying, "I've . . . I've . . . already called nine-one-one. The cops are going to be here any—"

But the Gallagher Girls didn't let him finish. The nine-one-one thing had been the totally wrong thing to say, because in a flash, two of the girls were on him, and I had to cry, "Eva, Courtney, no!"

Everyone was staring at me—Josh, who was surprised I wasn't tied up or dead; and all of the sophomores (besides Bex and Liz), who couldn't imagine why I would have stopped them from neutralizing someone who had such obvious honeypotness.

"Josh!" I snapped in a harsh whisper as I turned off the power to the tracking device and headed toward him. "What are you doing here?"

"I'm here to rescue you." Then he glanced around at my black-clad classmates. "Who are *they?*" he whispered.

"We're here to rescue her, too," Bex said.

"Oh," he said, and then nodded blankly. "There was a van . . . I saw you . . . I . . ."

"*That?*" I said with a wave of my hands. "It's a school thing." I tried to sound as casual as possible when I said, "Kind of like . . . hazing."

Josh might have believed me if the entire sophomore class hadn't been standing on a warehouse roof, dressed in black and wearing equipment belts.

"Cammie," he said, stepping closer, "first I find out you go to that school, and then you tell me you're leaving, and then I see you kicking like a madwoman and getting kidnapped or something." He took another step, accidentally knocking over an old piece of metal that then skidded off the side of the roof and crashed to the ground below.

Sirens started wailing. Flashing lights streaked across the ground below us. Liz looked down, then cried, "He tripped the alarm!"

But that didn't matter, because I couldn't see anything but Josh. I couldn't hear anything but the fear in his voice when he said, "Cammie, tell me the truth."

The truth. I could hardly remember what it was. I'd been eluding it for so long that it took me a moment to remember what it was and what had brought me to that rooftop.

"I *do* go to the Gallagher Academy. These are my friends." Behind me, my classmates were moving, preparing for the next phase of the mission. "And we have to go now."

"I don't believe you." He didn't sound hurt then—the words were a dare.

"What do I have to say?" I snapped. "Do I have to tell you that my father's dead, and my mom can't cook, and that these girls are the closest thing I have to sisters?" He looked past me to the girls of every size, shape, and race. "Do I have to say that you and I can't ever see each other again? Because it's true. It's all true." He reached out to touch me, but I jerked away, saying, "Don't come looking for me, Josh. I can't ever see you again." And then I looked into his eyes for the first time. "And you'll be better for it."

Bex handed me a piece of gear, but before I took it, I turned to face him one last time. "Oh," I said, "and I don't have a cat."

I turned to hide my tears and stared into the deep expanse of night that lay before me. I didn't stop to think about all that lay behind. Free of my secrets, free of my lies, I told myself I was doing what I was put on this earth to do. I ran. I jumped. I stretched out my arms, and for ten blissful seconds, I could fly.

Chapter twenty-eight

Okay, so it wasn't flying so much as skirting between two buildings on a zip line, but still, it felt good to be weightless.

Josh was behind me. I zoomed toward what lay ahead, and at that height and that speed, I didn't have a chance to look back. I touched down, and it felt natural to hear Eva tell Tina, "We're heading for the breaker boxes."

It was only right that Courtney should say, "Copy that," and drag Mick toward the fire escape on the west side.

We were Gallagher Girls on a mission—doing what we do best. So I didn't think about what had just happened, not even when Bex asked, "You okay?"

"I'm fine," I told her, and in that adrenaline-filled moment, it was true.

We ran to the south side, and Bex used a small tube that looks like a lipstick but really is a super-intense acidic cream. I totally don't recommend getting them mixed up, by the way, because, just as soon as Bex drew a big circle in the roof, the acid starting eating away, and thirty seconds later I was rappeling down into the warehouse below.

The building was a maze of tall metal shelves stacked with pallets. I imagined the beeping of forklifts as Bex and I crept through the south side of the building, trusting that our classmates were simultaneously creeping through the north.

"He's taller than I expected," Bex whispered as she waited for me to silently clear a corner.

"Yeah, whatev—"

But just then, a guy I recognized from the maintenance department jumped from a high shelf. He'd descended through the air like a big, black crow, but Bex and I had sensed him, felt his shadow. I stepped aside, and he landed with a thud against one of the shelves. He didn't even hesitate before spinning around to kick, but Bex was ready and slapped a Napotine patch right in the middle of his forehead. (I am really glad Dr. Fibs quit smoking, by the way, because, besides the obvious health benefits, the idea of putting tranquilizers on stickers is awesome.)

Bex and I were moving again through the dark maze when she said, "You're gonna find someone else. Someone even hotter. With even better hair!" *Lie*. But a nice one.

We crept farther down the aisle, carefully listening, sensing our surroundings (after all, if Mr. Solomon had called in favors from the maintenance department, then he was taking this finals thing *seriously*.)

"Beta team, how's it going?" I asked, but was met with static-y silence. Bex and I shared a worried glance. *This is not good.* "Charlie team?" Nothing from that end either.

I felt like a rat stuck in a maze, looking for a block of cheese. Every corner was dangerous. Every step could be a trap. So Bex and I looked at each other, recognition dawned, and we did what great spies always do: we looked up.

After climbing twenty feet to the top of the shelves, we could see men patrolling the paths beneath us as Bex and I moved stealthily above, drawing closer to the small office in the center of the building.

The office had interior walls that were probably twenty feet tall, far shorter than the warehouse roof that loomed, dark and cold, above us. We stopped and Bex held a pair of binocuglasses to her eyes, then handed them to me. "One guess who's sitting on the package?"

I peered into the small room and said, "Solomon."

Bex put her hand to her ear and said, "Beta team and Charlie team. We are in position. I repeat, Alpha team is—"

But before Bex could finish, I felt something grab my foot. I kicked, trying to free myself. I turned to Bex, but she was gone. There was scuffling on the ground. I turned, saw the beefy hand that held my ankle, heard boxes falling to the floor below.

I couldn't jerk free, and soon I was falling past the heavy metal shelves, so I reached out and grabbed one, and hung there for a moment, trying to turn my momentum and pull myself back up. But it was too late.

Something pulled again, and this time I hit the floor, felt

the cold, dusty concrete beneath my hands, and saw a pair of size fourteen work boots staring me in my face.

This is not good.

I tried to roll, to kick, to flip up and catch my opponent in the chin with my feet, but before I could budge, I realized my arms had stopped working.

"Come on, Cam," Bubblegum Guard said. "It's over, girl. I got you." He righted me and steered me around the corner, where Bex was being held by two maintenance guys (both of whom were bleeding).

"Nice going, though," Bubblegum Guard whispered as he dragged me toward the office door. Somehow, I don't think real international bad guys will be that nice. But I can hope.

I reeled through my options: damsel in distress, twisted ankle, fake seizure, head-butt to the nose? Something told me Bubblegum Guard wasn't going to be taken down by any of them. He had at least fifty pounds and fifteen years on me, but, as my mother says, I've always been a squirmer.

"I'm sorry, Ms. Morgan," Mr. Solomon said, strolling out of the office toward me. "But it's over. You don't have the disk. You have failed to meet your mission—"

It looked like it was over. He sounded like it was over. But, on cue, Liz cut the power and the lights.

Dark silhouettes flew from out of nowhere. It almost seemed to be raining Gallagher Girls. I wish I could include a blow-by-blow account, but everything happened too fast. Fists flew. Kicks struck home. I heard heavy bodies fall to the floor as Napotine patches made contact with skin.

The building must have been equipped with emergency lights, because, after a minute in the dark, an eerie yellow glow grew within the enormous space, and everything seemed to go still as the lights came on. I saw Bex level one of the guards and then bolt for the office, but just as she reached the threshold she must have tripped a motion detector, because an alarm sounded, and the room turned from office to prison as bars shot up from the floor, building a cage around the very thing we needed.

Bex banged against the bars, as behind her, Joe Solomon said, "Sorry, ladies, but I'm afraid this is the end of your mission." He shook his head. Instead of looking triumphant, he seemed sad, almost heartbroken. "I tried to tell you how important this is. I tried to get you ready, and now look at you." We were bloody and sore, but we were still standing, yet Mr. Solomon sounded guilty and disappointed. "How were you going to get out of here? What was your extraction plan? Were you really willing to sacrifice three quarters of your team for nothing?" He shook his head again and pulled away from us. "I don't want to see any of you next semester. I don't want that on my conscience."

"Excuse me, sir," I said. "But does that apply even if we have the disk?"

He laughed a quick, tired, barely audible laugh, reminding us all what our sisters have known for centuries— that men will always underestimate girls. Even Gallagher Girls.

"That disk," I said, pointing behind him to the cage that completely surrounded the small office except for the thin gaps where the floor opened up to allow the bars to shoot through. The space was far too small for a grown man to fit through. No, for that it would take a girl—preferably one the size of Anna Fetterman.

Dumbstruck, Mr. Solomon and the rest of his team stared as little Anna waved then slithered back through the gaps in the floor and out of sight. Some of the men bolted after her, but Joe Solomon stared on.

"Well," he said, "I guess—"

But before he could finish, a loud crashing sound filled the air. The room seemed full of dust and smoke and the sound of splintering lumber. Bubblegum Guard threw me against the wall, putting his body between me and harm as steel bent and shelves toppled, one right after another, falling like dominoes stacked in row.

It seemed like it took forever for Bubblegum Guard to let go of me. I think he was dazed—I know I definitely was. After all, it's not every day you A) break up with your secret boyfriend, B) get kidnapped by (sort of) former government operatives, and C) have the aforementioned secret boyfriend attempt to rescue you by driving a forklift through a wall.

"Cammie!" I heard Josh cry through the dust, but I couldn't answer him—not then. Mr. Solomon was on the floor. He had planned for every contingency but one—the persistence of a regular boy who has the misfortune of loving an exceptional girl.

"Cammie!" Josh said through the dust that was swarming around the forklift as he climbed down to stand atop the pile of rubble. "We. Need. To. Talk."

"Yes," said a voice behind me. I turned to see my mother standing there. My strong, beautiful, brilliant mother. "We do."

Mr. Solomon was stirring. Bubblegum Guard was fanning the dust out of the air, and Bex was grinning like this was the most fun she'd ever had in her entire life. It was over—the test, the lies, everything. It was over, so I did the only thing I could.

"Josh," I said, "I'd like you to meet my mom."

Chapter twenty-nine

After I had learned the truth about my parents, and before I came to the Gallagher Academy, the only time I wasn't worried was when they were both within my sight. I think that's when I started being The Chameleon. I'd creep into their bedroom and watch them sleep. I'd lie silently behind the sofa, listening to the sounds of the TV as they relaxed in the evening. But even for me, the night of the CoveOps final was a long one.

23:00 hours: Operatives return to headquarters and are instructed to go upstairs and go to bed.

23:40 hours: Tina Walters reports that Headmistress Morgan has locked herself in her office with The Subject.

01:19 hours: The Operative succeeds in getting all the sawdust and gunk out of her hair.

02:30 hours: Majority of sophomores stop studying for COW final and go to bed.

04:00 hours: The Operative still can't fall asleep.

The Operative realizes that the best-case scenario would involve a glass of "memory modification" tea and The Subject waking up in his own bed in a few hours without a single memory of what happened the night before. The Operative doesn't let herself think about the worst-case scenario.

At seven o'clock the next morning, I'd had enough of waiting, so I knocked on my mother's office door. I thought I was prepared for anything—that after the day I'd had before, nothing could knock me off guard ever again.

I was wrong.

"Hi," Josh said.

"What . . . Huh . . . How . . ." I could tell by the look on his face that he was seriously beginning to doubt my newly revealed genius status, but I couldn't help it—he should have been gone before then. I wasn't supposed to have to face him. We weren't supposed to have that awkward moment of standing crowded together in the doorway of my mother's office. The two halves of my life weren't supposed to collide.

"Were you here all night?" I asked when I finally regained my ability for coherent thought.

His eyes were red and heavy, but he didn't look like someone who was eager to go to sleep. In fact, he looked like someone who was never going to sleep again.

He rubbed his eyes. "Yeah, I called and told my mom I was staying at Dillon's. They . . . they didn't know anything about . . . They were cool with it."

"Yeah," I said. "We don't exactly show up on caller ID."

It wasn't supposed to be funny, but "Old Josh" would have laughed or smiled that slow, melting smile. "New Josh" just stood there—looking at me.

"Cammie." My mother's voice carried clearly through the doorway and echoed through the Hall of History. "Come in here, please."

I stepped inside, brushing against him for a moment that didn't last nearly long enough.

"I'll . . ." He motioned to the benches at the top of the stairs. "Your mom and that guy—they said I could wait."

But I didn't want him to wait. If he did, I'd have to look him in the eye; I'd have to say things that only make sense in a language even I don't know. I wanted him to walk away and not look back. But before I could say so, Mom said, "Cameron, now!" and I knew we were out of time. In so many ways.

She didn't hug and kiss me—which was strange. Not unexpected, but it gave seeing her an unfinished feeling, like I should stay standing by the door, waiting for her "How's it going, kiddo?" before I took a seat on the sofa and asked what was for supper. I glanced around and saw Mr. Solomon in the corner of the room. "Sleep well?" he asked.

"Not really." *Not a lie.*

"I enjoyed visiting with Josh," my mom said. "He seems nice." *He is.* "It was nice to meet him finally."

"Yeah, I . . ." Then I realized something was wrong. "Wait!"

Mom smiled at Mr. Solomon and—can you believe it—he actually smiled back. With teeth and everything! (Okay, so I might have thought he was kind of hot then. But only for a second or two.)

"Honey, you're good," Mom said to my look of utter disbelief. "But give us some credit."

Oh my gosh! I sank onto the leather sofa. "How . . ." There were so many ways to finish that sentence: how long had they known? How far were they willing to let me go? How did they find out?

"You've been very busy," Mom said. She sat down in one of the beautiful leather chairs across from me and crossed one perfect leg over the other.

"You mean you didn't wonder how we found you last night?" Mr. Solomon asked.

No, I hadn't wondered. Everything had happened so fast, and hours later I was still riding that same wave of emotion. I felt like an idiot—a great, big, hand-caught-in-the-cookie-jar fool.

"Cammie, this is not an ordinary school—it can't be, with such exceptional students. What you did was reckless and careless, and if you tried a stunt like that in the field, lives would be put at risk and operations could fail. You know that. Don't you?"

"Yes, ma'am."

"That being said, as someone with a good deal of experience"—she glanced at Mr. Solomon, who nodded—"it was a rather *impressive* display."

"It was?" I looked between the two of them, expecting a trapdoor to open up and send me zooming to the dungeon. "I'm not . . . in trouble?"

Mom tilted her head, weighing her words. "Let's just say, you've had one of the more extensive Covert Operations exercises this school has ever allowed."

"Oh," I said, and the word sounded heavy.

"But, Cam," Mom said, leaning forward, "why didn't you come to me?"

She sounded hurt. It was torture—the hard kind.

"I don't know." *Don't cry. Don't cry. Don't cry.* "I just . . ." It was too late; my voice was cracking. "I didn't want you to be ashamed of me."

"*Her* ashamed?" Mr. Solomon said, and it took me a split second to remember that he was even in the room. "You think *she* could have gotten away with as much as you did at your age?" He laughed, then smiled. "That wasn't your mom in you—that was your dad."

He stood and strolled to the window. I saw his reflection in the sunny glass as he spoke. "He always said you were going to be good." *Okay, so maybe he was still a little hot. . . .* "Cammie, I think I've been pretty hard on you this semester," Joe Solomon said, as if letting me in on a secret. "You know why?"

Because you hate me was the answer that sprang to mind, though I knew it wasn't the right one.

"I've already lost one member of the Morgan family I care about." He looked between me and my mom. "So I'd give about anything for you to never come into my classroom again." Shocked and hurt, I could do nothing but stare at him. He reached into his pocket and pulled out my form where I'd marked the Covert Operations box. "Are you sure you don't want to find a nice safe desk or lab somewhere?" I didn't answer, so after a moment he refolded the form and put it back in his pocket. "Well, if you're going to be in the field—you're going to be ready. I owe your old man that much." Sadness seeped into his voice, and for the first time I saw Joe Solomon as human. "I owe him more than that."

I glanced toward my mother, who gave him a sad, knowing smile.

"Have a good break, Cammie," Mr. Solomon said, sounding like his old self as he reached for the door. "Rest up. Next semester won't be the cakewalk you just had."

That was a cakewalk?! I wanted to scream, but Joe Solomon was already gone. I wanted answers from him. How well had he known my dad? Why did he come to the Gallagher Academy now? Why did I get the feeling there was more to the story?

But then my mom spoke, and I realized we were alone. My defenses fell, and I felt like I could curl up beside her and sleep straight through Christmas.

"Cammie," she said, moving to sit beside me. "I'm not glad you lied to me. I'm not glad you broke the rules, but there is one part of this that has made me very proud."

"The computer stuff?" I guessed. "Because, really, that was all Liz. I didn't—"

"No, kiddo. That's not it." She reached down and took

my hand. "Do you know that your dad and I weren't sure we wanted you to go to school here?"

I've heard a lot of crazy things in my life, but that one took my breath away. "But . . . you were a Gallagher Girl. . . . I'm a legacy. . . . It's . . ."

"Sweetheart," Mom stopped me. "When we came here, I knew I'd be taking away everything that isn't inside these walls. I didn't want this to be the only life you know." She smoothed my hair. "Your dad and I used to talk about whether this was the best place for you."

"But what . . . how did you decide?" I asked, but as soon as I had said the words, I knew it was a stupid question.

"Yeah, kiddo, when we lost your father I knew I had to get out of the field. . . ."

"And you needed a job?" I tried to finish for her.

She shook me off. "I needed to come home."

When did I start crying? I really didn't know. I really didn't care.

She smoothed my hair and said, "But the thing I worried most about was that you'd spend your childhood learning to be hard and strong and never learn that it's okay to be soft and sweet." She straightened beside me, forced me to look into her eyes. "Doing what we do, it doesn't mean turning off the part of yourself that loves, Cam. I loved your father. . . . I *love* your father. *And you*. If I thought you would have to give that up . . . to never know that . . . I would take you as far away from this place as we could go."

"I know," I said. *Not a lie.*

"Good. I'm glad you're smart enough to know that," she said, then pushed me away. "Now go on. You've got tests to take."

I ran my hands across my face, searching for stray tears, then I stood and headed toward the door. But before I could leave, she stopped me.

"It would have been okay, you know, kiddo? To mark that other box."

I looked back at her, and I saw not the headmistress or the spy or even the mother, but the woman I'd seen crying.

And just when I thought I couldn't love her more.

"I wouldn't touch that if I were you."

Josh spun around at the sound of my words. Still, his fingers were perilously close to Gilly's sword. "We're pretty good at keeping things protected around here," I said, inching closer.

He put his hands in his pockets. That was probably the safest place for them, but the gesture reminded me of the first night we'd met. I longed for that dark street, for the chance to do things over.

"So," he said. "A spy, huh?" His eyes never left the sword. I couldn't blame him. I didn't want to look at me, either.

"Yeah."

"That explains a lot."

"So they told you?" I asked.

He nodded. "Yeah, I got the grand tour."

Somehow, I found that really hard to believe, but I wasn't exactly in a position to say, *Did you see the nuclear-powered hovercraft we keep in the basement,* so I just nodded, too.

"Josh, you know you can't ever—"

"Tell anyone?" He looked at me. "Yeah, they told me."

"I mean, *ever,* Josh. *Ever.*"

"I know," he said. "I can keep a secret."

The words stung. They were supposed to.

There we were, in a room dedicated to secret lives and secret triumphs. He could see it all from where he stood. My sisterhood was bare to him. I was exposed, but there was more between us than ever before.

"I'm sorry I lied. I'm sorry I'm not . . . normal."

"No, Cammie, I get the spy thing," he said, spinning on me. "But you didn't just lie about where you go to school." His voice was harsh, but wounded. His eyes seemed almost bruised. "I don't even know who you are."

"Yes, you do," I said. "You know everything that matters."

"Your dad?" he asked.

I froze. "It's classified—what happened—I couldn't tell you. I wanted to, but—"

"Then just tell me he died. Tell me your mom can't cook and you're an only child. Don't . . . make up a family. Don't make up another life." Josh looked over the railing along the Hall of History, into the towering foyer of the Gallagher Mansion, and said, "What's so great about normal?"

I might have been the genius, but Josh was the one to see the truth. For a while there, I had needed another life, a trial life—normal on a temporary basis. The problem was looking into the wounded eyes of someone I cared about and telling him that I would never be free to really love him, because . . . well . . . then I'd have to kill him.

Then, I realized where we were—what he was looking at. JOSH KNOWS! I mentally screamed. There doesn't have to be any more lying. He's inside. He's one of us (kind of). He's . . .

But Josh was heading down the stairs. I bolted forward, yelling, "Wait, Josh. Wait! It's okay now. It's . . ."

When he reached the floor, he stopped and pulled his hand out of his pocket. "Do you want these?" I saw the earrings lying in his palm.

"Yes," I said, nodding, biting back tears. I flew down the stairs, and he shuffled them into my hands so quickly I never even felt his touch. "I love them. I didn't want to—"

"Sure." He walked farther away from me. I probably know a dozen different ways to subdue a guy Josh's size—not that I would have used any of them. (Okay, so I thought about it. . . .)

Oh my gosh, he's leaving, I thought—not knowing whether to feel sad at his loss or thrilled with the fact that we were letting him walk out that door—his memory of our secrets intact. Surely they're not going to let that happen, I wondered, unless they trust him . . . unless he's been cleared . . . unless someone decided that he didn't need to drink the tea and go to sleep and wake up feeling like he's had a crazy dream he can't remember.

Unless it's okay for me to love him.

He reached for the door, so I blurted, "Josh," knowing that if the Gallagher Academy was going to take a chance on him, I had to at least try to make things right. "I . . . I go to Nebraska over winter break. My grandparents live there—my dad's parents. But I'll be back."

"Okay," he said as he reached for the door. "I guess I'll see you around."

It was fast—like blink-or-you'll-miss-it fast—but Josh smiled at me—quickly, sweetly, and that was enough to let me know that he'd meant it when he said he'd be seeing me. More important, it proved that he'd be looking.

I was just starting to imagine what it was going to be like—a new year, a new semester, a new start with no secrets standing between us, but then he stopped and said, "Oh, tell your mom thanks for the tea."

He opened the door and walked outside. I stood in the middle of the empty foyer for a long time. After all, in the movies, the dramatic good-bye is often followed by the good-bye-er flying back through the door to sweep the good-bye-ee into a very dramatic, very sexy kiss. And if there was any dramatic, sexy kissing potential in my future, I wasn't going to sway from that spot.

I felt something soft and warm rub against my leg and looked down to see Onyx wrapping her tail around my ankle. She purred, consoling me, sounding like a very lucky cat, and I knew things had come full circle.

Behind me, girls started rushing down the stairs toward

the Grand Hall and a few last-minute study sessions before the first day of finals, but as they passed me, I knew what the main topic of conversation was going to be over breakfast. (You think regular girls love gossip—try Gallagher Girls!)

Still, I didn't mind their stares. Instead, I stood swaying in the current of bodies that was floating off to start the day, but I didn't budge until Bex appeared beside me.

"Hey." She shoved a book and a bagel into my hands. "Come on," she said with a tug at my arm. "We've got our COW final, you know. Liz made flash cards."

I followed my friend up the stairs, and I got lost in a sea of girls who were dressed like me, and were trained like I was, and who were entrenched in my same world.

Is this the world I would choose if I could go back—be ignorant and blissful and happy—if I could live a white picket life on a white picket street and be ignorant of the unpleasant deeds that have to be done in places most people can't find on a map? I don't know. Maybe I would if my mind was like an Etch A Sketch and I could shake it and erase all that I know. But I'm in too deep now. I know what goes bump in the night, and I know how to fight it.

Bex and I walked up the stairs. Then Liz joined our steps, then Macey. I don't know what's going to happen next semester. I don't know if Josh will ever talk to me again. I don't know what he'll remember, or what we'll face in CoveOps, or even what Mr. Smith will look like come September. But I know who will be beside me, and as every good spy knows—sometimes that's enough.